THE PENGUIN BOOK OF CRIME STORIES

PETER ROBINSON is the author of sixteen Inspector Banks novels, including his most recent book *Piece of My Heart,* as well as two non-series suspense novels, *Caedmon's Song* and *No Cure for Love. Strange Affair* was chosen as one of the best books of 2005 by *The Globe and Mail,* the *South Florida Sun-Sentinel,* and *January Magazine. Strange Affair* was also shortlisted for the *L.A. Times Book Award* for best crime fiction novel. Robinson has published a collection of short stories called *Not Safe After Dark.* His novels have been translated into over sixteen languages, and he has won a number of international awards, including the MWA Edgar, the CWA Dagger in the Library, the Martin Beck Award from Sweden, the Danish Palle Rosenkrantz Award, and the French Grand Prix de Littérature Policière. He has also won five Crime Writers of Canada Arthur Ellis Awards. Peter Robinson lives in Toronto, Canada, and Richmond, North York Shire.

Also by Peter Robinson

Caedmon's Song

No Cure for Love

Not Safe After Dark

Other Inspector Banks mysteries

Gallows View

A Dedicated Man

A Necessary End

The Hanging Valley

Past Reason Hated

Wednesday's Child

Final Account

Innocent Graves

Dead Right

In a Dry Season

Cold Is the Grave

Aftermath

The Summer That Never Was

Playing with Fire

Strange Affair

Piece of My Heart

Inspector Banks collections

Meet Inspector Banks
(*includes* Gallows View, A Dedicated Man, *and* A Necessary End)

Inspector Banks Investigates
(*includes* The Hanging Valley, Past Reason Hated, *and* Wednesday's Child)

The Return of Inspector Banks
(*includes* Innocent Graves, Final Account, *and* Dead Right)

THE PENGUIN BOOK OF
CRIME STORIES

SELECTED AND INTRODUCED BY

PETER
ROBINSON

PENGUIN
CANADA

PENGUIN CANADA

Published by the Penguin Group

Penguin Group (Canada), 90 Eglinton Avenue East, Suite 700, Toronto, Ontario, Canada
M4P 2Y3 (a division of Pearson Canada Inc.)

Penguin Group (USA) Inc., 375 Hudson Street, New York, New York 10014, U.S.A.
Penguin Books Ltd, 80 Strand, London WC2R 0RL, England
Penguin Ireland, 25 St Stephen's Green, Dublin 2, Ireland (a division of Penguin Books Ltd)
Penguin Group (Australia), 250 Camberwell Road, Camberwell, Victoria 3124, Australia
(a division of Pearson Australia Group Pty Ltd)
Penguin Books India Pvt Ltd, 11 Community Centre, Panchsheel Park, New Delhi – 110 017,
India
Penguin Group (NZ), 67 Apollo Drive, Rosedale, North Shore 0632, Auckland, New Zealand
(a division of Pearson New Zealand Ltd)
Penguin Books (South Africa) (Pty) Ltd, 24 Sturdee Avenue, Rosebank, Johannesburg 2196,
South Africa

Penguin Books Ltd, Registered Offices: 80 Strand, London WC2R 0RL, England

First published 2007

1 2 3 4 5 6 7 8 9 10   (RRD)

Introduction and selection copyright © Eastvale Enterprises, Inc.
The Copyright Acknowledgments on pages 253–254 constitute
an extension of this copyright page.

Manufactured in the U.S.A.

Library and Archives Canada Cataloguing in Publication data available upon request

ISBN-13: 978-0-14-305349-1
ISBN-10: 0-14-305349-3

Visit the Penguin Group (Canada) website at **www.penguin.ca**

Special and corporate bulk purchase rates available; please see
www.penguin.ca/corporatesales or call 1-800-810-3104, ext. 477 or 474

Contents

Introduction

by

PETER ROBINSON

I

Short stories are, by definition, short, and therein lies both their weakness and their strength. Most of the writers represented in this collection are novelists—many known for series detectives such as John Rebus, Harry Bosch and Tom Thorne—and a novelist has time to develop and explore characters, to illuminate themes and to pack a book with a great variety of incidents and settings. In a short story, you really don't have time to do that. Novels can sprawl and digress, but short stories have to stick to the point, keep things relatively simple and reach their denouements quickly. They can certainly create atmosphere and suspense, but quite often the action is limited to a short period of time and the characters can't be explored in any depth. Like poetry, where every word counts, the short story demands a very different approach from the writer than does the novel.

The crime story also presents special problems, and many of these can be linked to the need for the plot to hinge on a crime. Much mainstream fiction offers a "slice of life," a few pages of fine writing without pattern or resolution, but readers of crime stories usually expect a murder to occur and to be solved by a brilliant detective through the unveiling and interpretation of clues, along with the questioning of suspects and the occasional piece of brilliant and esoteric forensic knowledge. Often, readers expect a twist at the end—which gives rise to the only crime writer joke I have ever heard

(Q: How many crime writers does it take to screw in a light bulb? A: Two. One to screw it in and the other to give it a twist at the end).

This paradigm of the classic crime story was popularized by its early practitioners, especially Edgar Allan Poe, who is often reputed to have invented the genre with his three stories of "ratiocination" featuring Auguste Dupin: "The Murders in the Rue Morgue" (1841), "The Mystery of Marie Roget" (1842) and "The Purloined Letter" (1844). Over forty years later, Sir Arthur Conan Doyle published "A Study in Scarlet" in *Beeton's Christmas Annual* of 1887, and Sherlock Holmes and Dr. Watson were born. Though the many Sherlock Holmes stories that followed possessed elements of the thrilling and exotic adventure tales associated with *The Boy's Own Paper*, they are remembered most of all for Holmes's brilliant deductive powers. G.K. Chesterton's Father Brown was another early example of a popular fictional detective. Agatha Christie (1890–1976) published numerous stories featuring Belgian detective Hercule Poirot, Miss Marple and other detective characters between the wars; popular crime story writers of this Golden Age of detective fiction also included John Dickson Carr, Dorothy L. Sayers, S.S. Van Dine, Ellery Queen and Ngaio Marsh. A chief concern at this time was playing fair with the reader, and Monsignor Ronald Knox set up a "Decalogue" of rules to make sure this occurred. One of the most curious of his rules to readers in the present age is the fifth: "No Chinaman must figure in the story."

The popularity of the classic crime short story in Britain eventually declined, partly due to a drop in quality and partly due to the rising popularity of the novel in the 1930s and beyond. Most people agreed that Christie's Hercule Poirot novels were far better than her short stories featuring him, for example. On the other side of the Atlantic, a different, tougher and more realistic kind of detective story had come into being through the conjunction of the pulp magazines, the most famous of which was *Black Mask,* and the spectacular talents of Dashiell Hammett (1894–1961) and Raymond Chandler (1888–1959). Though neither could be said to have invented the hardboiled private detective (that honour generally goes to Carroll John Daly and his private eye, Race Williams), they certainly perfected the form, along with Ross Macdonald, and both were major crime writers. What Hammett achieved, according to Chandler's 1944 essay "The Simple Art of Murder," was to give "murder back to the kind of people that commit it for reasons, not with hand-wrought duelling pistols, curare, and tropical fish." In this sense, the stories and novels of Hammett and Chandler were a reaction against what they perceived to be the vapid and overly genteel world of the English crime story.

In some ways, of course, this world was no more or less real than the country manor of the British Golden Age stories. It soon generated its own conventions, and one mean street began to look and feel much like another, one cynical, romantic, world-weary private eye to sound like any other. But the differences between the two worlds could be quite extreme. The British relied on reason, class and gentlemanly courtesy, even in the face of murder, whereas the Americans relied on violence, wisecracks and the detective's ability to move within any level of society. While the police in British Golden Age stories are generally bumbling but benign nincompoops from the lower classes, the cops in Chandler's and Hammett's world are tough, cynical, brutal and corrupt tyrants.

The hardboiled stories, however, still have plenty of Golden Age elements, and they are filled with clues and clever crime-solving. Hammett's Continental Op is tough, no doubt about it, and the body count in novels such as *Red Harvest* is high, but he doesn't always solve crimes with his fists; nor does Philip Marlow, and even less so Ross Macdonald's Lew Archer. These men are deceptively urbane, witty and intelligent beneath their rough-and-ready surfaces. They have to show a certain kind of face to the world to do what they do, but what makes them particularly good at their jobs is what they manage to hide behind the wisecracks and bravado.

II

So how did we get from the Golden Age and the hardboiled detective to the stories in this collection? After the war, writers such as Margaret Millar, Ross Macdonald, Patricia Highsmith and Ruth Rendell introduced elements of psychology into crime fiction. The short story developed into a more psychologically complex genre, one not always overly reliant on clues, sudden twists and final reversals, and sometimes not reliant on them at all. While a writer may not be able to develop a sufficiently satisfying plot over twenty or thirty pages, he or she can certainly probe an obsession or examine the idea that, given the right circumstances, even the man next door is capable of murder.

Perhaps also after the horrors of the Second World War and the Holocaust, it was no longer desirable for many crime writers to produce neat, entertaining stories about solving murders, in which the criminal is punished, the loose ends are tied up and order is preserved. Writers had somehow to come to grips with the darkness in the human psyche. At this time, explorations of the criminal mind blossomed, and we even started to see descriptions of that mind at work, to find stories written, like some of those by Jim Thompson, from the criminal point of view. Sam Spade may have been cold and ruthless, but he had a code of honour to which he adhered. Many more recent characters in crime fiction, cops and criminals alike, are less morally anchored.

Also, in popular culture horror was never very far from crime—the main difference being the absence or presence of the supernatural, of vampires, werewolves and the like. A book such as Robert Bloch's *Psycho* bridges that gap in significant ways through its use of deviant psychology, its exploration of the twisted psychopathic mind of Norman Bates. We must also not forget the importance to crime fiction of filmmakers such as the Alfred Hitchcock of *Psycho, Vertigo* and *Rear Window* (itself based on a fine Cornell Woolrich short story) and such odd movies as *Peeping Tom,* along with the whole noir look and feel of many of the American crime movies and stories of the forties and fifties. If many movies took from the world of crime fiction, they certainly gave a lot back as well, to the extent, say, that *Chinatown* has often been mistakenly seen as a film of a great private eye novel when, in fact, it was an original screenplay by Robert Towne.

Eventually, crime writers were to look so deeply into the criminal mind that Thomas Harris came up with Hannibal Lecter, and James Lee Burke and John Connolly created villains who move so easily back and forth across the borders between horror and crime through their explorations of evil as a supernatural power that they have almost created a new genre in themselves. While murders still abound, of course, and detectives still seek clues, so much else is happening that the lines between the crime story and other kinds of fiction have become blurred, and the obligatory twist at the end has, in many cases, been replaced by irony, or even by a kind of dying fall.

Because of all this, crime short stories often go against a reader's expectations. If you are used to Eric Wright's Charlie Salter novels, for example, "Licensed Guide" will take you somewhere different. If you come to expect V.I. Warshawski novels from Sara Paretsky, then "Lily and the Sockeyes" will surprise you. George Pelecanos, known for his crime novels and his television writing for *The Wire,* has raised the bar, and his stories offer a glimpse of a world into which crime writers, and readers, rarely venture. Plots in many of the more contemporary stories don't end neatly, the loose ends are not tied up, and good people sometimes do bad things for the right reasons. The crime story today, then, is a many-faceted form, capable not only of surprising readers but of challenging them in ways beyond that of the crossword puzzle or mere exercise in logic, and, occasionally, of scaring the living daylights out of them. We even have, in the case of Robert J. Sawyer's "Biding Time," an overlap with the world of science fiction.

Not that we have left detection behind. Far from it—as the excellent stories from such diverse talents as Ian Rankin, Michael Connelly and John Harvey show, the crime story has simply grown along with the crime novel so that the old definitions no longer fit comfortably. From the wit and ingenuity of Robert Barnard to the graphic, tongue-in-cheek Southern Gothic of Karin Slaughter, the range is astonishing. But no one has entirely forgotten the old masters. Laura Lippman's "Easy as A-B-C," for example, is a modern homage to Poe, another denizen of Baltimore, and you won't have to look too far to find clues and detection aplenty among the authors here.

Whatever they might have become, though, short stories are still distinct and discrete entities, not mere slices of life or chapters of unfinished novels. Even if plot is no longer always paramount, the stories still demand the same sort of special discipline, attention to detail and devotion to craftsmanship that they always did.

III

One problem for writers is that most readers demand novels, and as a result there aren't many markets left for the crime short story these days. *Ellery Queen's Mystery Magazine*, *Alfred Hitchcock's Mystery Magazine* and *The Strand* persevere thanks to the heroic efforts of their respective editors and publishers. The U.S. crime anthology scene is healthy in the hands of experts such as Otto Penzler, Martin H. Greenberg and Edward D. Hoch, while Maxim Jakubowski and Martin Edwards keep the short story flag flying high in the U.K. Canada used to have an excellent series of anthologies called *Cold Blood*, edited by Peter Sellers (occasionally with John North) and published by Mosaic Press, but this series is sadly defunct. I am happy to be able to publish Peter's story "Avenging Miriam," winner of the *Ellery Queen's Mystery Magazine* Readers Award in 2001. More recently the Ottawa-based Ladies Killing Circle, which includes Mary Jane Maffini, has picked up some of the slack and published several anthologies, but unfortunately this group publishes only stories by women. Single-author short story collections would be rare indeed without the devotion of Doug Greene's Crippen & Landru, who have published volumes of stories by a number of the authors in this anthology, including Eric Wright.

As a result of the shrinking market, authors tend to devote themselves to writing novels and produce short stories only on request, often accepting a deadline far in the future that surprises them with its proximity when it finally comes due and not a word has been written! One outcome of this approach is that we tend to see more themed anthologies. In recent years collections of crime stories have been built around such subjects as Dickens, Shakespeare, love, the Bible, music, basketball, poker, NFL football and ocean cruises. One recent anthology, *Merry Band of Murderers*, even required its contributors to write a song to accompany their stories. These songs were recorded and a CD accompanied the book.

It can be quite a challenge for a crime writer to come up with a reworking of Shakespeare or Dickens or a modern twist on a Bible story that both echoes the original and works as a contemporary short story. The results are often very interesting. Another trend is for anthologies to be themed by gender, such as *Tart Noir*, or by place, as in the series that includes *Baltimore Noir* and *Brooklyn Noir*. The word *noir* is bandied about a lot in the crime fiction field these days, and I don't believe that half the people who use it know what it means—it just sounds cool—but there is no doubt that some of the stories in the noir-themed anthologies represented here do partake of its special qualities.

From the writer's point of view, a request for a short story on a theme, say, jazz or home renovations, both taxes the author's ingenuity and allows him or her a temporary escape from the chains of a series character. I have written only three or four Inspector Banks short stories because it is almost impossible to do the kinds of things I like to with his life and relationships in a short story, but writing short stories has freed me to explore many different characters and new places, such as Toronto, Paris and Florida, and to experiment with narrative points of view, such as first person. I have also been able to explore different historical periods, such as the Second World War and Victorian Yorkshire. All of this can be tremendously enjoyable for the author as well as quite challenging.

So the range of the crime short story today has expanded, yet the pleasure remains ultimately the same for the reader, that of being able to savour and finish something at one sitting. Remember, though, that anthologies are for dipping into as the mood takes you, in whatever order you want, and to read all these quickly from the first page to the last would be like eating a whole box of chocolates one after another. Not a good idea, though one that may be difficult to resist.

THE PENGUIN BOOK OF
CRIME STORIES

Sins of Scarlet

by

ROBERT BARNARD

CARDINAL PASCONA STOOD A LITTLE ASIDE from his fellow electors, observing the scene, conjecturing on the conversations that were animating every little knot of cardinals. The elderly men predominated, of course. The young men were not only in a minority, but they were unlikely to want any of their number to be elected. A long papacy was the last thing anybody wanted at this juncture. So instead of forming up into a clique of their own, they separated and mingled with the older men. They were all, in any case, related in some way or other to earlier popes, and their opinions for that reason tended to be discounted. That was unfair but understandable.

Cardinal Borromei.

That was the name that kept coming towards him, through the sticky and fetid air of the Chapel. It was clear to Pascona that opinion was drifting—had already drifted—in that direction. Borromei was related to a previous pope, like the young men, but his promotion to the rank of cardinal at the age of twenty-three was now so long ago that everybody had discounted it. He had proved his worth to the College by a long life of steady opinions, safe hands on the tiller, and general mediocrity. He was a man to ruffle no feathers, stir up no hornet's nests, raise no high winds.

Ideal.

Or ideal in the view of most of his fellow electors. And promising in other ways too: aged sixty-seven and obese from a fondness for rich and outré foods. That, and a partiality for the finest cognac, marked him out as likely to be present before long in the Chapel in mummified form only. Cardinal Pascona stepped down from the chapel stalls and began mingling with the knots of his fellows. The conversations were going as he had expected.

"The situation in France is becoming worrying," that old fool da Ponti was saying to a little group of like-minded ciphers. "Borromei has been used to a mediation role in Venice. Couldn't be bettered at the present time." He continued looking at him, and Pascona knew that any dissent would be discounted as the bile of an unsuccessful candidate. Everyone in the Conclave assessed Pascona as *papabile* but there was a distinct reluctance to vote for him.

"Absolutely," Pascona said with a smile. "A perfectly safe pair of hands, and accustomed to bringing peace to warring factions." He could not restrain himself from adding: "Though whether the Bourbons—fair-weather friends to us, at their best—deserve the services of the Church's best mediator is another matter. The unkind might suggest that they deserve to stew in a juice of their own making."

And he moved on, with a peaceful, delightful glide as if, having just dispensed a Christ-like wisdom, he was currently walking on air.

The bowls from their light supper were just being cleared away.

Pascona nodded in the direction of the robed and cowled figures who silently served them and waited for them to bring the silver goblets with their nightcaps in them. A vile red wine from Sicily in all probability. It was generally agreed among the cardinals that everything was done to make their stay incommunicado from the real world (if Rome and the Vatican was that) as unpleasant as possible. The aim of the Vatican officials was to persuade them to make a decision as quickly as they reasonably could so that a return to normality could be achieved. After all, for those officials, it was only a matter of one old man being succeeded by another old man. Nothing much happened during the last reign, and (unless a surprising choice was made) nothing much would happen in the next one.

Cardinal Pascona took up his goblet. It was indeed a vile wine, quite incredibly sour and thick. Prolonged indigestion or worse could well be the consequences for many of the elderly and infirm electors if they did more than sip at such muck. Confident in his own stomach the Cardinal drank, then went over to another group.

"It is a sobering thought," he injected into their small-talk that was by now a mere prelude to slumber, "that the world is waiting on our decision, but when the choice is announced everyone will say 'Who?'"

The cardinals smiled politely, though one or two of the smiles were sour. Not all of them liked to be thought totally insignificant in the wider scheme of things. Now the cowled figures were going round extinguishing the nests of candles on the walls. They rolled out the down mattresses and put on top of them a pillow and a pile of blankets hardly needed in the close atmosphere of the Sistine. Beside these bundles they put a nightlight. No great comforts for a long night. Cardinals removed their red robes and lay down in their substantial undergarments. Bones creaked as they levered themselves down. Cardinal Pascona took great care not to creak himself. He was still fit and active in every way. That ought to be noticed. He was not going to live for ever, but he had a few years yet in him, and good ones too.

He lay on his back looking up. Nothing could be seen of the ceiling, but in the murky light cast by the few remaining nightlights he could distinguish the contours of the Chapel. He had loved the Chapel since he had first seen it fifty years before. It spoke to him. Twenty years before, when he was barely forty, he had become part of a commission to report on the state of the Chapel, in particular on the state of Mazzuoli's restorations at the beginning of the century. Pascona had sat on the scaffolding day after day, eventually dressing as a workman, sharing their bread and wine, getting to *know* every inch of the ceiling and the altar wall and the *Last Judgement* fresco. The Commission had reported, but nothing had been done. Business as usual at the Vatican!

He altered the position of his bed so that his head was towards the altar. He did not want to think of the *Last Judgement*. Fine, terrifying, but the Christ was not his Christ—too commanding, too much an obvious man of action. A general, an organizer, that was Michelangelo's Christ. Whereas his was gentler, more of a healer, more forgiving, surely?

He lay in the darkness, his eyes fixed on the panels he could not see, recreating the scenes he knew so well, that had been imprinted on his soul some twenty years before. The drunken Noah, a rare scene of comedy, and to the right of that panel his favourite of all the *ignudi*—the naked men holding medallions. A boy-man, infinitely inviting, conscious of his own appeal—delightful, inexhaustible.

But then he let his eyes sweep across the darkness of the ceiling and fix on the central panel. The masterpiece among masterpieces in his opinion. The moment of creation. And in particular Adam: beautiful, languid before full awakening, holding hope and promise for all of Cardinal Pascona's tastes. And so like his own beloved Sandro! The yearning face, the beautiful body—it was as if Sandro had been created for him in the likeness of our first father.

6   ROBERT BARNARD

He slept.

He awoke next morning to the sounds of disturbance—shouting, choking, vomiting and groans. He leapt from his bed. The Chapel was now fully illuminated and he ran to a little group of cardinals in a circle, gazing down in consternation. In the middle of the circle, writhing on the stone floor, lay the obese figure of Cardinal Borromei. Pascona could only make out one word of his cries.

"Aiudo!"

He immediately took control.

"Help he must have. Summon a doctor!"

Cardinal da Ponti stepped in with his usual statement of the obvious.

"You know we cannot allow one in. The best we can do is get him out of the Chapel to be treated there."

"And that of course is what we must do."

"But he should be here. Today might be the day when ... And it might just be indigestion."

Cardinal Pascona paused, momentarily uncertain.

"Cardinal Borromei is someone who enjoys the pleasures of the table. But there have been few pleasures of the table on offer here in the Chapel. Spartan fare every day so far. The wine last night was disgraceful ..."

He was about to put aside his indecision and insist that the tormented man be removed and treated outside the Chapel when the whole body of cardinals was transfixed by a terrible cry. The flabby body on the floor arched, shuddered, then sank motionless back to the floor.

"È morto?" someone whispered.

Dead was certainly what he seemed to be. Cardinal Pascona knelt by the body, felt his chest, then put his face and ear close to his mouth. He shook his head.

"Dead," he said. "We must—with the permission of the Cardinal Chamberlain—remove the body. Then we must put out a statement to the waiting crowds. I think it should specify a *colpo di sangue* as the cause of death. A stroke."

"But it didn't look—"

Cardinal Pascona put up his hand and turned to Cardinal da Ponti.

"I specify that because it is easily understood by the least sophisticated member of the crowd. Everyone there will have had some family member—a grandfather, an uncle—who has died of a stroke. It is a question of getting the message across with the least fuss. If some amendment is needed after the doctors have examined him—so be it. But I do not anticipate any need for it."

"But a death in Conclave—and *such* a death: a man who, if I might put it so, was the *favourite*."

Cardinal Pascona was brusque in the face of such tastelessness.

"But what could be more likely? A large number of elderly men, shut up together in an unhealthy atmosphere, on a diet which—to put it mildly—is not what they are accustomed to. And the candidate in a state of extreme excitement. It has happened before, and it is a wonder that it hasn't happened more often."

The thought that there had been a precedent excited them all.

"Oh, *has* it happened?" asked Cardinal Morosi. Pascona ignored him. He addressed the whole College, summoned from their beds or from the *prima Colazione* by that terrible last cry.

"The need now is to remove, with all appropriate ceremonies and mourning, the deceased brother, and then to continue our deliberations. The world awaits our decision. We must not be found wanting at this crisis in our history, and that of the world."

It struck nobody that for Cardinal Pascona "the whole world" meant effectively the Western half of Europe. They busied themselves, summoned the waiting monks who were clearing away the breakfast things, and had Cardinal Borromei removed from the Chapel. Having someone willing and able to take charge enlivened their torpid and aging intellects, and they settled down to discussions in groups with zest and vigour. What was a death, after all, to men for whom it was only a beginning?

Yet, oddly, the initiative and address of Cardinal Pascona had an effect on the discussion which was the reverse of what might have been expected. Put bluntly (which it never was in this Conclave), it might have been summed up in the phrase "Who does he think he is?" The fact that they were all grateful to him for taking charge, were conscious that he had avoided several hours of indecision and in-fighting, did not stop them asking by what right he had taken control at that moment of crisis in the affairs of the Church.

"He takes a great deal too much on himself," one of them said.

And it did his chances no good at all.

For though Pascona was *papabile*, he was not the only one to be so. There had been a minor stir of interest in the early days of the Conclave in favour of Cardinal Fosco, Archbishop of Palermo. He was a man who had no enemies, usually spoke sense, and was two or three years on the right side of senility. True there was one thing against him. This was not the fact that he had something of an obses-sion about a rag-tag-and-bobtail collection of criminals in his native island. It was the Mafia this, the Mafia that the whole time, as if they were set to take over the world. That the cardinals shrugged off and suffered. But what was really against him in many cardinals' eyes was his height. He was barely five feet tall (or 1.5 metres, as the newfan-gled notions from France had it). Just to be seen by the crowd he would have to have several cushions on his throne when he went out on the balcony to bless the masses. It was likely to cause ridicule, and the Church was aware, since Voltaire, of how susceptible it was to wit, irony and proletarian laughter.

But suddenly, it seemed, Fosco was a decidedly desirable candidate.

Pascona watched and listened in the course of the day. Ballot succeeded ballot, with nothing so democratic as a declaration of the result. But the word went around: the vote for Fosco was inching up, that for Pascona slowly ebbing away. The Cardinal went around, talking to all and sundry with imperturbable urbanity—amiable to all, forswearing all controversy. He was among the first to collect his frugal evening meal. By then his mood was contemplative. He gazed benignly at the monks serving the *stufato*, then looked down in the direction of the Cardinal from Palermo. As he helped himself to the rough bread there was the tiniest of nods from one of the cowled heads.

"Dear Michelangelo, help one of your greatest admirers and followers," he prayed that night on his narrow bed. "Let the vote go to a follower of yourself, as well as a devout servant of Christ."

Before he slept his mind went not to the *ignudi*, nor to the awakening Adam in the great central panel, but away from the altar to the expelled Adam as, with Eve, and newly conscious of sin, he began the journey out of Paradise.

He smiled, as thoughts of Sandro and their forthcoming pleasures when they were united again warmed his aging body.

The morning was not a repeat of the day before.

Over breakfast there was talk, and before long it was time to take the first test of opinion, to find out whether straw should be added to the burning voting slips to make black smoke, or whether it should be omitted, to the great joy of the crowds in St. Peter's Square as the white smoke emerged. One cardinal had not risen from his bed, and he was the most important of all. Cardinal da Ponti went to shake him awake, then let out a self-suppressed gasp of dismay. The cardinals, oppressed by fear and horror, hurried over to the bed.

Cardinal Fosco lay, a scrap of humanity, dead as dead. He looked as if he could be bundled up, wrapped in a newssheet, and put out with the rubbish from the Conclave's meals.

"*Dio mio!*"

The reactions were various, but more than one started to say what was on everybody's minds.

"But he too was the—"

This time they hesitated to use the term from horse-racing. But one by one, being accustomed to bow to authority, they looked towards the man who, only yesterday, had set the tone and solved the problem of what should be done. Somehow Pascona, with his long experience of curias and conclaves, knew they would do that, and was ready. He cleared his throat.

"Fellow cardinals. Friends," he began. "Let us pray for our friend whom God has called to himself. And let us at the same time pray for guidance." There was a murmur of agreement, along with one or two murmurs of something else. After a minute's silence Cardinal Pascona resumed, adopting his pulpit voice.

"I believe we all know what must be done. I think God has spoken to us, each and every one, at this crisis moment—spoken as God always does speak, through the silent voice of our innermost thoughts." The cardinals muttered agreement, though most of them had had nothing in the interval for silent prayer that could honestly be called a thought. "He has told us that what must be thought of first at this most difficult moment is the Church: its good name, its primacy and power, and its mission to bring to God all waverers, all wrong-doers, all schismatics. It is the Church and its God-given mission that must be in the forefront of all our minds."

There was a more confident buzz of agreement.

"We are in a crisis, as I say, in the history of ours, the one true church. In the world at large doubt, distrust and rebellion seethe, distracting the minds of the unlettered, provoking the discontent of the educated. Ridicule, distrust of long-held beliefs, rebellion against the position of the natural leaders of Society—all these evils flourish today, as never before. At such a point any event—even an innocent and natural occurrence such as we witness here—" he gestured towards the human scrap on the bed—"will be taken up, seized upon as a cause of scandal and concern, distorted and blackened with the ingenuity of the Devil himself, who foments and then leads all such discontents and rebellions. Let us make our minds up, let us make our choice quickly, let us conceal what has happened until such a time as it can be announced and accepted as the natural event which in truth it was."

This time there was a positively enthusiastic reception for his words.

"Come my friends," resumed Pascona, delighted at the effect of his words, "let us get down to business. Let us vote, and let us vote to make a decision, and to present to the world a front of unity and amity. And let us treat our friend here with the respect that a lifetime of faithful service demands. Put a blanket over him."

It worked like a charm. A blanket was thrown over the body of the dead Cardinal Fosco, leaving his head showing. Not dead, only resting seemed to be the message. The living cardinals proceeded to a vote, and even before the last vote was in and counted it was clear that the straw would no longer be required: the smoke would be pure white.

The excitement was palpable. While they remained cloistered in the Chapel the other cardinals thumped Pascona on the shoulder and indulged in such bouts of kiddishness as were possible to a collection of men dominated by the dotards. After five minutes of this, and as the Chapel was penetrated by sounds of cheering from crowds in the Square, the new Pope proceeded to the passageway from the Chapel to St. Peter's, pausing at the door to look towards the altar and the massive depiction of the *Last Judgement* behind it. Magnificent, but quite wrong, he thought. And perhaps a silly superstition at that.

Then he proceeded into the upper level of the great Church, then along towards the door leading on to the balcony. He stopped before the throne, raised on poles like a sedan chair. He let the leading cardinals, led by the Cardinal Chamberlain and helped by the monks who had serviced the Conclave, robe him and bestow on him all the insignia of his new office. He behaved with impeccable graciousness.

"What name has Your Holiness decided to be known by?" asked the Chamberlain. Pascona paused before replying.

"I am conscious of the links of my mother's family to this great, this the *greatest* office. The fame of Alexander VI will live forever, but the name is too precious for me, and for the Church, for me to assume it. In truth it would be a burden. I shall leave that sacred name to my ancestor, and I shall take the name of the other Pope from her family. I shall be known as Calixtus IV."

The Chamberlain nodded.

From the Square there came sounds. Someone, perched somewhere, with good eyesight, must have been able to see through the open door of the balcony. A whisper, then a shout, had gone round.

"It's the Borgia. The Borgia!"

The fame of his mother's family easily eclipsed that of his father's. The tone of the shouts had fear in it, but also admiration, anticipation. What a time Alexander VI's had been! Bread and circuses, and lots of sex. Calixtus IV smiled to himself, then ascended the throne. As he was about to nod to the four carriers to proceed through the door and on to the balcony, one of the monks came forward with a bag of small coins, to scatter to the crowd below. As he handed the bag to the Pope, he raised his head and the cowl slipped back an inch or two. There was the loved face: the languid eyes of Michelangelo's Adam, the expression of newly awakened sensuality, and underneath the coarse robe the body, every inch of which Calixtus knew so well. He took the bag, and returned his gaze.

"*Grazie,* Ales-*Sandro,*" he said.

Stepping Up

by

MARK BILLINGHAM

I WAS NEVER CUT OUT to be the centre of attention. I never asked for it. I never enjoyed it.

Some people love all that though, don't they? They need to be the ones having their heads swelled and their arses licked; pawed at and fawned over. Some people are idiots, to be fair, and don't know what to do with themselves if they aren't smack in the middle of the fucking action.

Of course, there were times when I *did* get the attention, whether I wanted it or not. When things were going well and I won a title or two. I got it from men *and* women then, and you won't hear me say there was anything wrong with that. Blokes wanting to shake your hand and tarts queuing up to shake your other bits and pieces, well nobody's complaining about that kind of carry on, are they?

But *this*, though …?

The doctor had been banging on about exercise, especially as I was having such a hard time giving up the fags. It would help to get the old ticker pumping a bit, he said. Get your cholesterol down and shift some of that weight which isn't exactly helping matters, let's face it. You used to box a bit, didn't you, he said, so you shouldn't find it too difficult to get back in the swing of it. To shape up a little.

Piece of piss, I told him, then corrected myself when he smiled and straightened his tie.

"Cake, I meant. Sorry, Doc. Piece of cake."

I don't know which one of us I was kidding more.

I got Maggie's husband, Phil, to give me a hand and fetch some of my old gear out of the loft. We scraped the muck off the skipping rope and hung the heavy bag up in the garage. I thought I would be able to ease myself back into it, you know? Stop when it hurt and build things up slowly. Trouble was it hurt all the time, and the more I tried, the more angry I got that I'd let myself go to shit so badly; that I'd smoked so many fags and eaten so much crap and put so much booze away down the years.

"It was mum's fault for spoiling you," Maggie said. "If she hadn't laid on meat and two veg for you every day of her life, you *might* have learned to do a bit more than boil a bleeding egg. You wouldn't have had to eat so many take-aways after she'd gone …"

Once my eldest gets a bee in her bonnet, that's it for everyone. It was her that had nagged me into going to the doctor's in the first place, getting some exercise or what have you. So, even though the boxing training hadn't worked out, the silly mare had no intention of letting the subject drop.

One day, in the pub with Phil, I found out that I wasn't the only one getting it in the neck.

"Help me out, for Christ's sake," he said. "She won't shut up about it, how she thinks you're going to drop dead any bloody second. Just do *something*."

"Snooker?"

"Funny."

"Fucked if I know, Phil. There's nothing I fancy."

I'd told Mags I wouldn't go jogging and that was all there was to it. I've been there, so I know how that game works; shift a few pounds and fuck up your knee joints at the same time. Tennis wasn't for the likes of me and the same went double for golf, even though a couple of blokes in the pub had the odd game now and again. The truth is, I know you have to stick at these kind of things, and that's never been my strong suit. I had a talent in the ring, so I didn't mind putting the hours in, and besides, I had more … drive back then, you know? Day after day on a golf course or a sodding tennis court, just so I wouldn't look like a twat every time I turned out, didn't sound much fun.

Plus, there weren't that many people I could think of to play with, tell you the truth …

"There's a class," Phil said. "Down our local leisure centre. One night a week, that's all."

"Class?"

"Just general fitness, you know. Look it's only an hour and there's a bit of a drink afterwards. You'll be doing me a favour."

"Hmmm." I swallowed what was left of a pint and rolled my eyes, and that was it. That's how easily a misunderstanding happens and you get yourself shafted.

I should have twigged a couple of weeks later when Maggie came by to pick me up. On the way there I asked her where Phil was, was he coming along later and all that, and she looked at me like I'd lost the plot. See, I thought it was *his* class, didn't I? A few lads jumping about, maybe a quick game of five-a-side and then a couple of beers afterwards. When I walked out of that changing room in my baggy shorts and an old West Ham shirt, I felt like I'd been majorly stitched up. There was Maggie, beaming at me, and a dozen or so other women, and all of them limbering up in front of these little plastic steps.

A fucking *step* class. Jesus H …

And not just women, either, which didn't help a great deal. There were a couple of men there to witness the humiliation, which always makes it worse, right? You know what I'm talking about. There were three other fellas standing about, looking like each of them had gone through what I was going through right then. An old boy, a few years on me, who looked like he'd have trouble *carrying* his step. A skinny young bloke in a tight top, who I figured was queer straight away, and a fit-looking sort who I guessed was there to pull something a bit older and desperate.

Looking around, trying my hardest to manage a smile, I could see that most of the women were definitely in that category. Buses, backends, you see what I'm getting at? I swear to God, you wouldn't have looked twice at any of them.

Except for Zoe.

I MET HER FORTY-ODD YEARS BACK, when I was twenty-something and I'd won a few fights; one night when I was introduced to some people at a nightclub in Tottenham. Frank Sparks was doing pretty well himself at that time, and there were all sorts of faces hanging about. I wasn't stupid. I knew full well what was paying for Frank's Savile Row suit and what have you, and to tell you the truth, it never bothered me.

There weren't many saints knocking around anywhere back then.

Frank was friendly enough, and for the five or ten minutes I sat at his table, it was like we were best friends. He was one of those blokes with a knack for that, you know? Told me he was following my career, how he'd won a few quid betting on me, that kind of thing. He said there were always jobs going with him. All sorts of bits and pieces, you know, if things didn't work out or I jacked the fight game in or whatever.

I can still remember how shiny his hair was that night. And his teeth, and the stink of Aramis on him.

She was the sister of this bloke I used to spar with, and I'd seen her waiting for him at the back of the gym a few times, but it wasn't until that night in Tottenham that I started to pay attention. She was all dressed up, with different hair, and I thought she was an actress or a stripper. Then we got talking by the bar and she laughed and told me she was just Billy's sister. I said she was better looking than any of the actresses or strippers that were there guzzling Frank's champagne, and she went redder than the frock she was wearing, but I knew she liked it.

I saw her quite a bit after that in various places. She started going out with one of Frank Sparks' boys and wearing a lot of fancy dresses. I remember once, I'd just knocked this black lad over in the fourth round at Harringay. I glanced down, sweating like a pig, and she was sitting a few rows back smiling up at me, and the referee's count seemed to take forever.

YOU JUST GET ON THE THING, then off again; up and down, up and down, one foot or both of them, in time to the fucking music. Simple as that. You can get back down the same way you went up, or sometimes you turn and come down on the other side, and now and again there's a bit of dancing around the thing, but basically … you climb on and off a plastic step.

I swear to God, that's it.

Maybe, that first time, I should have just turned and gone straight back in that changing room. Caught a bus home. Maggie had that look on her face though, and I thought walking out would be even more embarrassing than staying.

So, I decided to do it just the once, for Mags, and actually, it didn't turn out to be as bad as I expected. It was a laugh as it goes, and at least I could do it without feeling like it was going to kill me. It was a damn sight harder than it looked, mind you, make no fucking mistake about *that*. I was knackered after ten minutes, but what with there being so many women in the class, I didn't feel like I had to compete with anyone, you know what I mean?

Ruth, the woman in charge, seemed genuinely pleased to see me when I showed up again the second week and the week after that. She teased me a bit, and I took the piss because she had one of those microphone things on her ear like that singer with the pointy tits. They were *all* quite nice, to be honest. A pretty decent bunch. I'd pretend to flirt a bit with one or two of the women, and I'd have a laugh with Anthony, who didn't bang on about being gay like a lot of them do, you know?

Even Craig seemed all right, to begin with.

The pair of us ended up next to each other more often than not, on the end of the line behind Zoe. Him barely out of breath after half an hour; me, puffing and blowing like I was about to keel over. The pair of us looking one way and one way only, while she moved, easy and sweet, in front of us.

One time, he took his eyes off her arse and glanced across at me. I did likewise, and while Ruth was shouting encouragement to one of the older ladies, the cheeky fucker winked, and I felt the blood rising to my neck.

I remember an evening in the pub with Maggie and Phil, a few weeks in, and me telling Maggie not to be late picking me up for the class. To take the traffic into account. She plastered on a smartarse smile, like she thought she'd cottoned on to something, but just said she was pleased I was enjoying myself.

IT ONLY TOOK ONE LUCKY PUNCH from a jammy Spaniard for every- thing to go tits up as far as the fighting was concerned. I had a few more bouts, but once the jaw's been broken, you're never quite as fearless. Never quite as stupid as you need to be.

Stupid as I had been, spending every penny I'd ever made, quick as I'd earned it.

With the place I was renting in Archway, the payments on a brand new Cortina, and sweet FA put by, it wasn't like I had a lot of choice when it came to doing door work for Frank Sparks. Besides, it was easy money, as it went. A damn sight less stressful than the ring anyway, and I certainly didn't miss the training. Your average Friday-night drunk goes down a lot easier than a journeyman light-heavyweight, but the fact is, I couldn't have thrown more than half a dozen punches in nearly a year of it. I was there to look as if I was useful, see, and that was fine. Like I said before, I was happier in the background and I think Frank was pretty pleased with the way I was handling things, because he asked me if I fancied doing a spot of driving.

And that's when I started seeing a lot more of her.

She wasn't married yet, but I'd heard it was on the cards. Her boyfriend had moved up through the ranks smartish, and was in charge of a lot of Frank's gambling clubs. Classy places in Knightsbridge and Victoria with cigarette girls and what have you. She used to go along and just sit in the corner drinking and looking tasty, but some of these sessions went on all night, and she'd always leave before her old man did.

So, I started to drive her.

I started to ask to drive her; volunteering quietly, you know? There were a couple of motors on call and we took it in turns at first. Then, after a few weeks, she asked for me, and it sort of became an arrangement.

In the image I still have of her, she's standing on a pavement, putting on a scarf as I indicate and drift across towards the curb. She's clutching a handbag. She waves as I pull up, then all but falls into the back of the Jag; tired, but happy as Larry to be on the way home.

In reality of course she was thinner, and drunker. Her eyes got flatter and the bleach made her hair brittle, and she was always popping some pill or other. That crocodile handbag rattled with them. The smile was still there though; lighting up what was left of her. The same as it was when I looked down through the ropes that time and saw her clapping.

When I felt as though I was the one who'd had the breath punched out of me.

HOW BLOODY OLD AM I?

It's a fair question, but I don't suppose it really matters. *Too* old, that's the point, isn't it? Too old to smoke and not worry about it; to put on a pair of socks without sitting down; to think about running for a bus.

Too old to feel immortal …

Like you'd expect, it was mostly Diet Coke and fizzy water in the pub afterwards. I had orange juice and lemonade myself, for the first week anyway, but Zoe drank beer from the off.

Ruth didn't give a monkey's what anyone did once the class was over, but there was one woman who didn't approve; who clearly enjoyed having another reason to dislike Zoe. She was glaring across at her from an adjoining table, one night a few weeks in, and I was giving it the old cow back with bells on.

"Maybe she's jealous because she secretly fancies you," Zoe whispered.

I pulled a face. "Christ, don't put me off me pint!"

She really enjoyed that one. Her laugh was low and dirty, and it still amazes me really, to think of it coming out of a mouth like hers. A face like that.

"She's just dried-up and bitter," I said. "Hates it that she's doing this to try and change how she looks, or what have you, while others don't really have to."

Zoe smiled, leaned a shoulder against mine. "Some people just don't know how to have fun, you know? Think their bodies are temples and all that."

"My body's more of a slaughterhouse these days," I said.

She enjoyed that one too. It felt fantastic to make her laugh. We shared a big packet of crisps, which really wound up the old bag on the next table. She left early, while Zoe and me and a few of the others stayed until they rang the bell, same as always. Ruth and Anthony were giggling by the jukebox, and Maggie kept an eye on me from a table near the door, where she sat clutching her mobile phone, waiting for Phil to come and pick the pair of us up.

"Why *do* you come?" I asked her. "It's not like you need to lose weight or anything. You seem pretty fit …"

She leaned a shoulder into mine. "You're sweet."

"I'm just saying."

She took another swig from her bottle. "I'm lazy," she said. "I need to make myself do things, get out and do something a bit off the wall, you know? Anyway, it's a laugh, don't you reckon?"

I did reckon, and I told her.

"I work in a stupid office," she said. "The people there are all right I suppose, but I don't want to see them after work or whatever. I think it's good to meet people who aren't anything like you are. People with different lives, you know? I tried a French class, but it was too hard, and the teacher was a bit stuck-up. This is much better. Much."

She had a voice it was easy to listen to. She certainly wasn't posh, but there wasn't really an accent either. Just soft and simple, you know?

"What about you?" she asked.

I said I was basically there to keep Maggie happy, and to try and get at least some of the old fitness back. I mentioned that I used to box a bit and she said that she could see it. That it was in the way I carried myself.

I had to hide my face in my glass, and I'd all but downed the rest of the pint by the time the blush had gone away.

"Someone needed a drink," she said.

There was a burst of high-pitched laughter from Ruth and Anthony, and when I looked across, I could see that Maggie had gone from a smartarse smile to something that looked like concern.

I went up to get the two of us refills, and exchanged nods with Craig who was deep in conversation with the woman behind the bar. He was smoking which made me deeply fucking envious. If Maggie hadn't been sitting by the door, I might well have ponced one.

"Enjoying yourself?" he said.

When the barmaid went to fetch the drinks, Craig span slowly round and leaned back against the bar. He looked across at Zoe for a minute, more maybe, then turned to me. His face said 'I *know*, I couldn't agree more, mate. But look at *me* and look at *you*.'

Or he might just have been asking me to pass the ashtray.

Oh fuck it, who knows?

HER OLD MAN *had a place in Battersea, on the edge of the park. There was a night I was driving her back from one of Frank's casinos, down through Chelsea towards Albert Bridge, when she started asking me all manner of funny questions.*

"Do you actually like any of them, though? Are any of them really your mates if you think about it?"

The gin had slowed her up a little. Thickened her voice, you know?

"Any of who?" I said.

She jerked a thumb back towards where we'd come from. "That lot. The boys. They're just people you work with, aren't they? Just blokes you knock around with, right, and I don't suppose any of them give a toss about you, either. Wouldn't you say?"

I shrugged and watched the road. It wasn't like I'd never heard her talking bollocks before. Next time she spoke, her voice had more breath in it, and she kept saying my name, but that's something else people do when they've had a couple, isn't it?

"It's just London, right?" she said. "Frank doesn't own stuff anywhere else, does he?"

"I don't know. I don't think so."

"I don't think so either."

"He's been up north on business, definitely. Manchester ..."

"It was only a few times," she said. "Just to meet people."

"Birmingham as well. I drove him to the station."

"He was just looking though, that's what I heard. Nothing came of it. It's all here really, don't you reckon?" She said my name again, slow with a question in it. Wanting me to agree with her. "Everyone's here, aren't they?"

I heard a song I knew she liked come on the radio and I turned it up for her. That girl who did Eurovision without any shoes on. I was waiting for her to start singing along, but when I looked in the rear-view I could see that her eyes were closed.

Her head was tipped back and her mascara was starting to run.

THINGS REALLY STARTED TO GO PEAR-SHAPED the time Zoe turned up looking like she did and Craig didn't turn up at all.

I hadn't admitted it to myself, not really, that the two of them were seeing each other outside the class, but I had to stop being stupid and face facts when I saw her walk in like that. It was like I suddenly knew all sorts of things at once. I knew that they'd got together, that everyone else had probably sussed it a damn sight faster than me, and I knew exactly what had happened to her face.

In class, I stepped that bit faster than usual. I stamped on and off that bastard thing, and it was automatic, like I could do it all day and I wasn't even thinking. Ruth said how well I was doing and when Zoe smiled at me, encouraging, I had to look away.

Afterwards, she didn't turn towards the pub with the rest of us, and when I saw that she was heading for the car-park, I moved to go after her. Maggie took hold of my arm and said something about getting a table. I told her I'd be there in a minute, to get one in for me, but she didn't look very happy.

I tried to get a laugh out of Zoe when I caught her up; made out like I was knackered, you know, from chasing after her, but she didn't seem to really go for it. "Do you not fancy it tonight then?" I said. "Not even a swift half?"

She was fetching her car-keys from her bag. Digging around for them and keeping her head down. "I've got an early start in the morning," she said. "New boss, you know?"

I nodded, told her that one wasn't going to hurt.

She caught me looking, not that I was trying particularly hard not to. It was like a plum that someone had stepped on around her cheek, and the ragged edges of it were the colour of a tea-stain. There was a half-moon of blood in her eye.

"I didn't know there was a cupboard open and I turned round into it," she said. "Clumsy bitch …"

"Shush …"

"I actually knocked myself out for a few seconds."

"Listen, it's all right," I said.

"What is?"

"Come and have one quick drink," I said. "Who am I going to share my salt and vinegar crisps with if you don't?"

It was as though she suddenly noticed that my hand was on her wrist, and she looked down and took half a step back. "I'll see you next week."

"Look after yourself." It came out as a whisper. I didn't really know what else to say.

She pressed the button on her car-keys and when the lights flashed and the alarm squawked, I saw her jump slightly.

In the pub, I couldn't blame Maggie for being off with me. I sat there with a face like a smacked arse, and I couldn't have said more than three words to anyone. After half an hour I'd had enough, and I asked her to call Phil, get him to fetch us early. That didn't go down too well either because she was having a laugh with Anthony, but I just wasn't in the mood for it.

As we were leaving, Ruth raised her glass and said something about me being her star pupil.

Zoe didn't turn up at all the following week.

WE WERE DRIVING, same as always. Seemed like, when it came to being close or what have you, that was the only time we ever really saw each other. Me in the front, her in the back.

"Go slowly, will you?" she'd said when she got in.

Obviously I was going to do what she wanted, right, and it was raining like a bastard anyway, so it wasn't like I could have put my foot down. Still, I wanted to get back to her place as quickly as I could. Don't get me wrong, I hated it when she got out of the car, hated it, but lately I'd taken to stopping somewhere after I'd dropped her off; soon as I'd got round the corner sometimes.

I'd pull over in the dark and sit quiet for a minute. Reach for a handkerchief. Throw one off the wrist, while I could still smell her in the car.

Sounds disgusting, I know, but it didn't feel like it back then.

I drove, slow like she wanted along the Brompton Road and down Sydney Street. Staring at the jaguar leaping from the end of the bonnet; the road slick, sucked up beneath it.

When I turned up the radio to drown out the squeak of the wipers, she leaned forward and asked me to switch it off.

Pissing down now. Clattering on the roof like tacks.

"There's people been talking to me," she said.

"What people?"

"They've been going over my options, you know?"

"What options?"

"The choices I've got."

I looked in the mirror. Watched her take a deep breath when she saw that I didn't understand.

"Billy's fucked up," she said. "Silly bugger's really gone and dropped himself in it."

Her brother. My ex-sparring partner. Always had been a bit of a tearaway.

"What's he done?" I asked. Prickles on my neck.

"He went for some flash Maltese fucker with a knife ..."

"Jesus."

"Didn't really do him too much harm, but they'll happily bump it up to attempted murder. Put him away for a few years unless I decide to help."

I knew who she was talking about now. Coppers were the same as anyone else at the end of the day. There were plenty of stupid ones, but enough of them with brains to make life interesting.

"There's only Billy and me," she said. "The bastards know how close we are."

She started to cry just a little bit then. I went inside my jacket for the handkerchief I'd be using later on, but she'd already pulled one out from her handbag. I'd heard the pills rattling as she rummaged for it.

I was taking us over the bridge by now. Gliding across it. The lights swung like a necklace up ahead and the rain was churning up the water on either side of me.

"It's not like I know a fat lot."

"Fat lot about what?" I said, but it was obvious what she was banging on about.

"Frank. Frank's business. All that."

All that.

"Obviously they think I know something." She raised her hands, let them drop down with a slap on to the leather seat. "Maybe I know enough."

Course she did; she wasn't stupid, was she? Enough to get her little brother out of the shit and herself slap bang in it.

I wanted to slam on the anchors and stop the car right there on the bridge. To reach into the back and shake her until her fillings came loose. I wanted to tell her that her brother was a pissy little waster, and that she shouldn't be such a daft bitch, and to say absolutely fuck all to anyone about fuck all.

I was the one that kept my mouth shut though, wasn't I? The one who just gripped the wheel that little bit tighter and manoeuvred the car like I was on my driving test. Checking the wing mirrors, hands at ten to two, watching my speed.

"I need to go away," she said.

Ten to two. Both eyes on the road …

"Somewhere abroad might be best. Somewhere hot, near the sea if I get a choice, but it might not have to be that far. Maybe Scotland or somewhere. I've tucked a bit away and I'm sure I can make a few bob later on. I can type for a kick-off."

Slowing for lights. No more than a mile away from the flat on the edge of the park. Checking the mirror and feathering the brake; moving down through the gears.

"I just don't feel like I can do it on my own, you know? That's the only bit I'm scared of, if I'm honest. It's pathetic I know, relying on someone like that, but the thought of nobody being there with me makes me feel sick, like I'm looking over the edge of something. I don't mean sex or whatever, but that's not out of the question either. It's mostly about having someone around who gives a toss, do you know what I mean?"

Waiting for the amber, willing that fucker to change.

"Someone who worries …"

She said my name, and it felt like I had something thick and bitter in my gullet.

Neither of us said anything else after that, but we were only five minutes away from the flat by then. The silence was horrible, make no mistake about that, but it just lay there until it sort of flattened out into something we were both willing to live with. Until she asked me to turn the radio back up.

When we pulled up, I got out to open her door, then climbed back in again quick without saying much of anything. When I looked up she was standing there by my door. She had an umbrella, but she never even bothered getting it out; just stood there getting pissed on, with the rain bringing her hair down, until thick strands of it were dead and dark against her face.

She was saying something. I couldn't hear, but I was looking at her mouth, same as always.

I thought she said: "It doesn't matter, Jimmy."

Then she put the tips of two fingers to her lips and pressed them against my window. They went white where she pressed, and I could still see the mark for a few minutes after I drove away.

I didn't stop the car where I normally did. Just kept going for a bit, trying to swallow and think straight. I drove up through Nine Elms and pulled in a mile or so past the power station.

Sat there and stared out across the shitty black river until it started to get light.

CRAIG LOOKED CONFUSED as much as anything when I walked round the corner. Grinned at him. It was half way through the morning, and him and a couple of older women in blouses and grey skirts had come out the back entrance of the bank for a crafty smoke.

"All right, mate?"

"Ticking along," I said. "You?"

It must have been there in my face or the way I spoke, because I saw the women stubbing out pretty long fag-ends, making themselves scarce. Neither of them so much as looked at him before they buggered off.

Craig watched his colleagues go, seemed to find something about it quite funny. He turned back to me, taking a drag. Shook his head.

"Sorry, mate. It's just a bit strange you turning up here, that's all. How d'you know where I worked?"

"Zoe must have said, last time she came to the class, you know?"

Something in his face that I couldn't read, but I didn't much care.

"How's she doing, anyway?" I said.

"Er, she's good, yeah."

"It was a shame she stopped coming, really. We were all saying how she made the rest of us work a bit harder, trying to keep up."

"She just lost interest I think. Me an' all, to be honest." Then a look that seemed to say they were getting their exercise in other ways, and one back from me that tried and failed to wipe it off his face.

It was warm and he was in shirt-sleeves. I was sweating underneath my jacket so I slipped it off, threw it across my arm.

"Are you feeling OK?"

"I'm fine," I said.

"You've gone a bit red."

I nodded, looked at the sweat patches under his arm and the pattern on his poxy tie.

He flicked his fag-end away. "Listen, I've got to get back to work …"

"Right."

"I'll say hello to Zoe, shall I?"

"How's her face?"

That took the smile off the fucker quick enough. Put that confused look back again, like he didn't know his arse from his elbow.

"It's fine now," he said. "She's all gorgeous again."

"Nasty, that was. Not seen many shiners worse than that one. Door wasn't it?"

"Cupboard door."

"Yeah, that's what's she said."

"She forgot it was open and turned round fast, you know? Listen—"

I was just looking at him by now.

"What?"

I knew I still had *that*. You never lose the look.

"What's your problem?"

Breathing heavily, a wheeze in it. For real some of it, like the red face, but I'd bunged a bit extra on top, you know. Laid it on thick just to get his guard down.

"I think maybe you ought to piss off now," he said.

I bent over, suddenly; dropped the jacket like I might be in some trouble. He stepped across to pick it up, like I wanted him to, which was when I swung a good hard right at his fat, flappy mouth.

I NEVER HAD HER in the car again after that night. Only saw her a couple of times as it goes, and even then, when she looked over, I always found something fascinating in the pattern on the carpet or counted the bits of chewing gum squashed onto the pavement.

Spineless cunt.

She went away some time after. I suppose I should say I was told she went away. It's an important distinction, right? Told like there was actually nothing to tell, but also like there wasn't much point me asking about it again or wasting any money on postcards.

A few years ago we were having a meal, me and one of the lads I used to knock about with back then. You have a curry and a few pints and you talk about the old days, don't you? You have a laugh.

Until her name came up.

He was talking about what he thought had happened and why. Wanted to know what I thought had gone on; fancied getting my take on it. You used to know her pretty well, didn't you, he said. That's what I heard, anyway. You used to be quite close to her is what somebody told me.

I had a mouthful of ulcers at that time. It was when my old girl was suffering, you know, and the doctor reckoned it was the stress of her illness that was causing it. Ulcers and boils, I had.

When he mentioned her name the first time, I started to chew on a couple of those ulcers. Gnawing into those bastards so hard it was making my eyes water, though my mate probably thought it was the vindaloo.

You used to be quite close to her, he said.

I bit the fuckers clean out then, two or three of them. I remember the noise I made, people in the restaurant turning round. I bent down over the table, coughing, and I spat them out into a serviette.

That more or less put the tin lid on our conversation, which was all right by me. My mate didn't say too much of anything after that. Well, we'd been talking about what was happening with me and my old lady before, and when he saw the blood in the napkin, maybe he was confused, you know, thought I was the one with the lung cancer.

IT WASN'T THE BEST PUNCH I ever threw, but it made contact and I concentrated on the blood that was running down his shirt-front as he swung me round and pushed me against the wall.

"What the fuck's your game, you silly old bastard?"

I tried to nut him and he leaned back, his arms out straight, holding me hard against the bricks.

"Take it easy."

I thought I felt something crack in his shin when I kicked out at him. I tried to bring my leg up fast towards his bollocks, but the pain in his leg must have fired him right up and his fists were flying at me.

It was no more than a few seconds. Just flailing really like kids, but Christ, I'd forgotten how much it hurts.

Every blow rang and tore and made the sick rise up. I felt something catch me and rip behind the ear; a ring maybe. Stung like fuck.

I swore, and kept kicking. I shut my eyes.

My fists were up, but it was all I could do to protect my face, so I can't have been doing him a lot of damage.

But I was trying.

When the gaps between the punches got a bit longer, I tried to get a dig or two in, just to keep my fucking end up, you know? That was when the background went blurry, and his face started to swim in front of me, but as far as I'm concerned that was down to the pain in my arm. It had bugger all to do with any punishment I might have taken.

The fucker hit me one more time, when I dropped my fists to clutch at my arm. It was all over then, more or less. But it was the pain in my chest that put me down, and not that punch.

Not the punch.

THERE'S ALWAYS A *SOMETHING* that gets you from one place to the next, right? That you're chasing after in some way, shape or form. Granted, some people are happy enough to let themselves get pissed along like a fag-end in a urinal, and yes, I know that some poor bastards are plain unlucky, but still …

OK, then, to be fair there's *usually* a something. For me, anyway, is all I'm saying. If I'm centre of attention right now, for all the wrong reasons, it isn't really down to anyone else, and I'm not going to feel sorry for myself.

That's more or less what I tried to say to Maggie and Phil when they came in, but they were in no fit state to listen, and I don't think I made myself very clear.

Fuck, they're *at* me again …

Loads of them, and I thought there was supposed to be a shortage. Poking and prodding. Talking over me like I'm deaf as well as everything else.

It's not pain exactly.

It's warm and wet and spreading through my arms and legs like I'm sinking into a bath or something. They've got those things you see on the TV out again, like a pair of irons on my chest. Like they're going to iron out my wrinkles.

Now they're going blurry either side of me, same as that fucker did when I was punching him. The sound's gone funny too.

And clear as you like, I can see her face. The stain around her eye and the purple bruise. The hair lying dead against her cheek in the rain.

Music as I step up and step up. Some tuneless disco rubbish while I'm sneaking looks at her in that tight leotard thing and Ruth bawls at me through her stupid microphone.

As I step up off the beach. With the sea coming up on to the sand behind me. Noisy, like the sigh of someone who's sick of waiting for something.

Stepping up on to the hot pavement, where she's stood waiting with a drink. That mouth, and her hair darker now and she looks magnificent. And we lean against each other and drink sangria at one of them places where you can sit outside.

The music's still getting louder, so I ask them to turn it up.

That song she likes on the radio.

The bird with the bare feet.

"I wonder if one day that, you'll say that you care.
If you say you love me madly, I'll gladly be there ... "

Angle of Investigation

by

MICHAEL CONNELLY

THEN

"This is all because of Manson," Eckersly said.

Bosch looked across the seat at his training partner, unsure of what he meant.

"Charles Manson?"

"You know, Helter Skelter and all of that shit," Eckersly explained. "They're still scared."

Bosch nodded, though he still didn't get it. He looked out the windshield. They were heading south on Vermont through territory unfamiliar to him. It was only his second day with Eckersly and his second on the job. Almost all of the neighbourhoods in Wilshire were unfamiliar to him but that was okay. Eckersly had been working patrol in the division for four years. He knew the neighbourhoods.

"Somebody doesn't answer the phone and back east they think Squeaky and the rest of Charlie's girls have broken in and chopped them up or something," Eckersly continued. "We get a lot of these 'check the lady' calls. Four years now and people still think L.A.'s been turned over to the nuts."

Bosch had been away from the world when Manson and his people had done their thing. So he didn't have a proper read on what the murders had done to the city. When he had come back from Vietnam he had felt an edginess in L.A. that had not been there before he left. But he didn't know whether that was because of the changes he had been through or the city had been through.

South of Santa Monica they took a left on Fourth Street and Bosch started reading numbers off of mailboxes. In a few seconds Eckersly pulled the squad car to a stop in front of a small bungalow with a driveway down the side to a single garage in the back. They both got out, Bosch taking his nightstick out of the plastic pipe on the door and sliding it into the ring on his equipment belt.

"Oh, you won't need that," Eckersly said. "Unless you want to use it to knock on the door."

Bosch turned back to the car to put the club back.

"Come on, come on," Eckersly said. "I didn't tell you to put it back. I just said you wouldn't need it."

Bosch hustled to catch up to him on the flagstone walkway leading to the front door. He walked with both hands on his belt. He was still getting used to the weight and the awkward bulk of it. When he had been in Vietnam his job was to go into the tunnels. He'd kept his body profile as trim as possible. No equipment belt. He carried all of his equipment—a flashlight and a forty-five—in his hands.

Eckersly had sat out the war in a patrol car. He was eight years older than Bosch and had that many years on the job. He was taller and heavier than Bosch and carried the weight and bulk of his equipment belt with a practised ease. He signalled to Bosch to knock on the front door, as if that took training. Bosch knocked three times with his fist.

"Like this," Eckersly corrected.

He rapped sharply on the door.

"Police, Mrs. Wilkins, can you come to the door, please?"

His fist and voice had a certain authority. A tone. That was what he was trying to teach his rookie partner.

Bosch nodded. He understood the lesson. He looked around and saw that the windows were all closed but it was a nice cool morning. Nobody answered the door.

"You smell that?" he asked Eckersly.

"Smell what?"

The one area where Bosch didn't need any training from Eckersly was in the smell of death. He had spent two tours in the dead zone. In the tunnels the enemy put their dead into the walls. Death was always in the air.

"Somebody's dead," Bosch said. "I'll check around back."

He stepped off the front porch and took the driveway to the rear of the property. The odour was stronger back here. To Bosch, at least. The dispatcher on the radio had said June Wilkins lived alone and hadn't answered phone calls from her daughter in Philadelphia for seven days.

There was a small enclosed yard with a clothesline stretching from the corner of the garage to the corner of the house. There were a few things hanging on the line, two silk slips and other women's undergarments. There were more clothing items on the ground, having fallen or been blown off the line. The winds came up at night. People didn't leave their clothes on the line overnight.

Bosch went to the garage first and stood on his toes to look through one of two windows set high in the wooden door. He saw the distinctive curving roofline of a Volkswagen Beetle inside. The car and the clothing left out on the line seemed to confirm what the odour already told him. June Wilkins had not left on a trip, simply forgetting to tell her daughter back east. She was inside the house waiting for them.

He turned to the house and went up the three concrete steps to the back door stoop. There was a glass panel in the door that allowed him to see into the kitchen and partway down a hallway that led to the front rooms of the house. Nothing seemed amiss. No rotting food on the table. No blood on the floor.

He then saw on the floor next to a trash can a dog food bowl with flies buzzing around the rotting mound inside it.

Bosch felt a quickening of his pulse. He took his stick out and used it to rap on the glass. He waited but there was no response. He heard his partner knock on the front door again and announce once more that it was the police.

Bosch tried the knob on the back door and found it unlocked. He slowly opened the door and the odour came out with an intensity that made him drop back off the stoop.

"Ron!" he called out. "Open door in the back."

After a moment he could hear his partner's equipment belt jangling as he hustled to the back, his footfalls heavy. He came around the corner to the stoop.

"Did you—oh, shit! That is rank! I mean, that is *bad!* We've got a DB in there."

Bosch nodded. He assumed DB meant dead body.

"Should we go in?" he asked.

"Yeah, we better check it out," Eckersly said. "But wait a second."

He went over to the clothesline and yanked the two slips off the line. He threw one to Bosch.

"Use that," he said.

Eckersly bunched the silken slip up against his mouth and nose and went first through the door. Bosch did the same and followed him in.

"Let's do this quick," Eckersly said in a muffled voice.

They moved with speed through the house and found the DB in the bathroom off the hallway. There was a clawfoot bathtub filled to the brim with still dark water. Breaking the surface were two rounded shapes at either end with hair splayed out on the water. Flies had collected on each as if they were lifeboats on the sea.

"Let me see your stick," Eckersly said.

Not comprehending, Bosch pulled it out of his belt ring and handed it to his partner. Eckersly dipped one end of the stick into the tub's dark water and prodded the round shape near the foot of the tub. The flies dispersed and Bosch waved them away from his face. The object in the water shifted its delicate balance and turned over. Bosch saw the jagged teeth and snout of a dog break the surface. He involuntarily took a step back.

Eckersly moved to the next shape. He probed it with the stick and the flies angrily took flight, but the object in the water did not move so readily. It was not free floating like the dog. It went down deep like an iceberg. He dipped the stick down further and then raised it. The misshapen and decaying face of a human being came up out of the water. The small features and long hair suggested a woman but that could not be determined for sure by what Bosch saw.

The stick had found leverage below the dead person's chin. But it quickly slipped off and the face submerged again. Dark water lapped over the side of the tub and both of the police officers stepped back again.

"Let's get out of here," Eckersly said. "Or we'll never get it out of our noses."

He handed the nightstick back to Bosch and pushed past him to the door.

"Wait a second," Bosch said.

But Eckersly didn't wait. Bosch turned his attention back to the body and dipped the stick into the dark water again. He pulled it through the water until it hooked something and he raised it up. The dead person's hands came out of the water. They were bound at the wrists with a dog collar. He slowly let them back down into the water again.

On his way out of the house, Bosch carried the stick at arm's length from his body. In the back yard he found Eckersly standing by the garage door, gulping down fresh air. Bosch threw the slip he had used to breathe through over the clothesline and came over.

"Congratulations, boot," Eckersly said, using the department slang for rookie. "You got your first DB. Stick with the job and it will be one of many."

Bosch didn't say anything. He tossed his nightstick onto the grass—he planned to get a new one now—and took out his cigarettes.

"What do you think?" Eckersly asked. "Suicide? She took the pooch with her?"

"Her hands were tied with the dog's collar," Bosch said.

Eckersly's mouth opened a little but then he recovered and became the training officer again.

"You shouldn't have gone fishing in there," he said sternly. "Suicide or homicide, it's not our concern anymore. Let the detectives handle it from here."

Bosch nodded his contrition and agreement.

"What I don't get," his partner said, "is how the hell did you smell that at the front door?"

Bosch shrugged.

"Used to it, I guess."

He nodded toward the west, as if the war had been just down the street.

"I guess that also explains why you're not puking your guts out," Eckersly said. "Like most rookies would be doing right now."

"I guess so."

"You know what, Bosch. Maybe you've got a nose for this stuff."

"Maybe I do."

NOW

Harry Bosch and his partner, Kiz Rider, shared an alcove in the back corner of the Open-Unsolved Unit in Parker Center. Their desks were pushed together so they could face each other and discuss case matters without having to talk loudly and bother the six other detectives in the squad. Rider was writing on her laptop, entering the completion and summary reports on the Verloren case. Bosch was reading through the dusty pages of a blue binder known as a murder book.

"Anything?" Rider asked without looking up from her screen.

Bosch was reviewing the murder book in consideration of it being the next case they would work together. He hadn't chosen it at random. It involved the 1972 slaying of June Wilkins. Bosch had been a patrolman then and had been on the job only two days when he and his partner at the time had discovered the body of the murdered woman in her bathtub. Along with the body of her dog. Both had been held under water and drowned.

There were thousands of unsolved murders in the files of the Los Angeles Police Department. To justify the time and cost of mounting a new investigation there had to be a hook. Something that could be sent through the forensic databases in search of a match: fingerprints, ballistics, DNA. That was what Rider was asking. Had he found a hook?

"Not yet," he answered.

"Then why don't you quit fooling with it and skip to the back?"

She wanted him to skip to the evidence report in the back of the binder and see if there was anything that could fit the bill. But Bosch wanted to take his time. He wanted to know all the details of the case.

It had been his first DB. One of many that would come to him in the department. But he'd had no part in the investigation. He had been a rookie patrolman at the time. He had to watch the detectives work it. It would be years in the department before it was his turn to speak for the dead.

"I just want to see what they did," he tried to explain. "See how they worked it. Most of these cases, they coulda-shoulda been cleared back in the day."

"Well, you have till I'm finished with this summary," Rider cautioned. "After that we better get flying on something, Harry."

Bosch blew out his breath in mock indignation and flipped a large section of summaries and other reports over in the binder until he got to the back. He then flipped the tab marked forensics and looked at an evidence inventory report.

"Okay, we've got latents, you happy?"

Rider looked up from her computer for the first time.

"That could work," she said. "Tied to the suspect?"

Bosch flipped back into the evidence report to look for the summary ascribed to the specific evidence logged in the inventory. He found a one-paragraph explanation that said a right palm print had been located on the wall of the bathroom where the body had been found. Its location was sixty-six inches from the floor and seven inches right of centre above the toilet.

"Well ..."

"Well, what?"

"It's a palm."

She groaned.

It was not a good hook. Databases containing palm prints were relatively new in law enforcement. Only in the last decade had palm prints been seriously collected by the FBI and the California Department of Justice. In California there were approximately 10,000 palms on file compared to the millions of fingerprints. The

Wilkins murder was thirty-three years old. What were the chances that the person who had left a palm print on the wall of the victim's bathroom would be printed two decades or more later? Rider had answered that one with her groan.

"It's still worth a shot," Bosch said optimistically. "I'll put in the SID request."

"You do that. Meantime, as soon as I'm done here I'll see if I can find a case with a real hook we can run with."

"Hold your horses, Kiz. I still haven't run any of the names out of the book. Give me today with this and then we'll see."

"Not good to get emotionally involved, Harry," she responded. "The Laura syndrome, you know."

"It's not like that. I'm just curious. It was sort of my first case."

"No, it wasn't."

"You know what I mean. I remember thinking she was an old lady when the detectives gave me the run down on it. But she was only forty-six. I was half her age so I thought anybody forty-six was old and had a good run of it. I didn't feel too bad about it."

"Now you do."

"Forty-six was too young, Kiz."

"Well, you're not going to bring her back."

Bosch nodded.

"I know that."

"You ever seen that movie?"

"*Laura?* Yeah, I've seen it. Detective falls in love with the murder victim. You?"

"Yeah, but it doesn't hold up too well. Sort of a parlour room murder case. I liked the Burt Reynolds take on it in the eighties. *Sharky's Machine.* With Rachel Ward. You seen it?"

"I don't think so."

"Had Bernie Casey in it. When I was a youngster I always thought he was a fine looking man."

Bosch looked at her with a raised eyebrow.

"Before I switched teams," she said. "Then I rented it a couple years ago and Bernie didn't do it for me. I liked Rachel Ward."

Her bringing up her sexuality seemed to put an uneasiness between them. She turned back to her computer. Bosch looked down at the evidence report.

"Well, we know one thing," he said after a while. "We're looking for a left-handed man."

She turned back to looking at him.

"How do you know that?"

"He put his right hand on the wall over the toilet."

"And?"

"It's just like a gun, Kiz. He aimed with his left hand because he's left-handed."

She shook her head dismissively.

"Men ..."

She went back to work on her computer and Bosch went back to the murder book. He wrote down the information he would need to give to the latent prints section of the Scientific Investigation Division in order for a tech to look up the palm print in their files. He then asked if Rider wanted him to pick her up a coffee or a soda from the cafeteria while he was floating around the building. She said no and he was off. He took the murder book with him.

BOSCH FILLED OUT the comparison request forms and gave them to a print tech named Larkin. He was one of the older, more experienced techs. Bosch had gone to him before and knew that he would move quickly with the request.

"Let's hope we hit the jackpot, Harry," Larkin said as he took the forms.

It was true that there was always a sense of excitement when you put an old print into a computer and let it ride. It was like pulling the lever on a slot machine. The jackpot payoff was a match, a cold hit in police parlance.

After leaving SID Bosch went to the cafeteria for a cup of coffee and to finish reading through the murder book. He decided he could handle the constant background noise of the cafeteria better than he could handle the intrusive questions from Kiz Rider.

He understood where his partner was coming from. She wanted to choose their cases dispassionately from the thousands that were open. Her concern was that if they went down a path in which Bosch was exorcizing ghosts or choosing cases with personal attachments then they would burn out sooner rather than later.

But Bosch was not as concerned. He knew that passion was a key element in any investigation. Passion was the fuel that kept his fire burning. So he purposely sought the personal connection or short of that, the personal outrage, in every case. It kept him locked in and focused. But it wasn't the Laura syndrome. It wasn't the same as falling in love with a dead woman. By no means was Bosch in love with June Wilkins. He was in love with the idea of reaching back across time and catching the man who had killed her.

THE KILLING of June Wilkins was as horrible as it was cunning. The woman was bound hands and feet with a dog collar and a leash and then drowned in the tub. Her dog was treated to the same death. The autopsy showed no bruising or injuries on Wilkins suggestive of a struggle. But analysis of blood and tissue samples taken during autopsy indicated that she had been drugged with a substance called ketamine hydrochloride, a veterinary sedative that acts as a paralyzing agent. It meant that it was likely that Wilkins was conscious but unable to move her muscles to fight or defend herself when she was submerged in the water in the bathtub. Analysis of the dog's blood found that the animal had been drugged with the same substance.

A textbook investigation followed the murder but it ultimately led to no arrests or the identification of a suspect. June Wilkins had lived alone. She had been divorced and had one child, a college student who went to school in Philadelphia. June worked as an assistant to a casting director in an office in a building at Hollywood and Vine, but had been on a two-week vacation at the time of her death.

No evidence was found that she'd had an ongoing romantic relationship or that there were any hard feelings from a former relationship. It appeared to neighbours, acquaintances, co-workers and family members that the love of her life was her dog, a miniature poodle named Frenchy.

The dog was also the focus of her life. He was of pure breed and the only travel Wilkins did in the year most recent to her death had been to attend dog shows in San Diego and Las Vegas where Frenchy competed. The second bedroom of her bungalow had been converted into a grooming salon where ribbons from previous dog shows lined the mirrors.

The original investigation was conducted by partners Joel Speigelman and Dan Finster of Wilshire Division. They began with a wide focus on Wilkins' life and then narrowed in on the dog. The use of the veterinary drug by the killer and the killing of the dog suggested some connection to that aspect of the victim's life. But that avenue soon hit a dead end when the detectives found no indication of a dispute or difficulty involving Wilkins in the competitive world of dog shows. They learned that Wilkins was considered a harmless novice in that world and was neither taken seriously by her competitors nor competitive in nature herself. The detectives also learned that Frenchy, though a purebred animal, was not a champion calibre dog, and the ribbons he took home were more often than not awarded for simply competing, not winning.

The detectives changed their theory and began to consider the possibility that the killer had purposely misdirected the investigation toward the dog show angle. But what the correct angle of investigation should have been was never determined. The investigation stalled. The detectives never linked the palm print on the bathroom wall to anyone, and lacking any other solid leads the case was pushed into the wait-and-see pile. That meant it was still on the desk but the investigators were waiting for something to break—an anonymous tip, a confession or even another murder of similar method. But nothing came up and after a year it was moved off the table and into the archives to gather dust.

While reading through the binder Bosch had written down a list of names of people who had come up in the investigation. These included family members, neighbours and co-workers of the victim as well as acquaintances she encountered through veterinary services and the dog shows she attended.

In most cases Speigelman and Finster had asked for birth dates, addresses and even social security numbers while conducting their interviews. It was standard operating procedure. Their thoroughness back then would now help Bosch when he ran every name from the list through the crime computer.

When finished reading Bosch closed the murder book and looked at his list. He had collected thirty-six names to run through the computer. He knew he had the names and the palm print and that was about it. He could also run ketamine hydrochloride through the computer to see if it had come up in any other investigations since 1972.

He decided that if nothing came out of the three angles of investigation he would drop the case, admit defeat to his partner and press on to the next case that had a valid hook.

As he finished his coffee, he thought about the palm print. There had been no analysis of it other than to measure its location on the wall and have it ready for comparison to suspects that might come up in the investigation. But Bosch knew that there was more to it than that. If the print was sixty-six inches up the wall that meant it was likely that the man who had left it was over six feet tall. He came to this conclusion because he knew that if the suspect leaned forward to brace himself while urinating he would probably put his hand on the wall at shoulder level or slightly above. Add a foot in height for his neck and head and you have a man ranging from six-two to six-six in total height. A tall left-handed man.

"That narrows it down," Bosch said to himself, noting his own sarcasm.

He got up, dumped his coffee cup and headed out of the cafeteria. On the elevator up to five he thought about the times he had leaned his hand on the wall over a toilet. He was either drunk, middle-of-the-night sleepy or burdened by something besides a heavy bladder. He wondered which of these conditions had fit the tall, left-handed man.

Most of the police department's civilian offices were on the fifth floor along with the Open-Unsolved Unit. He passed the unit's door and went down to the Personnel Department. He picked up contact information on Speigelman, Finster and his old partner, Eckersly. In years past such information would be jealously guarded. But under order from the office of the Chief of Police, detectives with the Open-Unsolved Unit were given carte blanche because it was part of investigatory protocol to contact and interview the original investigators of a case that had been re-opened.

Eckersly, of course, was not one of the original investigators. He was only there on the morning they had found the lady in the tub. But Bosch thought it might be worth a call to see if he remembered that day and had any thoughts on the re-investigation of the case. Bosch had lost contact with Eckersly after he completed his street training and was transferred out of Wilshire Division. He assumed he was no longer on the job and was not mistaken. Eckersly had pulled the plug at twenty years and his pension was sent to the town of Ten Thousand Palms, where he was the police chief.

Nice move, Bosch thought. Running a small town police force in the desert and collecting an LAPD pension on the side. Every cop's dream.

Bosch also noted the coincidence of Eckersly now living in a town called Ten Thousand Palms and the fact that Bosch was currently running an angle through a database of 10,000 palm prints.

RIDER WAS NOT AT HER DESK when Bosch got back to the unit. There was no note of explanation left on his desk and he figured she had simply taken a break. He sat at her desk and looked at her laptop. She had left it on but had cleared the screen before leaving the office. He pulled the list of names out of the murder book and connected to the National Crime Index Computer. He didn't have his own computer and was not highly skilled in the use of the Internet and most law enforcement databases. But the NCIC had been around for years and he knew how to run names on it.

All thirty-six names on his list would have been run through existing databases in 1972 and cleared. What he was looking for now was whether any of the thirty-six people had been arrested for any kind of significant or similar crime in the years after the June Wilkins murder.

The first name he entered came back with multiple hits for drunk driving arrests. This didn't particularly get Bosch excited but he circled the name on the list anyway and moved on. No hits came up on the next seven and he crossed them out. The next name after that scored a hit with an arrest for disturbing the peace. Bosch circled it but again was not feeling the tug of a hook yet.

The process continued with most of the names coming up clean. It wasn't until he entered the twenty-ninth name that Bosch looked at the screen and felt a tightness grip his chest.

The twenty-ninth name was Jonathon Gillespie. He had been described in the murder book as a dog breeder who sold miniature poodles in 1972. He had sold the dog Frenchy to June Wilkins two years before her death and was interviewed by Speigelman and Finster when they were trying to run down the dog show angle on the case. According to the NCIC records, Gillespie went to prison on a rape charge in 1981 and served six years in prison. He was now a registered sexual offender living in Huntington Beach. There had been no other arrests since 1981. He was now sixty-eight years old.

Bosch underlined the name on the list and wrote down the case number. It had an LAPD prefix. Though he immediately wanted to go to work on Gillespie, he finished running the rest of the names through the NCIC database first. He got two more hits, one for a DUI and one for a hit-and-run accident with injuries. He circled the names to keep with his procedure but was not excited about them.

Before signing out of the NCIC system he switched over to the crime-tracking database and entered ketamine hydrochloride into the search window. He got several hits back, all within the last fifteen years, and learned that the substance was being used increasingly as a date rape drug. He scrolled through the cases listed and didn't see anything that linked them to June Wilkins. He logged off the database to begin his pursuit of Jonathon Gillespie.

Closed cases from 1981 had gone to microfiche archives and the department was slowly moving backwards and entering case information into the department's computerized database. But 1981 was too far back. The only way Bosch would be able to look at the sexual assault case that had sent Gillespie to prison would be to go to the records archives, which were housed over at Piper Tech, the storage facility and air squadron base at the edge of downtown.

Bosch went to his side of the desk and wrote a note to Rider telling her he had come up with a hot angle and was chasing it through Piper Tech. The phone on his desk started to ring. He finished the note and grabbed the phone while standing up to reach the note over to Rider's desk.

"Open-Unsolved, this is Bosch."

"Harry, it's Larkin."

"I was just going to call you."

"Really? Why?"

"I have a name for you."

"Funny, I have a name for you. I matched your palm and you're not going to like it."

"Jonathon Gillespie."

"What?"

"Jonathon Gillespie."

"Who is that?"

"That's not your match?"

"Not quite."

Bosch sat back down at his desk. He pulled a pad over in front of him and got ready to write.

"Who did you come up with?"

"The palm print belonged to one of ours. Guy must have left it while at the crime scene. Sorry about that."

"Who is it?"

"The name is Ronald Eckersly. He worked for us sixty-five to eighty-five, then he pulled the pin."

Bosch almost didn't hear anything else Larkin said.

"... shows that he was a patrol lieutenant upon retirement. You could go to personnel and get a current location if you need to talk to him. But it looks like he might have just screwed up and put his hand on the wall while he was at the scene. Back then they didn't know anything about crime scene protocol and some of these guys would—hell, about twenty years ago I was dusting a homicide scene and one of the detectives who had been there all night started frying an egg in the dead guy's kitchen. He said, 'he ain't gonna miss it and I'm goddamn starved.' You believe that? So no matter how hard you drill into them not to touch—"

"Thanks, Larkin," Bosch said. "I've got to go."

Bosch hung up, grabbed the note off Rider's desk and crumpled it in his hand. He took his cell phone off his belt and called Rider's cell number. She answered right away.

"Where are you?" Bosch asked.

"Having a coffee."

"You want to take a ride?"

"I've got the case summary to finish. A ride where?"

"Ten Thousand Palms."

"Harry, that's not a ride. That's a journey. That's at least ninety minutes each way."

"Get me a coffee for the road. I'll be right down."

He hung up before she could protest.

ON THE DRIVE OUT Bosch told Rider about the moves he had made with the case and how the print had come back to his old partner. He then recounted the morning he and Eckersly had found the lady in the tub. Rider listened without interrupting, then had only one question at the end.

"This is important, Harry," she said. "You are dealing with your own memory and you know from case experience how faulty memories can be. We're talking thirty-three years ago. Are you sure there wasn't a moment that Eckersly couldn't have put his hand on the wall?"

"Yeah, like he might've leaned against the wall and taken a leak while I didn't notice."

"I'm not talking about taking a leak. Could he have leaned against the wall when you found the body, like he got grossed out or sick and leaned against the wall for support?"

"No, Kiz. I was in that room the whole time he was. He said, 'Let's get out of here,' and *he* was the first one out. He did not go back in. We called in the detectives and then stood outside keeping the neighbours away when everybody showed up."

"Thirty-three years is a long time, Harry."

Bosch waited a moment before responding.

"I know this sounds sad and sick but your first DB is like your first love. You remember the details. Plus ..."

He didn't finish.

"Plus what?"

"Plus my mother was murdered when I was a kid. I think it's why I became a cop. So finding that woman—my second day on the job—was sort of like finding my mother. I can't explain it. But what I can tell you is that I remember being in that house like it was yesterday. And Eckersly never touched a thing in there, let alone put his hand on the wall over the toilet."

Now she was silent for a long moment before responding.

"Okay, Harry."

TEN THOUSAND PALMS was on the outskirts of Joshua Tree. They made good time and pulled into the visitor parking space in front of the tiny police station shortly before one. They had worked out how they would handle Eckersly in the last half hour of the drive.

They went in and asked a woman who was sitting behind a front counter if they could speak with Eckersly. They flashed the gold and told her they were from the Open-Unsolved Unit. The woman picked up a phone and communicated the information to someone on the other end. Before she hung up a door behind her opened and there stood Ron Eckersly. He was thicker and his skin a dark and worn brown from the desert. He still had a full head of hair that was cut short and silver. Bosch had no trouble recognizing him. But it didn't appear that he recognized Bosch.

"Detectives, come on back," he said.

He held the door and they walked into his office. He was wearing a blue blazer with a maroon tie over a white shirt. It did not appear to Bosch that he had a gun on his belt. Maybe in a little desert town a gun wasn't needed.

The office was a small space with LAPD memorabilia and photographs on the wall behind the desk. Rider introduced herself and shook Eckersly's hand and then Bosch did the same. There was a hesitation in Eckersly's shake and then Bosch knew. Instinctively, he knew. He was holding the hand of June Wilkins' killer.

"Harry Bosch," Eckersly said. "You were one of my boots, right?"

"That's right. I came on the job in seventy-two. We rode Wilshire patrol for nine months."

"Imagine that, one of my boots coming back to see me."

"Actually, we want to talk to you about a case from seventy-two," Rider said.

As planned, she took the lead. They took seats and Bosch once again tried to determine if Eckersly was armed. There was no telltale bulge beneath the blazer.

Rider explained the case to Eckersly and reminded him that he and Bosch had been the patrol officers who discovered the body. She asked if he remembered the case at all.

Eckersly leaned back in his desk chair, his jacket falling to his sides and revealing no holster or weapon on his belt. He looked for an answer on the ceiling. Finding nothing, he leaned forward and shook his head.

"I'm drawing a blank, Detectives," he said. "And I'm not sure why you would come all the way out here to ask an old patrol dog about a DB. My guess is we were in and out, and we cleared the way for the dicks. Isn't that right, partner?"

He looked at Bosch, his last word a reminder that they had once protected each other's back.

"Yes, we were in and out."

"But we have information—newly developed information—that you apparently had a relationship with the victim," Rider said matter of factly. "And that this relationship was not brought to light during the initial investigation."

Eckersly looked closely at her, wondering how to read the situation. Bosch knew this was the pivotal moment. If Eckersly was to make a mistake, it would be now.

"What information?" Eckersly asked.

"We're not at liberty to discuss it, Chief," Rider responded. "But if you have something to tell us, tell us now. It would be best for you to clear this up before we go down the road with it."

Eckersly's face cracked into a smile and he looked at Bosch.

"This is a joke, right? Bosch, you're putting her up to this, right?"

Bosch shook his head.

"No joke," Bosch said. "You're in a spot here, Chief."

Eckersly shook his head as if uncomprehending of the situation.

"You said Open-Unsolved, right? That's cold case stuff. DNA. This a DNA case?"

Bosch felt things tumbling into place. Eckersly had made the mistake. He had taken the bait and was fishing for information. It wasn't what an innocent man would do. Rider felt it too. She leaned toward his desk.

"Chief, do you mind if I give you a rights warning before we go further with this?"

"Oh, come on," Eckersly protested. "You can't be serious. What relationship?"

Rider read Eckersly the standard Miranda rights warning from a card she pulled out of a pocket in her blazer.

"Chief Eckersly, do you understand your rights as I have read them?"

"Of course I understand them. I've only been a cop for forty years. What the hell is going on here?"

"What's going on is that we are giving you the opportunity to explain the relationship you had with this woman. If you choose not to cooperate then it's not going to work out well for you."

"I told you. There was *no* relationship and you can't prove there was. That body had been in that tub for a week. From what I heard, it practically came apart when they were taking it out of there. You got no DNA. Nobody even knew about DNA back then."

Rider made a quick glance toward Bosch and this was her signal that he could step in if he wanted. He did.

"You worked Wilshire for four years before that morning," Bosch said. "Did you meet her on patrol? When she was out walking the dog? Where did you meet her, Chief? You told me you were working solo for four months before I was put in the car with you. Is that when you met her? When you were out working alone?"

Eckersly angrily grabbed the phone out of its cradle on his desk.

"I still know some people at Parker Center. I'm going to see if they are aware of what you two people are doing. Coming to *my* office to accuse me of this crap!"

"If you call anyone, you better call your lawyer," Bosch said.

Eckersly slammed the phone back down into its cradle.

"What do you want from me? I did not know that woman. Just like you, I saw her for the first time floating with her dog in the bathtub. First *and* last time. And I got out of there as fast as I goddamn could."

"And you never went back in."

"That's right, boot. I never went back in."

There, they had him.

"Then how come your palm print was on the wall over the toilet?"

Eckersly froze. Bosch read his eyes. He remembered the moment he had put his hand on the wall. He knew they had him.

Eckersly glanced out the office's only window. It was to his left and it offered a view of a fire department equipment yard. He then looked back at Bosch and spoke in a quiet voice.

"You know how often I wondered when somebody like you would show up here … how many years I've been waiting?"

Bosch nodded.

"It must have been a burden," he said without sympathy.

"She wanted more, she wanted something permanent," Eckersly said. "Christ, she was fifteen years older than me. She was just a patrol pal, that's what we called them. But then she got the wrong idea about things and when I had to set her straight she said she was going to make a complaint about me. She was going to go to the captain. I was married back then. I couldn't …"

He said nothing else. His eyes were downcast. He was looking at the memory.

Bosch could put the rest of it together. Eckersly hatched a plan that would throw the investigation off, send it in the wrong direction. His only mistake being the moment he put his hand on the wall over the toilet.

"You have to come with us now, Chief," Rider said.

She stood up. Eckersly looked up at her.

"With you?" he said. "No, I don't."

With his right hand he pulled open the desk drawer in front of him and quickly reached in with his left. He withdrew a black steel pistol and brought it up to his neck.

"No!" Rider yelled.

Eckersly pressed the muzzle deep into the left side of his neck. He angled the weapon upward and pulled the trigger. The weapon's contact against his skin muffled the blast. His head snapped back and blood splattered across the wall of police memorabilia behind him.

Bosch never moved in his seat. He just watched it happen. Pretty soon the woman from the front counter came running in and she screamed and held her hands up to her mouth.

Bosch turned and looked at Rider.

"That was a long time coming," he said.

LAURA WAS ALREADY RENTED at Eddie's Saturday Matinee so Bosch rented *Sharkey's Machine* instead. He watched it at home that night while drinking beer and eating peanut butter sandwiches, and trying to keep his mind away from what had happened in Eckersly's office. It wasn't a bad movie, though he could see almost everything coming. Burt Reynolds and Bernie Casey made pretty good cops and Rachel Ward was the call girl with a heart of gold. Bosch saw what Burt saw in her. He thought he could easily fall in love with her too. Call girl or not, dead or alive.

Near the end of the movie there was a shootout and Bernie Casey got wounded. Bleeding and out of bullets, he used a Zen mantra to make himself invisible to the approaching shooter.

It worked. The shooter walked right by him and Bernie lived to tell about it. Bosch liked that. At the end of the movie he remembered that moment the best. He wished there was a Zen chant he could use now so Ronald Eckersly could just walk on by him too. But he knew there was no such thing. Eckersly would take his place with the others that came to him at night. The ones he remembered.

Bosch thought about calling Kiz and telling her what he thought of the movie. But he knew it was too late and she would get upset with him. He killed the TV instead and turned off the lights.

Just Friends

by

JOHN HARVEY

THESE THINGS I REMEMBER about Diane Adams: the way a lock of her hair would fall down across her face and she would brush it back with a quick tilt of her head and a flick of her hand; the sliver of green, like a shard of glass, high in her left eye; the look of surprise, pleasure and surprise, when she spoke to me that first time—"And you must be, Jimmy, right?": the way she lied.

It was November, late in the month and the night air bright with cold that numbed your fingers even as it brought a flush of colour to your cheeks. London, the winter of fifty-six, and we were little more than kids then, Patrick, Val and myself, though if anyone had called us that we'd have likely punched him out, Patrick or myself at least, Val in the background, careful, watching.

Friday night it would have been, a toss-up between the Flamingo and Studio 51, and on this occasion Patrick had decreed the Flamingo: this on account of a girl he'd started seeing, on account of Diane. The Flamingo a little more cool, a little more style; more likely to impress. Hip, I suppose, the word we would have used.

All three of us had first got interested in jazz at school, the trad thing first, British guys doing an earnest imitation of New Orleans; then, for a spell, it was the Alex Welsh band we followed around, a hard-driving crew with echoes of Chicago, brittle and fast, Tuesday nights the Lyttelton place in Oxford Street, Sundays a club out at Wood Green. It was Val who got us listening to the more modern stuff, Parker 78s on Savoy, Paul Desmond, the Gerry Mulligan Quartet.

From somewhere, Patrick got himself a trumpet and began practising scales and I kicked off playing brushes on an old suitcase while saving for the down payment on a set of drums. Val, we eventually discovered, already had a saxophone—an old Selmer with a dented bell and a third of the keys held on by rubber bands: it had once belonged to his old man. Not only did he have a horn, but he knew how to play. Nothing fancy, not yet, not enough to go steaming through the changes of "Cherokee" or "I Got Rhythm" the way he would later, in his pomp, but tunes you could recognize, modulations you could follow.

The first time we heard him, really heard him, the cellar room below a greasy spoon by the Archway, somewhere the owner let us hang out for the price of a few coffees, the occasional pie and chips, we wanted to punch him hard. For holding out on us the way he had. For being so damned good.

Next day, Patrick took the trumpet back to the place he'd bought it, Boosey and Hawkes, and sold it back to them, got the best price he could. "Sod that for a game of soldiers," he said, "too much like hard bloody work. What we need's a bass player, someone half-decent on piano, get Val fronting his own band." And he pushed a bundle of fivers into my hand. "Here," he said, "go and get those sodding drums."

"What about you?" Val asked, though he probably knew the answer even then. "What you gonna be doin'?"

"Me?" Patrick said. "I'm going to be the manager. What else?"

And, for a time, that was how it was.

Private parties, weddings, bar mitzvahs, support slots at little clubs out in Ealing or Totteridge that couldn't afford anything better. From somewhere Patrick found a pianist who could do a passable Bud Powell, and, together with Val, that kept us afloat. For a while, a year or so at least. By then even Patrick could see Val was too good for the rest of us and we were just holding him back; he spelled it out to me when I was packing my kit away after an all-nighter in Dorking, a brace of tenners eased down into the top pocket of my second hand Cecil Gee jacket.

"What's this?" I said.

"Severance pay," said Patrick, and laughed.

Not the first time he paid me off, nor the last.

But I'm getting ahead of myself.

That November evening, we'd been hanging round the Bar Italia on Frith Street pretty much as usual, the best coffee in Soho then and now; Patrick was off to one side, deep in conversation with a dark-skinned guy in a Crombie overcoat, the kind who has to shave twice a day and wore a scar down his cheek like a badge. A conversation I was never meant to hear.

"Jimmy," Patrick said suddenly, over his shoulder. "A favour. Diane, I'm supposed to meet her. Leicester Square tube." He looked at his watch. "Any time now. Go down there for me, okay? Bring her to the club; we'll see you there."

All I'd seen of Diane up to that point had been a photograph, a snapshot barely focused, dark hair worn long, high cheek bones, a slender face. Her eyes—what colour were her eyes?

"The tube," I said. "Which exit?"

Patrick grinned. "You'll get it figured."

She came up the steps leading on to Cranbourne Street and I recognized her immediately; tall, taller than I'd imagined, and in that moment—Jesus!—so much more beautiful.

"Diane?" Hands in my pockets, trying and failing to look cool, blushing already. "Patrick got stuck in some kind of meeting. Business, you know? He asked me to meet you."

She nodded, looking me over appraisingly. "And you must be Jimmy, right?" Aside from that slight flaw, her eyes were brown, a soft chocolaty brown, I could see that now.

Is it possible to smile ironically? That's what she was doing. "All right, Jimmy," she said. "Where are we going?"

When we got to the Flamingo, Patrick and Val had still not arrived. The Tony Kinsey Quintet were on the stand, two saxes and rhythm. I pushed my way through to the bar for a couple of drinks and we stood on the edge of the crowd, close but not touching. Diane was wearing a silky kind of dress that clung to her hips, two shades of blue. The band cut the tempo for "Sweet and Lovely," Don Rendell soloing on tenor.

Diane rested her fingers on my arm. "Did Patrick tell you to dance with me, too?"

I shook my head.

"Well, let's pretend that he did."

Six months I suppose they went out together, Diane and Patrick, that first time around, and for much of that six months, I rarely saw them one without the other. Towards the end, Patrick took her off for a few days to Paris, a big deal in those days, and managed to secure a gig for Val while he was there, guesting at the *Chat Qui Pêche* with René Thomas and Pierre Michelot.

After they came back I didn't see either of them for quite a while: Patrick was in one of his mysterious phases, doing deals, ducking and weaving, and Diane—well, I didn't know about Diane. And then, one evening in Soho, hurrying, late for an appointment, I did see her, sitting alone by the window of this trattoria, the Amalfi it would have been, on Old Compton Street, a plate of pasta in front of her, barely touched. I stopped close to the glass, raised my hand and mouthed "Hi!" before scuttling on, but if she saw me I couldn't be sure. One thing I couldn't miss though, the swelling, shaded purple, around her left eye.

A week after this Patrick rang me and we arranged to meet for a drink at the Bald Faced Stag; when I asked about Diane he looked through me and then carried on as if he'd never heard her name. At this time I was living in two crummy rooms in East Finchley—more a bed-sitter with a tiny kitchen attached, the bathroom down the hall—and Patrick gave me a lift home, dropped me at the door. I asked him if he wanted to come in but wasn't surprised when he declined.

Two nights later I was sitting reading some crime novel or other, wearing two sweaters to save putting on the second bar of the electric fire, when there was a short ring on the downstairs bell. For some reason, I thought it might be Patrick, but instead it was Diane. Her hair was pulled back off her face in a way I hadn't seen before, and, a faint finger of yellow aside, all trace of the bruise around her eye had disappeared.

"Well, Jimmy," she said, "aren't you going to invite me in?"

She was wearing a cream sweater, a coffee-coloured skirt with a slight flare, high heels which she kicked off the moment she sat on the end of the bed. My drums were out at the other side of the room, not the full kit, just the bass drum, ride cymbal, hi-hat and snare; clothes I'd been intending to iron were folded over the back of a chair.

"I didn't know," I said, "you knew where I lived."

"I didn't. Patrick told me."

"You're still seeing him then?"

The question hung in the air.

"I don't suppose you've got anything to drink?" Diane said.

There was a half bottle of Bell's out in the kitchen and I poured what was left into two tumblers and we touched glasses and said, "Cheers." Diane sipped hers, made a face, then drank down most of the rest in a single swallow.

"Patrick ..." I began.

"I don't want to talk about Patrick," she said.

Her hand touched the buckle of my belt. "Sit here," she said.

The mattress shifted with the awkwardness of my weight.

"I didn't know," she said afterwards, "it could be so good."

You see what I mean about the way she lied.

PATRICK AND DIANE got married in the French church off Leicester Square and their reception was held in the dance hall conveniently close by; it was one of the last occasions I played drums with any degree of seriousness, one of the last times I played at all. My application to join the Metropolitan Police had already been accepted and within weeks I would be starting off in uniform, a different kind of beat altogether. Val, of course, had put the band together and an all-star affair it was—Art Ellefson, Bill LeSage, Harry Klein. Val himself was near his mercurial best, just ahead of the flirtations with heroin and free form jazz that would sideline him in the years ahead.

At the night's end we stood outside, the three of us, ties unfastened, staring up at the sky. Diane was somewhere inside, getting changed.

"Christ!" Patrick said. "Who'd've fuckin' thought it?"

He took a silver flask from inside his coat and passed it round. We shook hands solemnly and then hugged each other close. When Diane came out, she and Patrick went off in a waiting car to spend the night at a hotel on Park Lane.

"Start off," Patrick had said with a wink, "like you mean to continue."

We drifted apart: met briefly, glimpsed one another across smoky rooms, exchanged phone numbers that were rarely if ever called. Nine years later I was a detective sergeant working out of West End Central and Patrick had not long since opened his third night club in a glitter of flash bulbs and champagne; Joan Collins was there with her sister, Jackie. There were ways of skirting round the edges of the law and, so far, Patrick had found most of them: favours doled out and favours returned; backhanders in brown envelopes; girls who didn't care what you did as long as you didn't kiss them on the mouth. Diane, I heard, had walked out on Patrick; reconciled, Patrick had walked out on her. Now they were back together again, but for how long?

When I came off duty, she was parked across the street, smoking a cigarette, window wound down.

"Give you a lift?"

I'd moved up market but not by much, an upper floor flat in an already ageing mansion block between Chalk Farm and Belsize Park. A photograph of the great drummer, Max Roach, was on the wall; Sillitoe's *Saturday Night and Sunday Morning* next to the Eric Amblers and a few Graham Greenes on the shelf; an Alex Welsh album on the record player, ready to remind me of better times.

"So, how are things?" Diane asked, doing her best to look as if she cared.

"Could be worse," I said. In the kitchen, I set the kettle to boil and she stood too close while I spooned Nescafé into a pair of china mugs. There was something beneath the scent of her perfume that I remembered too well.

"What does he want?" I asked.

"Who?"

"Patrick, who else?"

She paused from stirring sugar into her coffee. "Is that what it has to be?"

"Probably."

"What if I just wanted to see you for myself?"

The green in her eye was bright under the unshaded kitchen light. "I wouldn't let myself believe it," I said.

She stepped into my arms and my arms moved around her as if they had a mind of their own. She kissed me and I kissed her back. I'd like to say I pushed her away after that and we sat and drank our coffee like two adults, talked about old times and what she was going to do with her life after the divorce. She was divorcing him, she said: she didn't know why she hadn't done it before.

"He'll let you go?"

"He'll let me go."

For a moment, she couldn't hold my gaze. "There's just one thing," she said, "one thing that he wants. This new club of his, someone's trying to have his licence cancelled."

"Someone?"

"Serving drinks after hours, an allegation, nothing more."

"He can't make it go away?"

Diane shook her head. "He's tried."

I looked at her. "And that's all?"

"One of the officers, he's accused Patrick of offering him a bribe. It was all a misunderstanding, of course."

"Of course."

"Patrick wonders if you'd talk to him, the officer concerned."

"Straighten things out."

"Yes."

"Make him see the error of his ways."

"Look, Jimmy," she said, touching the back of her hand to my cheek, "you know I hate doing this, don't you?"

No, I thought. No, I don't.

"Everything has a price," I said. "Even friendship. Friendship, especially. And tell Patrick, next time he wants something, to come and ask me himself."

"He's afraid you'd turn him down."

"He's right."

When she lifted her face to mine I turned my head aside. "Don't let your coffee get cold," I said.

Five minutes later she was gone. I sorted out Patrick's little problem for him and found a way of letting him know if he stepped out of line again, I'd personally do my best to close him down. Whether either of us believed it, I was never sure. With or without my help, he went from rich to richer; Diane slipped off my radar and when she re-emerged, she was somewhere in Europe, nursing Val after his most recent spell in hospital, encouraging him to get back into playing. Later they got married, or at least that's what I heard. Some lives took unexpected turns. Not mine.

I STAYED ON in the Met for three years after my thirty and then retired; tried working for a couple of security firms, but somehow it never felt right. With my pension and the little I'd squirrelled away, I found I could manage pretty well without having to look for anything too regular. There was an investigation agency I did a little work for once in a while, nothing too serious, nothing heavy, and that was enough.

Patrick I bumped into occasionally if I went up west, greyer, more distinguished, handsomer than ever; in Soho once, close to the little Italian place where I'd spotted Diane with her bruised eye, he slid a hand into my pocket and when I felt where it had been there were two fifties, crisp and new.

"What's this for?" I asked.

"You look as though you need it," he said.

I threw the money back in his face and punched him in the mouth.

Two of his minders had me spread-eagled on the pavement before he'd wiped the mean line of blood from his chin.

At Val's funeral we barely spoke; acknowledged each other but little more. Diane looked gaunt and beautiful in black, a face like alabaster, tears I liked to think were real. A band played "Just Friends," with a break of thirty-two bars in the middle where Val's solo would have been. There was a wake at one of Patrick's clubs afterwards, a free bar, and most of the mourners went on there, but I just went home and sat in my chair and thought about the three of us, Val, Patrick and myself, what forty years had brought us to, what we'd wanted then, what we'd done.

I scarcely thought about Diane at all.

JACK KILEY, that's the investigator I was working for, kept throwing bits and pieces my way, nothing strenuous like I say, the occasional tail job, little more. I went into his office one day, a couple of rooms above a bookstore in Belsize Park, and there she sat, Diane, in the easy chair alongside his desk.

"I believe you two know each other," Jack said.

Once I'd got over the raw surprise of seeing her, what took some adjusting to was how much she'd changed. I suppose I'd never imagined her growing old. But she had. Under her grey wool suit her body was noticeably thicker; her face was fuller, puffed and cross-hatched around the eyes, lined around the mouth. No Botox; no nip and tuck.

"Hello, Jimmy," she said.

"Diane's got a little problem," Jack said. "She thinks you can make it go away." He pushed back from his desk. "I'll leave you two to talk about it."

The problem was a shipment of cocaine that should have made its way seamlessly from the Netherlands to Dublin via the UK. A street value of a quarter of a million pounds. Customs and Excise, working on a tip-off, had seized the drug on arrival, a clean bust marred only by the fact the coke had been doctored down to a mockery of its original strength; a double shot espresso from Caffè Nero would deliver as much of a charge to the system.

"How in God's name," I asked, "did you get involved in this?"

Diane lit a cigarette and wafted the smoke away from her face. "After Val died I went back to Amsterdam, it's where we'd been living before he died. There was this guy—he'd been Val's supplier …"

"I thought Val had gone straight," I said.

"There was this guy," Diane said again, "we—well, we got sort of close. It was a bad time for me. I needed …" She glanced across and shook her head. "A girl's got to live, Jimmy. All Val had left behind was debts. This guy, he offered me a roof over my head. But there was a price."

"I'll bet." Even I was surprised how bitter that sounded.

"People he did business with, he wanted me to speak for him, take meetings. I used to fly to Belfast, then, after a while, it was Dublin."

"You were a courier," I said. "A mule."

"No. I never carried the stuff myself. Once the deal was set up, I'd arrange shipments, make sure things ran smoothly."

"Patrick would be proud of you," I said.

"Leave Patrick out of this," she said. "This has nothing to do with him."

I levered myself up out of the seat; it wasn't as easy as it used to be. "Nor me." I got as far as the door.

"They think I double-crossed them," Diane said. "They think it was me tipped off Customs; they think I cut the coke and kept back the rest so I could sell it myself."

"And did you?"

She didn't blink. "These people, Jimmy, they'll kill me. To make an example. I have to convince them it wasn't me; let them have back what they think's their due."

"A little difficult if you didn't take it in the first place."

"Will you help me, Jimmy, yes or no?"

"Your pal in Amsterdam, what's wrong with him?"

"He says it's my mess and I have to get myself out of it."

"Nice guy."

She leaned towards me, trying for a look that once would have held me transfixed. "Jimmy, I'm asking. For old time's sake."

"Which old time is that, Diane?"

She smiled. "The first time you met me, Jimmy, you remember that? Leicester Square?"

Like yesterday, I thought.

"You ever think about that? You ever think what I would have been like if we'd been together? Really together?"

I shook my head.

"We don't always make the right choices," she said.

"Get somebody else to help you," I said.

"I don't want somebody else."

"Diane, look at me for fuck's sake. What can I do? I'm an old man."

"You're not old. What are you? Sixty-odd? These days sixty's not old. Seventy-five. Eighty. That's old."

"Tell that to my body, Diane. I'm carrying at least a stone more than I ought to; the tendon at the back of my left ankle gives me gyp if ever I run for a bus and my right hip hurts like hell whenever I climb a flight of stairs. Find someone else, anyone."

"There's nobody else I can trust."

I TALKED TO JACK KILEY about it later; we were sitting in the Starbucks across the street, sunshine doing its wan best to shine through the clouds.

"What do you know about these types?" Jack asked. "This new bunch of cocaine cowboys from over the old Irish Sea?"

"Sod all," I said.

"Well, let me give you a bit of background. Ireland has the third highest cocaine use in Europe and there's fifteen or twenty gangs and upwards beating the bollocks off one another to supply it. Some of them, the more established, have got links with the IRA, or did have, but it's the newer boys that take the pippin. Use the stuff themselves, jack up an Uzi or two and go shooting; a dozen murders in Dublin so far this year and most of the leaves still on the fucking trees."

"That's Dublin," I said.

Jack cracked a smile. "And you think this old flame of yours'll be safe here in Belsize Park or back home in Amsterdam?"

I shrugged. I didn't know what to bloody think.

He leaned closer. "Just a few months back, a drug smuggler from Cork got into a thing with one of the Dublin gangs—a disagreement about some shipment bought and paid for. He thought he'd lay low till it blew over. Took a false name and passport and holed up in an apartment in the Algarve. They found his body in the freezer. Minus the head. Rumour is whoever carried out the contract on him had it shipped back as proof."

Something was burning deep in my gut and I didn't think a couple of antacid tablets was going to set it right.

"You want my advice, Jimmy?" he said, and gave it anyway. "Steer clear. Either that or get in touch with some of your old pals in the Met. Let them handle it."

Do that, I thought, and there's no way of keeping Diane out of it; somehow I didn't fancy seeing her next when she was locked away on remand.

"I don't suppose you fancy giving a hand?" I said.

Jack was still laughing as he crossed the street back towards his office.

AT LEAST I DIDN'T have to travel far, just a couple of stops on the Northern Line. Diane had told me where to find them and given me their names. There was some kind of ceilidh band playing in the main bar, the sound of the bodhran tracing my footsteps up the stairs. And, yes, my hip did ache.

The McMahon brothers were sitting at either end of a leather sofa that had seen better days, and Chris Boyle was standing with his back to a barred window facing down on to the street. Hip-hop was playing from a portable stereo at one side of the room, almost drowning out the traditional music from below. No one could accuse these boys of not keeping up with the times.

There was an almost full bottle of Bushmills and some glasses on the desk, but I didn't think anyone was about to ask me if I wanted a drink.

One of the McMahon brothers giggled when I stepped into the room and I could see the chemical glow in his eyes.

"What the fuck you doin' here, old man?" the other one said. "You should be tucked up in the old folks' home with your fuckin' Ovaltine."

"Two minutes," Chris Boyle said. "Say what you have to fuckin' say then get out."

"Supposin' we let you," one of the brothers said and giggled some more. Neither of them looked a whole lot more than nineteen, twenty tops. Boyle was closer to thirty, nearing pensionable age where that crew was concerned. According to Jack, there was a rumour he wore a colostomy bag on account of getting shot in the kidneys coming out from the rugby at Lansdown Road.

"First," I said, "Diane knew nothing about either the doctoring of the shipment, nor the fact it was intercepted. You have to believe that."

Boyle stared back at me, hard-faced.

One of the McMahons laughed.

"Second, though she was in no way responsible, as a gesture of good faith, she's willing to hand over a quantity of cocaine, guaranteed at least eighty per cent pure, the amount equal to the original shipment. After that it's all quits, an even playing field, business as before."

Boyle glanced across at the sofa then nodded agreement.

"We pick the point and time of delivery," I said. "Two days time. I'll need a number on which I can reach you."

Boyle wrote his mobile number on a scrap of paper and passed it across. "Now get the fuck out," he said.

Down below, someone was playing a penny whistle, high-pitched and shrill. I could feel my pulse racing haphazardly and when I managed to get myself across the street, I had to take a grip on a railing and hold fast until my legs had stopped shaking.

WHEN JACK LEARNED I was going through with it, he offered to lend me a gun, a Smith & Wesson .38, but I declined. There was more chance of shooting myself in the foot than anything else.

I met Diane in the parking area behind Jack's office, barely light enough to make out the colour of her eyes. The cocaine was bubble-wrapped inside a blue canvas bag.

"You always were good to me, Jimmy," she said, and reaching up, she kissed me on the mouth. "Will I see you afterwards?"

"No," I said. "No, you won't."

The shadows swallowed her as she walked towards the taxi waiting out on the street. I dropped the bag down beside the rear seat of the car, waited several minutes, then slipped the engine into gear.

The place I'd chosen was on Hampstead Heath, a makeshift soccer pitch shielded by lines of trees, a ramshackle wooden building off to one side, open to the weather; sometimes pickup teams used it to get changed, or kids huddled there to feel one another up, smoke spliffs or sniff glue.

When Patrick, Val and I had been kids ourselves there was a murdered body found close by and the place took on a kind of awe for us, murder in those days being something more rare.

I'd left my car by a mansion block on Heath Road and walked in along a partly overgrown track. The moon was playing fast and loose with the clouds and the stars seemed almost as distant as they were. An earlier shower of rain had made the surface a little slippy and mud clung to the soles of my shoes. There was movement, low in the under-growth to my right hand side, and, for a moment, my heart stopped as an owl broke, with a fell swoop, through the trees above my head.

A dog barked and then was still.

I stepped off the path and into the clearing, the weight of the bag real in my left hand. I was perhaps a third of the way across the pitch before I saw them, three or four shapes massed near the hut at the far side and separating as I drew closer, fanning out. Four of them, faces unclear, but Boyle, I thought, at the centre, the McMahons to one side of him, another I didn't recognize hanging back. Behind them, behind the hut, the trees were broad and tall and close together, beeches I seemed to remember Val telling me once when I'd claimed them as oaks. "Beeches, for God's sake," he'd said, laughing in that soft way of his. "You, Jimmy, you don't know your arse from your elbow, it's a fact."

I stopped fifteen feet away and Boyle took a step forward. "You came alone," he said.

"That was the deal."

"He's stupider than I fuckin' thought," said one or other of the McMahons and laughed a girlish little laugh.

"The stuff's all there?" Boyle said, nodding towards the bag.

I walked a few more paces towards him, set the bag on the ground, and stepped back.

Boyle angled his head towards the McMahons and one of them went to the bag and pulled it open, slipping a knife from his pocket as he did so; he slit open the package, and, standing straight again, tasted the drug from the blade.

"Well?" Boyle said.

McMahon finished running his tongue around his teeth. "It's good," he said.

"Then we're set," I said to Boyle.

"Set?"

"We're done here."

"Oh, yes, we're done."

The man to Boyle's left, the one I didn't know, moved forward almost to his shoulder, letting his long coat fall open as he did so, and what light there was glinted dully off the barrels of the shotgun as he brought it to bear. It was almost level when a shot from the trees behind struck him high in the shoulder and spun him round so that the second shot tore through his neck and he fell to the ground as good as dead.

One of the McMahons cursed and started to run, while the other dropped to one knee and fumbled for the revolver inside his zip-up jacket.

With all the gunfire and the shouting I couldn't hear the words from Boyle's mouth, but I could lip read well enough. "You're dead," he said, and drew a pistol not much bigger than a child's hand from his side pocket and raised it towards my head. It was either bravery or stupidity or maybe fear that made me charge at him, unarmed, hands outstretched as if in some way to ward off the bullet; it was the mudded turf that made my feet slide away under me and sent me sprawling headlong, the two shots Boyle got off sailing over my head before one of the men I'd last seen minding Patrick in Soho stepped up neatly behind Boyle, put the muzzle of a 9mm Beretta hard behind his ear and squeezed the trigger.

Both the McMahons had gone down without me noticing; one was already dead and the other had blood gurgling out of his airway and was not long for this world.

Patrick was standing back on the path, scraping flecks of mud from the edges of his soft leather shoes with a piece of stick.

"Look at the state of you," he said. "You look a fucking state. If I were you I should burn that lot when you get home, start again."

I wiped the worst of the mess from the front of my coat and that was when I realized my hands were still shaking. "Thanks, Pat," I said.

"What are friends for?" he said.

Behind us his men were tidying up the scene a little, not too much. The later editions of the papers would be full of stories of how the Irish drug wars had come to London, the Celtic Tigers fighting it out on foreign soil.

"You need a lift?" Patrick asked, as we made our way back towards the road.

"No, thanks. I'm fine."

"Thank Christ for that. Last thing I need, mud all over the inside of the fucking car."

WHEN I GOT BACK to the flat I put one of Val's last recordings on the stereo, a session he'd made in Stockholm a few months before he died. Once or twice his fingers didn't match his imagination, and his breathing seemed to be giving him trouble, but his mind was clear. Beeches, I'll always remember that now, that part of the Heath. Beeches, not oaks.

Havanightmare

by

JOSÉ LATOUR

DARKNESS WAS IN FULL FLIGHT to the east when Megan Olwin rested her forearms on the teak rail enclosing the liner's floodlit upper deck. She took a deep breath and let her gaze sweep over the little puffs of water that danced on the choppy sea ahead before peering at the black horizon and overcast sky. Enjoying the wind's playful fondling of her shoulder-length brown hair and the misty brine dampening her face, the woman wondered how the ship could remain so steady in the swell caused by what she judged to be an advancing cold front. Megan Olwin had no idea that the *New Galaxy* was equipped with fin stabilizers protruding from its sides below the water to reduce the roll. In fact, she ignored everything about the design and construction of luxury ocean liners. She didn't know she was standing on the covering of the captain's bridge deck; that the tall, elongated white structure behind her hid sophisticated navigational and communication systems, and that precisely at 07:09 on February 9, 1997, the vessel was plowing ahead at twenty-three knots.

MEGAN OLWIN was on her fourth Caribbean holiday. One snowy January evening, the thirty-four-year-old biochemist, who was born, raised, and presently living in Vermont, had found in her day's mail a brochure from her travel agent. On her three previous tours she had gotten smug satisfaction out of fancying her friends shovelling snow from their doorsteps as she—bikini-clad in dark sunglasses—basked in the sun along the strand of emeralds known as the Lesser Antilles, sometimes on a sandy beach close to a port of call, more frequently by the ship's pool. From Grenada to the Virgin Islands, she had observed with interest the differences among small multiracial communities with African, Spanish, French, and English ancestries.

This time she had signed up for a cruise starting in Puerto Plata that would take her to Havana, Cancún, and Santiago de Cuba before returning to the Dominican Republic. As she began limbering up for her usual early morning jog, Megan was about to admit a serious error of judgement in her choice of attire. Sailing by Cuba's northern coast, she was much closer than she originally realized to the huge masses of frigid air.

Not wanting to return to her cabin for warmer clothing, she sighed in resignation, turned left, and started to trot. She wore a crimson crew-neck pullover, black satin skating shorts, and well-worn sneakers. The port course took her by the children's playground, past the pool, sun decks, tennis court, and funnel. She rounded the deck's stern section by the starboard walkway, reached her starting point, and began a second lap.

She was hoping for a gorgeous sunny day, but it seemed a bleak prospect by the time she slowed down to a walk thirty minutes later.

To port, a low rocky coastline could be guesswork behind the fine mist that was created by the smashing waves that climbed geyser-like to impressive heights. To starboard, the cold front seemed more menacing under the weak sunlight that was filtered by low-hung clouds. Gripping the rosewood banister of a beautiful, wide stairway, Megan Olwin returned to the cozy ambience of the ship's passageways and felt glad for it. A few moments later she unlocked the door of her first-class cabin, went in, closed it, and, just as she was headed for the shower, came face to face with a tall, swarthy man pointing a gun at her.

"Sorry lady," the man said with a heavy Spanish accent. "Next three days you do as I say or die."

FIVE HOURS LATER a perplexed Megan realized she wouldn't be able to hold out for another five minutes and wondered if some sort of plastic covering protected the mattress. Still in her jogging outfit, arms alongside her torso, wrists and ankles tied to the legs of the bed, her head was propped on a pillow to favour the observation of a seventeen-inch TV set tuned to CNN. Her lips were sealed with a three-inch-wide strip of adhesive tape that had a dime-size hole at center to allow breathing, should her nose get stuffed. Unable to control her bladder any longer, Megan felt the warm urine dampening her buttocks up to her waist.

She knew the *New Galaxy* was moored to the port of Havana's passenger pier. The cruise program said they would arrive at the Cuban capital around 9 A.M. and, according to the news channel, it was 11:25. Besides, she recognized the berthing manoeuvre from previous trips. As she lay on her bed, she kept her eyes closed, hoping to impress on the kidnapper her scorn. When she felt the ship slowing down, she visualized the launch detaching itself from a larger vessel to bring the pilot on board. As the *New Galaxy* positioned itself by the pier, she conjured up ropes being thrown, imagined hearing the air-operated ladder hiss along the liner's side, and envisioned sweaty, half-naked natives dancing to some local tune to appropriately welcome those bringing much-needed greenbacks.

What she couldn't picture was the present whereabouts of her kidnapper. Megan had no way of knowing that the man had gone ashore donning a white plastic cap, sunglasses, an outmoded, light-green long-sleeved shirt, a shoulder bag, tight tan slacks, and brown lace-up shoes—an attire which singled him out among the flock of tourists in garish shirts, Bermuda shorts, and assorted headgear. But when a mere three blocks from the pier he lagged behind the group pacing off Old Havana's Plaza de Armas, turned onto San Ignacio Street, and joined the locals hurrying along narrow sidewalks and stone-paved streets, the kidnapper became one more fish in the shoal. Walking briskly and oblivious of the surroundings, he covered the distance between the House of Africa and a bank of public phones on San Rafael Street in less than twenty minutes. From a hip pocket, the man produced a few Cuban coins, dropped one in the slot and dialed a number.

For close to ten minutes, he talked in whispers, his lips brushing the mouthpiece, his face a study in mood swings. Dropping a five-cent coin every three minutes, he alternately looked depressed, hopeful, and overjoyed. One moment he was begging; the next ordering. For a while he reasoned, listened to the other party, and then argued intensely before coming out on top. Before hanging up, a broad smile lit up his face, and nodding contentedly he returned the handset to its hook.

The kidnapper sighed deeply, took off his sunglasses and, suppressing a smile, looked around as if he just now realized where he was. Leisurely he strolled around what fifty years before had been Havana's downtown, now a mishmash of well-provisioned state shops where only dollar-bearing customers were admitted, and old department stores sparsely stocked with low-quality products sold for pesos. But the man didn't seem to mind dilapidated façades, the litter on the asphalt, or the drizzle that began to fall. He looked enraptured by something that had nothing to do with the neighbourhood, though for a passerby he would have seemed engrossed in the widely varying architectural styles all around him.

Precisely at that same moment back on the ship, Megan was recalling that the kidnapper had groaned, "I'll be back in a few hours," before grabbing the DO NOT DISTURB sign from the coffee table, opening the main door, slipping the sign on the passageway side of the handle, and leaving the cabin. Megan had no idea what a "few hours" meant to the kidnapper. The *New Galaxy* would leave Havana at midnight, so she still might have to wait twelve hours before seeing the motherfucker again. Or longer. Suppose the spic shacked up with some broad, or got coked-out or drunk somewhere? And she was very hungry. A tendency to chubbiness had made Megan a standard card-bearer for Weight Watchers since her teens, and her supper had consisted of Norwegian salmon poached in tarragon sauce, three celery sticks, and half a bottle of Calistoga. She had asked for and got a glass of water a little after eight A.M. and fear had kept her stomach quiet, but now it rumbled demandingly.

The asshole had pledged not to harm her without volunteering explanations. After tying her up in bed—at which point Megan was absolutely certain she would be raped—the creep sat on a deep chair, wiped the sweat from his face with a perfumed handkerchief, and heaved a sigh of relief. "I give you my word nothing's gonna happen to you if you do as I say," he stated. Megan was considerably mollified, not so much by the promise as by some undercurrent of sincerity in his voice.

"Why are you doing this to me?" she asked.

The man shook his head several times and forced a smile the way adults do when dodging a too-complicated answer that would satisfy a child's curiosity. Then he said, "Where's your passport and boarding pass?"

Megan fixed her gaze to the cabin's teak-panelled bulkhead directly ahead to exercise her only possible rebellion: silence. Then Megan had made the mistake of crying out "help" at the top of her lungs. With a panther-like leap, the man pried open her mouth and shoved a perfumed, moistened handkerchief inside. Then he produced from a shopping bag a roll of adhesive tape and surgical scissors, and set about doing what had been undeniably planned beforehand.

Megan Olwin realized the severity of what was happening to her after she listened to the two o'clock news summary: three so-called anti-terrorism experts discussed the Japanese ambassador's residence in Lima, Peru. Basically, they stated that some acts of terrorism are not defensible. Sometimes terrorists win. *Who was this guy? What did he want? I might die at the hands of this nut, Megan reasoned, or have a fear-induced heart attack, or starve to death before some cabin boy starts wondering about the number of days that that particular sign has been on that particular doorknob.*

What had she accomplished in life? She hadn't unlocked some transcendental effect or structure or mechanism or protein or hormone, had never published a paper in the *Journal of Biological Chemistry*, had failed in her marriage, had no children, few friends, was estranged from her parents, and the guy she was dating didn't seem to know that women have a clitoris. Tears rolled down her temples, and when her nose got blocked she almost admired the kidnapper's foresight. Drowning in self-pity, her sobs gradually slowed to regular breathing and she fell asleep.

By late afternoon the kidnapper was enjoying a leisurely stroll along the Prado promenade in the company of a nice-looking white woman in her early thirties. She donned a white linen shawl-collar blouse, a neutral-coloured, ankle-length split skirt, and ill-fitting sandals. Her accessories included a Panama hat, dark sunglasses, gold studs in her earlobes, and a stainless wristwatch with an art deco dial.

She held a purse with both hands as if it contained something extremely valuable. Only her underwear wasn't Megan's.

The couple walked among a crowd getting ready for the evening's carnival. Small kiosks served all sorts of snack foods and beverages, dancers and musicians, dressed alike for the *comparsas*, hurried to their meeting places, early birds swilled beer from huge waxed paper glasses, and many youngsters weaved through slow-paced or stationary spectators. The smell of food overcame the perfumes emanating from people in their Sunday best, and the temperature had dropped to a comfortable seventy degrees.

Even tourists remained unnoticed, but the woman sauntering along with the kidnapper seemed jittery. Occasionally he would say something to her, and she would quickly nod or shake her head without uttering a single word.

At Central Park they turned left to cross a wide, stone-paved space that had obviously been a street in the past, and entered the Floridita, a favourite watering hole for visiting foreigners. Huddled together, exchanging whispers and smiles like reunited lovers, they each had two daiquiris.

In moments of silence they glanced at the mural—flanked by two beautiful bronze lamps—depicting the port of Havana in the eighteenth century. The man ordered a ham and cheese sandwich to go before asking for the cheque. On her way out the woman pulled up the slingback straps on her sandals.

Night had fallen. The couple turned onto Obispo Street and shuffled by the display windows of the stores. Young and lean police officers kept hookers and peddlers of "genuine" Havana cigars at bay. Trying to improve his tourist impersonation, at each block the man pointed to some odd element as if seeing it for the first time: a bush flourishing on a two-hundred-year-old tile roof, beams propping up a crumbling façade, an art gallery. Relaxed by the drinks, the woman smiled fleetingly at some of his remarks.

When they reached the waterfront promenade known as Malecón, the woman tensed. Keeping their pace slow and casual like typical passengers of a pleasure cruise, the kidnapper did all the talking in primitive English. When they approached the entrance of the pier, the woman unclasped her purse, and with trembling hands, showed Megan's boarding pass and passport to the two security guards blocking the way. One of them searched for the name in the alphabetically arranged nine-page list on his clipboard before checking it off. The other compared the passport's photo with the passenger and seemed satisfied. She got waved in. The kidnapper also showed his documents and gained admittance. The woman wavered and cupped her hand over her eyes. The kidnapper held her by the right arm and guided her along. Both sentries frowned. The kidnapper rolled his neck and smiled.

"One drink too many," he said to the watchmen in English. Met with ignorant stares, the kidnapper mimicked drinking from a bottle. The guards laughed and turned their backs as the couple hotfooted it onto the *New Galaxy*.

MEGAN OLWIN was trying to concentrate on Larry King's suspenders when she heard a rustle. Turning her head she saw the kidnapper enter the cabin. The man threw the latch, dropped a small paper bag on the couch, and approached his victim with a few strides. He jerked the adhesive tape from her mouth, and just as Megan was about to let out a cascade of selected profanities, the man dropped to his knees and started kissing her forehead and cheeks and chin and temples. *Oh boy*, Megan thought in horror when the rum in his breath reached her nostrils, *now the drunk bastard feels like pussy*. But with the same suddenness the kidnapper paused, sniffed, and looked around embarrassed.

"Sorry, Megan," he said. "I didn't ..."

At a loss for words, the man began untying a very confused Megan. In a few seconds, she had gone from lame resignation to a raving mad, frightened person frustrated by her inability to figure out what was going on.

Massaging her wrists, she started for the bathroom.

"I stand in door," the man announced blocking her path. "Don't hurry—an hour maybe—but don't close door and don't scream."

Thirty-five minutes later, after scarfing down the Floridita sandwich, Megan Olwin sat in a deep chair facing her kidnapper. She rubbed lotion on her wrists and ankles. The man had been decent enough to turn the vinyl-covered mattress upside down, substitute the soiled sheets with the bedspread, and hand her the fresh underwear, oversized black T-shirt, and jeans she had asked for from behind the shower curtain. Sitting on the couch across from Megan, the stubble and sheen of grease on his face revealed that he hadn't taken a shower before changing into the white slacks, light-blue Oxford shirt, and navy-blue blazer he wore. Dark circles under his eyes added a touch of exhaustion to his unkempt appearance, but the man looked alert, and the gun by his side was a good dissuader.

Beneath her anger, fear, and frustration, Megan's curiosity pulsed. Her rational mind and scientific training demanded an explanation, although she realized the futility of asking for it. She suspected this was no run-of-the-mill criminal or commonplace crime. The man hadn't even asked for her money, traveller's cheques, or credit cards, and as far as she could surmise, they had remained untouched. And the nonsensical kissing spree on his return, as though he was exulting over some incredible achievement. Megan replaced the lid on the bottle of lotion and turned her eyes to the double window near the bed, where she saw a beam of light from a lighthouse move across a pitch black sky.

Maybe he'd fall asleep on the couch, Megan speculated. It would be her chance to slip out. Except there was a strong possibility the schmuck would tie her down again should he feel sleepy. She knew she should pretend to sleep, make him feel confident, but after close to twelve hours lying on her back the idea did not appeal to her. They sat in silence for a few more minutes before Megan remembered the *Vanity Fair* she hadn't had time to read.

"I have a magazine somewhere in that chest of drawers," she said, pointing to the piece of furniture. "Can I get it? Read a while?"

Grabbing the gun, the kidnapper stood up, found the publication, and handed it to Megan. She appeared absorbed in a long piece on the Middle East peace process. As eleven o'clock approached, the ship started droning a little louder, pulling the man out of his state of reverie. He got up and walked to the windows, and gazed out intently. He seemed so deeply engrossed in contemplation that Megan started getting up very slowly. Halfway through the motion, the man turned and stared Megan down—literally. She returned her attention to the magazine.

At midnight, as the *New Galaxy* set out from the pier, the kidnapper chuckled. People could be heard laughing and talking loudly in the passageway. As the ship sailed away, the lighthouse beam disrupted the soft illumination inside the cabin. About half an hour later, the engines slowed down. Megan closed the magazine and imagined the pilot returning to his launch. Two or three minutes later the ship registered an almost imperceptible vibration when, freed from all tutelage, it rode ahead hugging the shore. The exhausted-looking man returned to the couch and plopped down. From the inner breast pocket of his blazer, he pulled out a sheaf of papers which he unfolded.

"Three pages," he said looking Megan right in the eye. "I can't speak English well. Understand? Yes. Talk myself? No. So I sit and write this. Library, bilingual dictionary, I sit down, take time, I make sense. Tonight, I read to you first page. Okay?"

Megan nodded.

The man lowered his gaze to the page and read:

"Doing to you what I did was the only way to rescue my wife. My wife is now on board. She is in my cabin. She does not know what I did to you. I have no quarrel with you and I have no intention of harming you. But I cannot let you free yet. You would denounce me to the shipmaster, to the officers. I would be charged with kidnapping and sent back to Cuba with my wife. I will be shot or sentenced to thirty years in prison. My wife will go to prison too. That is why I cannot let you free yet. You will be free a couple of hours after we disembark in Cancun. I give you my word. Before I say goodbye I will read you the other two pages. Now, please, lay down. I have to tie you up again. I will sleep here too, so no gag. Do not scream. If you need anything call me. Thank you."

The man folded the pages and returned them to his pocket. Megan was staring at him open-mouthed. The kidnapper let out a prodigious yawn.

"I can't believe this is happening to me," she said.

"Oh yes," the man said. "Believe, yes, believe."

FOR MEGAN OLWIN, the next thirty-nine hours crawled along like a caterpillar on crutches. Resigned to her fate, she read and watched reruns on the TV, taking comfort from the fact that the sky remained cloudy and frequent squalls sent rivulets trickling down the window-panes. Nobody would be swimming in the pool or sunning on the sun deck.

Boredom set in because she believed the kidnapper. *Cuba* had been a household word when she was growing up. Her parents, like many couples, got carried away during the October 1962 missile crisis, and she belonged to the scores of babies born between thirty-six and forty-two weeks later. After learning this in her early teens, Megan had always been interested in the island, and knew about the one-way human flow, split families, and trading embargo that stubbornly remained one of the thorns in America's side. The story the man told was probably true, Megan concluded. She just happened to be the woman on board with the right age and physical appearance. There was a high probability she wouldn't be shot or harmed if she behaved.

The kidnapper quickly established a routine. Each time he left the cabin, he first bound her hands and feet, and sealed her mouth with a new strip of adhesive tape. When he slept on the couch there was no gag. If he was just sitting around, which was most of the time, Megan was free to move about the cabin as she wished, save for closing the bathroom door from the inside.

Cabin stewards posed the biggest dilemma to the kidnapper and were Megan's permanent hope. The man realized that ignoring the polite knocks would arouse suspicion and had opened the cabin door twice, just a crack, to accept fresh linens and the replenishment of toiletries. He had declined offers to tidy up with substantial tips, conspiratorial winks, and charming smiles, intimating that recent acquaintances had become lovebirds and wished to be left alone.

What neither he nor Megan knew was that that same afternoon two different stewards, one assigned to first-class and another caring for second-class passengers, had made odd reports to the chief steward about travellers that apparently never left their quarters. One steward described a Spanish-speaking lady who ordered triple breakfasts, lunches, and suppers from a cabin that was supposed to be occupied by a lone gentleman. The other report was of a first-class cabin which was supposed to be occupied by an American from which a tall, dark-hued man had twice sent back the cleaning girl and never ordered food.

The ship's security chief was both prudent and knowledgeable. He had been with the *New Galaxy* for six years and had witnessed more cabin swaps than stars on cloudless nights. He knew that part of the fare the ship's passengers paid bought discretion, and he was also convinced that 99.9 percent of what looks remarkable, strange, or suspicious turns out to have very simple and innocent explanations. But he was also well aware he should make sure nothing was really wrong.

To play it by the book, at 15:52 hours on February 11, a Tuesday, when the *New Galaxy* was one hour away from its Mexican port of destination, he took up the matter with the captain. Sitting comfortably in the posh suite assigned to Number One, the two men in white starched uniforms with black-and-gold braided insignia of rank, sipped tea and discussed the awkward situation. The captain remembered the shapely American who boarded his ship in Puerto Plata; now that she had been brought to his attention, he found it strange that he had not seen her since. His subordinate reported that the man who had answered the phone in cabin 111 said that Ms. Olwin was taking a nap, didn't want to be disturbed, and would the caller leave his name and cabin number? The security officer added that nobody answered the phone in cabin 224, in spite of the fact that two hours earlier a Latin lady had admitted an attendant delivering three substantial meals. The decision was made to keep a discreet observation on both compartments and to take a peek as soon as the dwellers went ashore.

Forty-five minutes later, just as a Mexican pilot gained admittance onto the ship's bridge, the buoyant kidnapper sitting on the couch of cabin 111 unfolded the two pages he had just taken out and started reading to his victim, resignedly sitting in the same deep chair.

"Now I will try to win your forgiveness, and your complicity too. Everything I will tell you is true, every word. My father was a fisherman, he owned a twenty-foot launch and I started going out to sea with him when I was seven. I learned to love the sea. When my time came to fulfill my military service I chose the Cuban Coast Guard. I stayed after completing my tour of duty, studied hard, became the skipper of a fourteen-foot patrol boat eight years later. I was a young Communist, I looked forward to becoming a Party militant. We

were supposed to watch out for the Miami pirates that would sail to Cuba to open fire against our people, but all I saw were drug smugglers, fishing parties and rafters trying to reach the Florida Keys. Our orders were to pick up rafters and take them back. I must have picked up two thousand rafters. Men were sent to prison, women and children almost always were sent home. I started wondering, conversed with my only friend on board, the boat engineer. One day I lost my patience when the political officer was giving me a lecture and I asked to him 'What is wrong with what we are doing? Why so many poor people risk their lives to get out of here?' It was a mistake. Three weeks later a stolen tug carrying sixty people was sunk by three other tugs. Forty persons drowned; twenty were children.

"I said to myself 'I do not want to be party to this.' My engineer and I talked things over. One late evening we took our boat out. A scheduled maintenance had been completed and we were supposed to make a test, check if everything was okay. We set out to Key West and asked for political asylum.

"I could not take my wife with me. There was no way to get her on board, but I planned to send for her as soon as possible. I know the Cuban government hears Miami radio stations and reads Miami press, so I did not give interviews because I figured maybe if I said the truth, brag about our defection, they would not grant her permission to leave Cuba. I kept my mouth shut. A year ago she got a visa from the American embassy in Havana. I sent her the money for all that was needed: birth certificate, marriage certificate, medical examinations, passport, everything. But she was refused permission to leave. An immigration official told her that if I had been man enough to steal a patrol boat, I should be man enough to return to Cuba and smuggle her out because she would never be given permission to leave.

"I was left no choice. I am a man. I love my wife. I owed it to her. So I conceived this plan. I am sorry for you. But even if you forgive me now I have to tie you up again…"

"No, listen up," Megan said as she uncoiled from the deep chair.

"Shut up, sit down," the kidnapper snapped. "Let me finish." And for the second time he stared Megan down.

He resumed reading:

"I have to tie you up again because I cannot run the risk of being deceived by you. There is too much at stake. I promise that we will leave Cancun in less than an hour after disembarking, but before leaving I shall phone the police and tell them that you are here, tied and gagged.

"I said I wanted your complicity because besides wanting you to understand why I did this to you, I ask you not to tell to the Mexican authorities what I just told you. Not to tell about my wife, not to say that I am a Cuban and to delay reporting your lost passport for a few hours. If you do this, you will make it easier for us to get away. If you do not, I will understand. Now, please, lay down on the bed, please."

ON THE UPPER DECK of the *New Galaxy*, a security guard in civilian clothes drew the walkie-talkie to his mouth and pressed the send key.

"The man in the blue blazer and the woman in the white blouse are going down the ladder. Over."

The security officer and the chief steward slipped a master key in the lock of cabin 111 and opened the door. Without a word they gently stepped inside the small living area and looked around, footsteps muted by the thick, plush carpet. Behind the partition they found Megan in bed. Both men rushed forward. The chief steward carefully removed the adhesive tape as the security officer began untying what he recognized as fishermen's bends.

"Are you all right?" the steward asked Megan.

"I guess so," she said feeling her hands.

"Untie her legs," the security officer instructed. "I'm gonna get the son of a bitch."

"No, wait!" Megan shouted.

Paying no heed, the security officer picked up the radio from the rug and left the cabin. Once in the passageway he broke into a run.

Free at last, Megan rushed out, leaving the slack-jawed chief steward behind. She stopped in the passageway to get her bearings, looked both ways and chose the stairway to the upper deck. From there she saw the security officer going down the ladder two steps at a time. A hundred yards away her kidnapper, holding a woman by the elbow, was reaching the end of the pier. On the other side of a tall chain-link fence stood a building that housed Mexican immigration and customs. The security officer hit the ground and sprinted after the couple.

"Nooo!" Megan cried at the top of her lungs.

The wind blew in the right direction, and the swarthy man turned his head for an instant. He pushed the woman in the white blouse forward, pulled out a gun and turned to face his pursuer. Passengers around him scattered in all directions. The security officer stopped dead in his tracks and lay down on the concrete. To Megan's left, a man in civilian clothes was excitedly babbling into a walkie-talkie.

The woman in the white blouse crossed the fence after looking back several times, and a hand pulled her inside the Mexican compound. The swarthy man turned away from the ship and approached the fence. Two Mexican security guards with guns drawn came out the building shouting something that Megan couldn't hear. Holding his gun at waist level, the swarthy man seemed frozen for an instant, as if considering something. Megan saw three flashes and heard three pops. The swarthy man fell and after a few spasmodic kicks lay still.

Megan's vision blurred and she felt two trickles warming her cheeks.

Easy as A-B-C

by

LAURA LIPPMAN

ANOTHER HOUSE COLLAPSED TODAY. It happens more and more, especially with all the wetback crews out there. Don't get me wrong. I use guys from Mexico and Central America, too, and they're great workers, especially when it comes to landscaping. But some other contractors aren't as particular as I am. They hire the cheapest help they can get and the cheapest comes pretty high, especially when you're excavating a basement, which has become one of the hot fixes around here. It's not enough, I guess, to get the three-story rowhouse with four bedrooms, gut it from top to bottom, creating open, airy kitchens where grandmothers once smoked the wallpaper with bacon grease and sour beef. It's not enough to carve master bath suites from the tiny middle rooms that the youngest kids always got stuck with. No, these people have to have the full family room, too, which means digging down into the old dirt basements, sending a river of mud into the alley, then putting in new floors and walls. But if you miscalculate by even an inch—boom. You destroy the foundation of the house. Nothing to do but bring the fucker down and start carting away the bricks.

It's odd, going into these houses I knew as a kid, learning what people have paid for sound structures that they consider mere shells, all because they might get a sliver of a water view from a top-floor window or the ubiquitous rooftop deck. Yeah, I know words like ubiquitous. Don't act so surprised. The stuff in books—anyone can learn that. All you need is time and curiosity and a library card, and you can fake your way through a conversation with anyone. The work I do, the crews I supervise, that's what you can't fake because it could kill people, literally kill them. I feel bad for the men who hire me, soft types who apologize for their feebleness, whining: *I wish I had the time.* Give those guys a thousand years and they couldn't rewire a single fixture or install a gas dryer. You know the first thing I recommend when I see a place where the "man of the house" has done some work? A carbon monoxide detector. I couldn't close my eyes in my brother-in-law's place until I installed one, especially when my sister kept bragging about how handy he was.

The boom in South Baltimore started in Federal Hill twenty-five years ago, before my time, flattened out for a while in the '90s, but now it's roaring again, spreading through south Federal Hill and into Riverside Park and all the way up Fort Avenue into Locust Point, where my family lived until I was ten and my grandparents stayed until the day they died, the two of them, side by side. My grandmother had been ailing for years and my grandfather, as it turned out, had been squirrelling away various painkillers she had been given along the way, preparing himself. She died in her sleep and, technically, he did, too. A self-induced, pharmaceutical sleep, but sleep nonetheless. We found them on their narrow double bed, and the pronounced rigor made it almost impossible to separate their entwined hands. He literally couldn't live without her. Hard on my mom, losing them that way, but I couldn't help feeling it was pure and honest. Pop-pop didn't want to live alone and he didn't want to come stay with us in the house out in Linthicum. He didn't really have friends. Mee-maw was his whole life and he had been content to care for her through all her pain and illness. He would have done that forever. But once that job was done, he was done, too.

My mother sold the house for $75,000. That was a dozen years ago and boy did we think we had put one over on the buyers. Seventy-five thousand! For a house on Decatur Street in Locust Point. And all cash for my mom, because it had been paid off forever. We went to Hausner's the night of the closing, toasted our good fortune. The old German restaurant was still open then, crammed with all that art and junk. We had veal and strawberry pie and top-shelf liquor and toasted grandfather for leaving us such a windfall.

So imagine how I felt when I got a referral for a complete redo at my grandparents' old address and the real estate guy tells me: "She got it for only $225,000, so she's willing to put another hundred thousand in it and I bet she won't bat an eyelash if the work goes up to $150,000."

"Huh," was all I managed. Money-wise, the job wasn't in my top tier, but then, my grandparents' house was small even by the neighbourhood's standards, just two stories. It had a nice-size backyard, though, for a rowhouse. My grandmother had grown tomatoes and herbs and summer squash on that little patch of land.

"The first thing I want to do is get a parking pad back here," my client said, sweeping a hand over what was now an overgrown patch of weeds, the chain-link fence sagging around it. "I've been told that will increase the value of the property ten, twenty thousand."

"You a flipper?" I asked. More and more amateurs were getting into real estate, feeling that the stock market wasn't for them. They were the worst of all possible worlds, panicking at every penny over the original estimate, riding my ass. You want to flip property for profit, you need to be able to do the work yourself. Or buy and hold. This woman didn't look like the patient type. She was young, dressed to the nines, picking her way through the weeds in the most impractical boots I'd ever seen.

"No, I plan to live here. In fact, I hope to move in as quickly as possible, so time is more important to me than money. I was told you're fast."

"I don't waste time, but I don't cut corners," I said. "Mainly, I just try to make my customers happy."

She tilted her head, gazing at me through naturally thick and black eyelashes. It was the practised look of a woman who had been looking at men from under her eyelashes for much of her life, sure they would be charmed. And, okay, I was. Dark hair, cut in one of those casual, disarrayed styles, darker eyes that made me think of kalamata olives, which isn't particularly romantic, I guess. But I really like kalamata olives. With her fair skin, it was a terrific contrast.

"I'm sure you'll make me very happy," was all she said.

I GUESS HERE is where I should mention that I'm married, going on eighteen years and pretty happily, too. I realize it's a hard concept to grasp, especially for a lot of women, that you can be perfectly happy, still in love with your wife, maybe more in love with your wife than you've ever been, but it's been eighteen years and a young, firm-fleshed woman looks up at you through her eyelashes and it's not a crime to think: *I like that.* Not: *I'd like to hit that,* which I hear the young guys on my crews say. Just: *I like that, that's nice, if life were different I'd make time for that.* But I had two kids and a sweet wife, Angeline, who'd only put on a few pounds and still kept her hair blond and long, and was pretty appreciative of the life my work had built for the two of us. So I had no agenda, no scheme going in. I was just weak.

But part of Deirdre's allure was how much she professed to love the very things whose destruction she was presiding over, even before I told her that the house had belonged to my grandparents. She exclaimed over the wallpaper in their bedroom, a pattern of tiny yellow roses, even as it was steamed off the walls. She ran a hand lovingly over the banister, worn smooth by my younger hands, not to mention my butt a time or two. The next day it was gone, yanked from its moorings by my workers. She all but composed an ode to the black-and-white tile in the single full bath, but that didn't stop her from meeting with Charles Tile Co. and choosing a Tuscany-themed medley for what was to become the master bath suite. (Medley was their word, not mine. I just put the stuff in.)

She had said she wanted the job fast, which made me ache a little, because the faster it went, the sooner I would be out of her world. But it turned out she didn't care about speed so much once we got the house to the point where she could live among the ongoing work—and once her end-of-the-day inspections culminated with the two of us in her raw, unfinished bedroom. She was wilder than I had expected, pushing to do things that Angeline would never have tolerated, much less asked for. In some part of my mind, I knew her abandon came from the fact that she never lost sight of the endpoint. The work would be concluded and this would conclude, too. Which was what I wanted as well, I guess. I had no desire to leave Angeline or cause my kids any grief. Deirdre and I were scrupulous about keeping our secret, and not even my longtime guys, the ones who knew me best, guessed anything was up. To them, I bitched about her as much as I did any client, maybe a little more.

"Mouldings?" my carpenter would ask. "Now she wants mouldings?" And I would roll my eyes and shrug, say: "Women."

"Mouldings?" she asked when I proposed them.

"Don't worry," I told her. "No charge. But I saw you look at them."

And so it was with the appliances, the countertops, the triple-pane windows. I bought what she wanted, billed for what she could afford. Somehow, in my mind, it was as if I had sold the house for $225,000, as if all that profit had gone to me, instead of the speculator who had bought the house from my mother and then just left it alone to ripen. Over time, I probably put ten thousand of my own money into those improvements, even accounting for my discounts on material and my time, which was free. Some men give women roses and jewellery. I gave Deirdre a marble bathroom and a beautiful old mantle for the living room fireplace, which I restored to the wood-burning hearth it had never been. My grandparents had one of those old gas-fired logs, but Deirdre said they were tacky and I suppose she was right.

Go figure—I've never had a job with fewer complications. The weather held, there were no surprises buried within the old house, which was sound as a dollar. "A deck," I said. "You'll want a rooftop deck to watch the fireworks." And not just any deck, of course. I built it myself, using teak and copper accents, helped her shop for the proper furniture, outdoor hardy but still feminine, with curvy lines and that *verdi gris* patina she loved so much. I showed her how to cultivate herbs and perennials in pots, but not the usual wooden casks. No, these were iron, to match the décor. If I had to put a name to her style, I guess I'd say Nouvelle New Orleans—flowery, but not overly so, with genuine nineteenth-century pieces balanced by contemporary ones. I guess her taste was good. She certainly thought so and told me often enough.

"If only I had the pocketbook to keep up with my taste," she would say with a sigh and another one of those sidelong glances, and the next thing I knew I'd be installing some wall sconce she simply had to have.

One twilight—we almost always met at last light, the earliest she could leave work, the latest I could stay away from home—she brought a bottle of wine to bed after we had finished. She was taking a wine-tasting course over at this restaurant in the old foundry. A brick foundry, a place where men like my dad had once earned decent wages, and now it housed this chichi restaurant, a gallery, a health club, and a spa. It's happening all over Locust Point. The old P&G plant is now something called Tide Point, which was supposed to be some high-tech mecca, and they're building condos on the old grain piers. The only real jobs left in Locust Point are at Domino and Phillips, where the red neon crab still clambers up and down the smokestack.

"Nice," I said, although in truth I don't care much for white wine and this was too sweet for my taste.

"Vigonier," she said. "Twenty-six dollars a bottle."

"You can buy top-shelf bourbon for that and it lasts a lot longer."

"You can't drink bourbon with dinner," she said with a laugh, as if I had told a joke. "Besides, wine can be an investment. And it's cheaper by the case. I'd like to get into that, but if you're going to do it, you have to do it right, have a special kind of refrigerator, keep it climate controlled."

"Your basement would work."

And that's how I came to build her a wine cellar, at cost. It didn't require excavating the basement, luckily, although I was forever bumping my head on the ceiling when I straightened up to my full height. But I'm 6'3" and she was just a little thing, no more than 5'2", barely one hundred pounds. I used to carry her to bed and, well, show her other ways I could manipulate her weight. She liked me to sit her on the marble counter in her master bath, far forward on the edge, so I was supporting most of her weight. Because of the way the mirrors were positioned, we could both watch, and it was a dizzying infinity, our eyes locked into our own eyes and into each other's. I know guys who call a sink fuck the old American Standard, but I never thought of it that way. For one thing, there wasn't a single American Standard piece in the bathroom. And the toilet was a

Canadian model, smuggled in so she could have the bigger tank that had been outlawed in interest of water conservation. Her shower was powerful, too, a stinging force that I came to know well, scrubbing up afterwards so Angeline couldn't smell where I had been.

The wine cellar gave me another month—putting down a floor, smoothing and painting the old plaster walls. My grandparents had used the basement for storage and us cousins had played hide-and-seek in the dark, a made-up version that was particularly thrilling, one where you moved silently, trying to get close enough to grab the others in hiding, then rushing back to the stairs, which were the home-free base. As it sometimes happens, the basement seemed larger when it was full of my grandparents' junk. Painted and pared down, it was so small. But it was big enough to hold the requisite refrigeration unit and the custom-made shelves, a beautiful burled walnut, for the wines she bought on the advice of the guy teaching the course.

I WAS DONE. There was not another improvement I could make to the house, so changed now it was as if my family and its history had been erased. Deirdre and I had been hurtling toward this day for months and now it was here. I had to move on to other projects, ones where I would make money.

Besides, people were beginning to wonder. I wasn't around the other jobs as much, and I also wasn't pulling in the kind of money that would help placate Angeline over the crazy hours I was working. Time to end it.

Our last night, I stopped at the foundry, spent almost forty bucks on a bottle of wine that the young girl in the store swore by. Cakebread, the guy's real name. White, too, because I knew Deirdre loved white wines.

"Chardonnay," she said, wrinkling her nose.

"I noticed you liked whites."

"But not Chardonnay so much. I'm an ABC girl—Anything But Chardonnay. Dennis says Chardonnay is banal."

"Dennis?"

She didn't answer. And she was supposed to answer, supposed to say: *Oh, you know, that faggot from my wine-tasting class, the one who smells like he wears strawberry perfume.* Or: *That irritating guy in my office.* Or even: *A neighbour, a creep. He scares me. Would you still come around, from time to time, just to check up on me?* She didn't say any of those things.

She said: "We were never going to be a regular thing, my love."

Right. I knew that. I was the one with the wife and the house and the two kids. I was the one who had everything to lose. I was the one who was glad to be getting out, before it could all catch up with me. I was the one who was careful not to use the word love, not even in the lighthearted way she had just used it. Sarcastic, almost. It made me think that it wasn't my marital status so much that had closed off that possibility for us, but something even more entrenched. I was no different from the wallpaper, the banister, the garden. I had to be removed for the house to be truly hers.

My grandmother's parents had thought she was too good for my grandfather. They were Irish, shipworkers who had gotten the hell out of Locust Point and moved uptown, to Charles Village, where the houses were much bigger. They looked down on my grandfather just because he was where they once were. It killed them, the idea that their precious youngest daughter might move back to the neighbourhood and live with an Italian, to boot. Everybody's got to look down on somebody. If there's not somebody below you, how do you know you've travelled any distance at all in your life? For my dad's generation, it was all about the blacks. I'm not saying it was right, just that it was, and it hung on because it was such a stark, visible difference. And now the rules have changed again, and it's the young people with money and ambition who are buying the houses in Locust Point, and the people in places like Linthicum and Catonsville and Arbutus are the ones to be pitied and condescended to. It's hard to keep up.

My hand curled tight around the neck of the wine bottle. But I placed it in its berth in the special refrigerator, gently, as if I were putting a newborn back in its bed.

"One last time?" I asked her.

"Of course," she said.

She clearly was thinking it would be the bed, romantic and final, but I opted for the bathroom, wanting to see her from all angles. Wanting her to see me, to witness, to remember how broad my shoulders are, how white and small she looked when I was holding her against my chest.

When I moved my hands from her hips to her head, she thought I was trying to position her mouth on mine. It took her a second to realize that my hands were on her throat, not her head, squeezing, squeezing, squeezing. She fought back, if you could call it that, but all her hands could find was marble, smooth and immutable. Yeah, that's another word I know. Immutable. She may have landed a few scratches, but a man in my work gets banged up all the time. No one would notice a beaded scab on the back of my hand, or even on my cheek.

I put her body in a trash bag, covering it with lime leftover from a landscaping job. Luckily, she hadn't been so crazed that she wanted a fireplace in the basement, so all I had to do was pull down the fake front I had placed over the old hearth, then brick her in, replace the fake front. It wasn't planned, not a moment of it, but when it happened, I knew what to do, as surely as I know what to do when a floor isn't level or a soffit needs to be closed up so birds can't get in.

Her computer was on, as always, her e-mail account open because she used cable for her Internet, a system I had installed. I read a few of her sent messages, just to make sure I aped her style, then typed one to an office address, explaining the family emergency that would take me out of town for a few days. Then I sent one to "Dennis," angry and hate-filled, accusing him of all kinds of things, telling him not to call or write. Finally, I cleaned the house best I could, especially the bathroom, although I didn't feel I had to be too conscientious. I was the contractor. Of course my fingerprints would be around. The last thing I did was grab that bottle of Chardonnay, took it home to Angeline, who liked it just fine, although she would have fainted if she knew what it cost.

Weeks later, when Deirdre was officially missing and increasingly presumed dead according to the articles I read in the *Sunpapers*, I sent a bill for the projects that I had done at cost, marked it "Third and Final Notice" in large red letters, as if I didn't know what was going on. She was just an address to me, one of a half-dozen open accounts. Her parents paid it, even apologized for their daughter being so irresponsible, buying all this stuff she couldn't afford. I told them I understood, having kids of my own, Joseph Jr. getting ready for college next year. I said I was so sorry for what had happened and that I hoped they found her soon. I do feel sorry for them. They can't begin to cover the monthly payments on the place, so it's headed toward foreclosure. The bank will make a nice profit, as long as the agents gloss over the reason for the sale; people don't like a house with even the hint of a sordid history.

And I'm glad now that I put in the wine cellar. Makes it less likely that the new owner will want to dig out the basement. Which means there's less chance of a collapse, and less likelihood that they'll ever find that little bag of bones in the hearth.

Wake Up Little Suzie

by

MARY JANE MAFFINI

NOW THAT POPS wasn't there to keep an eye on things, it was all up to Suze. Someone had to make sure Mike Jr. learned his times tables and saved his paper route money for a winter jacket. Someone had to check Mom didn't fall asleep with her cigarette still burning and get them booted out of another apartment. Suze didn't mind. She taught Mike Jr. her best arithmetic tricks and showed him how to tie knots and read maps so he could get his Cub badges. She was a light sleeper, so it wasn't so hard to get up and check the sofa for smouldering butts. Pops always said you do what you have to.

She kept the calendar with the due dates for the rent and the electricity and picked up the money from the trust account at the bank and delivered the envelopes with the exact amount in them to the right places at the right time. Every two weeks she paid the bills for their grocery orders at Morrison's.

Suze made sure she led her Grade Five class (average 98.2%) because, like Pops used to say, you don't ever give the nuns one more thing to look down their long noses at you over.

She'd had her troubles with the nuns, especially Mother St. Basil, who used to say rotten things to her in front of the class and make mean hints about Mom and her boyfriends. Especially after the time Officer Collins came to the school to ask Suze and Mike Jr. about Arvie. Mother St. Basil was always making a big show of sending Suze to wash her hands and saying things like "dirt attracts dirt." Suze knew what she meant, and so did everyone else in the class.

But now she had Miss deLorentis for Grade Six. Miss deLorentis never said a whisper about how Suze was dressed or what was in her lunch pail. She only cared about what kind of person you were, and not who your mother was. Suze hoped Miss deLorentis never found out that she signed all her own report cards. Miss deLorentis was perfect, with her shiny black hair, huge dark eyes, plaid skirts, tiny ankles and polished leather pumps. She wished Pops could have met Miss deLorentis.

But Pops was pushing up the daisies, as Arvie had just reminded her. "You can't go snivelling to your grandfather now that he's six feet under," Arvie would say with a smirk. Suze bit her tongue so she wouldn't tell Arvie that if Pops was alive, there'd be no way a bum like you could have moved in with Mom. Mom would have slapped her right across the face if Suze talked to Arvie like that. Mom thought Arvie was fun and full of surprises. Suze didn't like those surprises.

Like now, Arvie sneaking up on her while she was frying up baloney and heating a can of peas for supper.

"You're sitting on a fortune, Suze? Know what that means?"

Suze didn't have to know what it meant. If it came out of Arvie's mouth, there was something dirty about it. "That's disgusting. I hope Mom hears you."

But Mom couldn't hear anything. She was playing her three new forty-fives, and she just kept dancing in the front room while Arvie supposedly got her a Captain Morgan's Dark with Coke. She loved the Everly Brothers and so had Suze, until Arvie had started singing "Wake Up Little Suzie" in that creepy way and ruined it for her.

Mom called out from the front room. "Get in here, Arvie, I'm putting on 'Little Darlin'." It would have felt good to hear Mom laugh, except Arvie was getting too close again. Buckingham cigarettes and beer on his breath, and the smell of grease to keep his hair in the duck's ass. Sweat from his open shirt. Suze was stuck by the stove, with him pressing in, stuck feeling his belly on her back. One of these days, she was going to throw up.

"Hey, Mike Jr.," she said, whipping the frying pan off the burner, "what are you doing back so soon?" Arvie whirled just long enough for Suze to duck by him and park herself in the front room. "Mom, I got two really big tests coming up, and I'll be studying tonight, so don't anybody bother me. Okay? Fathers of Confederation. Middle names and everything. And provincial capitals, including the Northwest Territories and the Yukon. So I won't open my door, even if you knock on it. Anyway, I'll have the Hit Parade on, I won't even hear you."

Mom kept dancing all by herself. "Get that stinking baloney out of here. And make sure Mike Jr. goes to bed all right."

Suze tried to lean close and whisper so Arvie couldn't hear. It wasn't such a great idea for Arvie to know everything. It wouldn't be the first time he'd been through Mike's stuff when Mom got past her third dark and dirty. Suze was pretty sure that's when Pop's war medals went missing. "He's at the Cub sleep-out tonight. You know that. I'm doing his paper route for him tomorrow."

Mom gave her a small shove. "Watch your feet, Suze."

Pops always said that Mom used to be fine. It was only after Mike Sr. passed away she went a bit foolish. He could hardly blame her, no husband and two kids. What would Pops say if he saw Mom the way she was now, with her hair bleached nearly white and her red lipstick, wearing tight Capris and her banlon sweater opened to the third button? She used to have mouse-coloured hair like Suze, and she used to be just as skinny. They both had freckles, but now Mom's were buried in pancake makeup.

Suze ate her supper at the dinette set with her back to the wall and her eye on the door in case Arvie came back. That was the reason Suze didn't have much stomach for the fried baloney and peas, even with tons of Heinz.

She ducked into Mike Jr.'s bedroom, which was really a storage closet, and felt around under the lumpy mattress, but no luck. It took a while for her to find the purple Crown Royal bag full of quarters, dimes and nickels stuffed into Mike Jr.'s Davy Crockett hat. She shoved the bag under her blouse. It wasn't fair that Mike Jr. got stuck without a window and had to do his homework at the kitchen table when Suze had a desk. Pops had built it himself. It had gotten a bit beat up in the last three moves, but it was still good once she put a pile of books where the leg had broken off.

Outside Mike Jr.'s room, she spotted Arvie leaning against the wall in the dark end of the hallway. "You going out tonight, Suze? You got someplace special in mind?"

Her heart jumped. She didn't see how he could know anything, but he did have that slippery grin on his lips, and she often caught him following her. Of course, she always gave him the slip, but it wasn't that easy. Pops used to say, keep your head up and don't let them see you sweat. She made sure she didn't run, just moved normally, until she closed her own door behind her and clicked the lock. She could still smell Arvie, even though he wasn't there. That was bad, having his smell in her head.

She listened, just in case Arvie was going to pull something tricky. After three dark and dirties, Mom could be passed out any minute. But it was quiet. And she had a Yale lock, bought with her summer baby walking money. She turned on the radio, Top 100, nice and loud. She slipped on her Mary Maxim sweater and hooked the rope on the radiator and opened the window. She hung on tight and shinnied down to the shed roof below. The rope always burnt her hands. She grabbed the rainspout on the side of the back porch and made it to the ground in two jumps, just missing Mike Jr.'s Red Rider wagon ready for the papers in the morning. Carrying all of Mike Jr.'s paper route money unbalanced her a bit. Maybe someday they'd move to a first floor apartment where you didn't have to practically break your neck to sneak out.

Suze loved this kind of night. The wind whipped the trees. The leaves whispered. The ones that had fallen crunched underfoot. Someone had been burning leaves in their yard. A couple of times she thought she heard something scurrying in the bushes. Just in case, she picked up a brick from the side of the Thompsons' house, where they were building a garage. They could afford to build a garage, but they never gave Mike Jr. so much as a nickel tip for the paper, and they cheated Suze when she walked the baby.

Sometimes it was good to have a brick on you. She kept away from the streetlights as she headed down the street. She stepped out of the way of the sandwich board sign on the sidewalk outside Viger's Variety Store. Mr. Viger was always yelling at kids when they bumped into it. She didn't mind being in the shadows. It was only a half moon, but she knew the way, could have found where she was headed in the pitch dark. Even though it was October, a bunch of Protestant kids were still slamming balls around as she passed the Tennis Club. In spite of the bright lights on the court, no one turned to watch her hurry by on the path behind. She checked twice over her shoulder then slid down the ravine and got herself over the brook and up the hill. You had to watch out on that path. If you weren't careful, you could bump into a rubbydub or find your way blocked by some older boys with that look in their eyes. Just in case, Suze kept the brick in her hand. And she could disappear through the trees like a puff of fog if she had to. Tonight the path was clear. She scrambled over the rocks, jumped the five-foot wrought iron fence and landed on the soft lawn.

The cemetery. It made a lot of people nervous, but Suze had always liked it, even more so now that Pops was there. Normally Suze would have stopped to check out the freshly dug grave in the next plot. But tonight she needed to get to Pops first. She cleared a few crunchy oak leaves from the front of Pop's gravestone. She checked that the little chrysanthemum she'd planted was still alive. They were supposed to bloom right through until November. Suze didn't have a lot of luck with the plants she brought to Pops, but she was working hard to get the hang of taking care of them. Next maybe she'd try to find some holly or something nice for Christmas. She didn't think the gardener at St. Francis of Assisi would miss one more plant.

She plunked herself down and leaned back onto the smooth slab of the monument and closed her eyes. It felt good, and no wonder. One hundred percent imported Italian granite. Soft grey with peach streaks running through it. Pops had told her all about the granite when they buried Mike Sr. The details made the difference. Dimensions. Shape. Choice of stone. Lettering. Pops favoured Gothic.

Cost more than his Desoto, he used to say, but his boy was worth it. The plot too cost a bomb, but Pops said you can't take it with you, but you sure can lie in it. Gramma's name was there first. Greta Mabel Hagan, beloved wife of Joseph, 1906–1950. Suze didn't really remember much about Gramma. Then, of course, Michael Gerard Hagan, 1932–1955. Every time Pops took them to visit, he'd make her and Mike Jr. swear on that grave they were never going to park their sorry butts within fifteen feet of a motorcycle. And last there was

Pops himself, Joseph Alexander Hagan 1902–1957. Suze was saving up to have "beloved grandfather" added, in Gothic.

The week after they buried Pops, Suze had spent a lot of time checking out the surfaces of every headstone in the cemetery, running her hands along their satin surfaces, comparing their thickness, design, tracing the different kind of lettering, admiring the sculptures on the fancy ones. This was the best by far. Pops had done a good job. He had classy neighbours too. The McCurdys on the left and the Hetheringtons on the right, even though Pops never had much use for the Hetheringtons. Still, they were important people.

Pop had always kept up with the news, and Suze made sure he got it. And she asked for advice too. Pops loved giving advice.

"Half moon tonight, Pops. You can see the big dipper. Nice weather, a bit cool. Things are good at school, and Mike Jr. got a ninety on his spelling test. But I got a problem with Arvie. He took Mom's cigarette money twice this month, and she's drinking a lot more with him around, and I caught him snooping through Mike Jr.'s room so many times already. He even follows me when I've got the rent. I had to duck through Chapman's lumberyard to get away from him. So I figured you wouldn't mind if I stashed Mike Jr.'s jacket money here under your chrysanthemum so that Arvie doesn't get his mitts on it."

Of course, Pops wouldn't mind something like that. She didn't mention Arvie rubbing up against her all the time and barging into the bathroom when she was in the tub. There wasn't anything Pops could do about it, and there was no point in worrying him.

Learn to pick your battles, Pops always said.

"Good news, Pops. You're going to have more company next door. Mrs. Hetherington from down Parker Street. You know her, she always went to the seven o'clock mass with that black hat on with the feather. You always said she thought she was Mrs. God. Her funeral's tomorrow at eleven. I heard the Monsignor saying the Mass. I imagine it will be a big deal, not as big as yours, of course." The Bishop himself had said Pop's funeral mass, since Pops had been big in the Knights of Columbus, so he wouldn't begrudge Mrs. Hetherington her Monsignor, even if he never could stand her when she was alive.

After Suze had filled him in on the news in the neighbourhood, usually she just sat there, relaxing, enjoying the quiet, leaning against the granite. Sometimes, if it had been a long day, she fell asleep. This time she jerked awake when she heard a soft thud from behind the headstone. She sat up. The wind? A raccoon? Gravediggers?

She smelled him before she saw him.

"Wake up, Little Suzie," Arvie said.

"I'm not asleep." Suze tried to keep her own voice calm, because she hadn't planted Mike Jr.'s money yet.

"How come you're playing hard to get?"

Suze thought fast. Arvie sounded drunk. Drunk enough to be mean, but not drunk enough to stumble over his own feet.

"You heard me," Arvie slithered around to the front of the gravestone. "Are you some kind of tease? There's a name for girls like you." His eyes glittered in the dark.

"Who's that behind you?" Suze said.

"You little slut, I'm not falling for that again," Arvie said.

Suze grabbed Mike Jr.'s money and scrambled behind the gravestone. She got to her feet and ran like hell. She zigged and zagged the way the boys did on the football field. Arvie was breathing hard and swearing. Suze was used to running, and she got as far as the McCurdys' plot, then she jumped over three small crosses of the Clancy babies, hoping Arvie would injure himself on them. But Arvie must have played football, because he seemed to catch on to her tricks. Her lungs were bursting, and she tried to think—if she got to the path and close enough to the tennis court, maybe some of the Protestant kids would hear her if she could scream loud enough. Even a rubbydub would have looked good at that moment. Arvie couldn't do anything with anyone watching. She doubled back and headed towards the fence with the path on the other side of it, coming up close to Pop's grave, when Arvie launched himself. He slammed her behind the knees. She got a mouthful of damp earth from Mrs. Hetherington's freshly dug grave when she hit the ground.

He was heavy and strong. Suze couldn't move out from under him, couldn't breathe. Arvie lifted himself long enough to flip her over.

"You know you've been asking for it," he said.

You do what you have to, Pops would have said.

It seemed like Suze's arm had a mind of its own, like it belonged to someone else. It seemed like slow motion watching the arm arc and the old Crown Royal bag with Mike Jr.'s paper route money make a perfect half circle before it slammed into Arvie's temple. Slow motion as the bag opened and nickels, dimes and quarters scattered around the open grave, clinking. Suze was floating somewhere else, watching.

She lay still for a long time with him on top of her, twitching. He made a noise like a gurgling drain. It seemed like an hour before she was able to push him off.

Suze crawled a few feet and was sick in the McCurdys' rose bushes. When she finally got her legs to stop shaking and forced herself to look, Arvie had stopped gurgling. He lay there, the side of his head a new shape. Suze gathered up what she could find of Mike Jr.'s scattered collection of quarters, nickels and dimes and tried to think. What would Pops do?

MISS DELORENTIS understood about the funeral. She squeezed Suze's hand. Her black eyes shone.

"Of course, you must go. Especially an old family friend. And no, you won't need to make up anything you miss afterwards. You're so far ahead. Your detailed map of the provinces was magnificent. You really have what it takes."

Suze put on her navy sweater and her Black Watch kilt. She borrowed Mom's little black veil with the bow on it. Mom was passed out on the sofa, so she didn't need to make up a lie.

The funeral went all right. Suze didn't think the Monsignor had nearly as much class as the Bishop. The Hetheringtons didn't seem all that upset. Pops would enjoy hearing about that. He once said that Mrs. Hetherington had the temperament of a wasp and the face of a basset hound and the mind of a cesspool. Suze arrived at the cemetery shortly after the hearse and watched the six pall bearers slowly lower the mahogany coffin with the shiny brass handles into the open hole. When it settled in, each member of the Hetherington family threw a handful of earth onto the coffin. Five grown-up sons, each with the same sloping shoulders and unhappy eyes as the father. None of the Hetheringtons had started to cry at that point, and it didn't look like they were about to. They were not people who looked good in black. No one put a flower on the coffin like Suze and Mike Jr. had with Pops. Suze didn't expect they would engrave "beloved" on Mrs. Hetherington's stone. Suze shook Mr. Hetherington's small dry hand before she left. "I'm sorry for your loss," she said.

AT THE DESK, Officer Collins looked up with surprise. "Look what the cat dragged in, will ya, Reg."

"Here comes trouble," said the other cop, who had a pockmarked face.

They were both grinning, but Suze managed not to grin back at them.

"Something wrong, Suze?" Officer Collins said.

"My mom's boyfriend has gone off, and she's real worried about him. I wondered if you can do something to find him."

"You mean that Arvie Penny?"

"A bad penny always turns up," Officer Collins said.

Suze waited until they stopped laughing. "She's scared something bad might have happened to him."

The other cop said, "I imagine it did. But I'll tell you, she's better off without Arvie Penny. And so are you kids. Trust me."

"Can you put out a bulletin? On the radio?"

"Get a load of that, will you, Reg. A bulletin."

"That's a laugh and a half. Look, that bum is probably stepping off the bus in Toronto now, planning to hole up with some little piece of jailbait."

"Watch your language, Reg. There's not much we can do about it, Suze. Remember I warned you about him? We don't have him in the cell. Tell her to call us if he comes back."

"Okay," said Suze.

"Maybe we can toss him behind bars for her," Officer Collins said.

"I know he's not the greatest guy but, even so, can you do a search or something?"

"I wish we could help you, Suze, but we're having a busy time of it here. We got a lot of petty theft and vandalism going on. Things disappearing, building materials, flowers, shrubs, lots of crazy things. Someone dumped a load of dirt in the nuns' station wagon over at the convent."

"Well, whatever you could do to find him would be appreciated," Suze said.

"Never gives up. God, you're just like the old man. Ain't she, Reg?"

"Your grandfather all over. Same eyes, same attitude. Too bad you're not a boy, you'd make a hell of an officer when you grow up, just like Joe."

"So listen, Suze," Officer Collins said. "If he never shows up, your mom's lucky and so are you. Good riddance to bad rubbish."

"Thanks anyway," said Suze. You gotta get your ducks in a row, Pops always said.

"QUARTER MOON TONIGHT, Pops. You can see both the dippers. There's a bit of frost in the air. The Protestant kids finally quit playing tennis. I'm sorry for the inconvenience about your new neighbour. I did what I had to, and I hope it doesn't bother you too much." Suze was leaning up against the cool front of the gravestone, bringing Pops up to date. "They say eternity's a long time, and it's bad enough you got to put up with Mrs. Hetherington right next door, let alone Arvie buried right underneath her. I was pretty worried they'd find him before they buried her. I did a good job covering him up. I used the sign from Viger's Variety, it was just the right size and heavy enough in case he stiffened up. I levelled the space around him with some bricks from the Thompsons' and put enough dirt on top to hide everything. The hardest part was getting rid of the extra soil so the mound wasn't too high after they covered the coffin. I'm glad I had Mike Jr.'s wagon. You always told me to watch out for the details. Lucky not everyone's good with details like you. No one noticed the hole was only about five feet. I know you wouldn't approve of some of what I did, but remember what you told me about making tough choices when you have to.

"Mom's still drinking too much and crying most of the time. She says she's going to leave us here for a while and go to Toronto looking for him. That might be good. We won't have to worry about fires in the sofa. Mike Jr. got his citizenship badge and his winter jacket. I got a hundred per cent on the Great Lakes and Canada's exports. You would like Miss deLorentis a lot. She says I've got what it takes. I think she's right. I think I'll have what it takes to be a cop like you when I grow up."

Lily and the Sockeyes

by

SARA PARETSKY

WHEN CLEMENTINE DUVAL TOOK THE JOB of managing public relations for the Vancouver Sockeye baseball team, the sports side of town buzzed. Nepotism, some said. After all, if her father hadn't been Hall of Fame shortstop Leon DuVal, the Sockeyes would never have talked to her. True, she was an athlete in her own right—women's NCAA strike-out leader when she played softball for the University of Kansas. True, she'd studied journalism and covered sports for several local papers for five years. But still—a woman handling the press for a men's pro team? If Leon hadn't bought a piece of the Sockeyes, the sportswriters said, it would never have happened.

Other tongues clacked about WXJ sportscaster Jimmy-Bob Reedy. Sixty if he was a day, fat, slack-lipped, with hands he couldn't keep to himself, he'd been chased out of Los Angeles by an angry Dodger franchise. Five years later, he had somehow ingratiated himself with the Sockeye front office and was the lead announcer on both television and radio. While loyal fans—and hapless colour man Carlos Edwards—flinched, Jimmy-Bob lost track of the ball-strike count, forgot who was at bat, mispronounced names and droned on about his latest fishing trip.

Three WXJ women staffers had quit after doing technical back-up for him. The station and the front office gave handsome severance pay to stop possible attempted-rape charges, but the tales were known widely among sportswriters. How, they wondered, would Clementine react if Jimmy-Bob copped a feel? Known for her slow curve and her fast temper, she might well break his nose. However much that might please the fans, it wouldn't endear her to the front office.

The team gave Clementine mixed reviews. The fact that her college pitching stats were better than their two-million-dollar Cy Young starter was gleefully repeated in the papers. When Jason Colby gave up a walk and three consecutive doubles in a crucial game with Philadelphia, Jimmy-Bob talked on the air about little else for days.

"Why Carlos," he'd say to his long-suffering back-up, "our cute little Clementine could of got us out of that inning without a scratch. You see her working with the boys at batting practice? You should a caught her from behind on her follow-through." Followed by a wet-lipped laugh.

Clementine had pitched for batting practice a couple of times as a publicity gimmick. She had a decent fastball and a good curve, but no one—least of all herself—thought she was any competition for Jason Colby. But the Cy Young winner was having a bad year, and he couldn't laugh off Jimmy-Bob's sniping. Even though he knew it wasn't Clementine's fault, he reacted by refusing her efforts to set up interviews and keep relations running smoothly with the press until his rhythm returned.

She had more success with young players still trying to prove themselves. She'd bring them over to her father's apartment for dinner, and they would sit stiffly on their chairs listening to Leon discourse on fielding and hitting: it couldn't hurt their chances in the majors for Leon DuVal to know who they were.

The other person who wasn't crazy about Clementine's sports career was her grandmother. Lily DuVal, a notable actress in her day, still carried considerable punch in film and theatre circles. She had no use for sports, and had never understood why her son wanted to go into baseball when she'd lined up a couple of movie parts for him. Her daughter-in-law had even less love of baseball and had walked out on Leon and two-year-old Clementine. Lily took in her grand-daughter and tried to instill in her a hatred of baseball and a love of theatre. Alas, neither took.

When Clementine graduated from college, she returned to the city to live with her grandmother in Lily's twenty-room mansion in suburban Fisherman's Cove. Lily, who adored her, swept magnificently through the house in emerald-studded caftans, entertained the theatre and the press with panache, and loftily ignored her grand-daughter's calling. "Clementine is in entertainment," she would tell people, smiling maliciously.

Lily was a vegetarian and a single-malt whiskey drinker. Loch Ness Distillers flew in crates of twenty-three-year-old Glen Moray whiskey for her from Scotland. Some people said that she and Sir Malcolm Darrough, Loch Ness's chairman, had been more than close friends in the thirties. All Lily would say was she judged a man by his taste in single malts, not how far he could hit a silly white ball.

Other dear friends said that despite her famed hatred of baseball, Leon got his start with the Sockeyes because of Lily's "friendship" with Sockeye owner Teddy Wolitzer. After Clementine had been around the Sockeye dugout and front office for three months, she naturally heard these stories, which lost none of their zest to the tellers for being forty years old. With the same straightforward action that characterized her fastball, she asked Lily about it one night at dinner.

"I hope it's not true," she said, her mouth full of lentil salad (with endive, tomatoes and onions—a summer treat, Lily called it). "I mean, he may have been the world's biggest charmer when he was thirty, Granny, but he's almost as disgusting as Jimmy-Bob Reedy. And almost as fat, too. Around the newsroom, they call him Teddy Bear, not because he's cute, you know, but because of his paws. I believe the stories they tell about him and Jason Colby's daughter. He's just the type, you know."

Lily raised her plucked eyebrows as high as the line of her brilliantly dyed turquoise hair. "Really, Clementine. Isn't it bad enough that you bring home earned-run averages and at-bats, without dredging up all this ancient—and very dull—gossip? Could we change the topic, please? How's your *Jock-Talk* program going?"

This was Lily's name for Clementine's boldest PR venture to date. Clementine had done the traditional—bat days, glove days, autograph days ad nauseam. But she believed baseball's great untapped market was the woman spectator. In a survey of the ten most popular sports among women, baseball wasn't even ranked, while football was fourth behind tennis, ice-skating and gymnastics. How to get women interested in baseball? She had talked it over with Lily.

"Impossible!" her grandmother had snorted. "The only thing even remotely appealing about baseball is the bodies of the players. And even those are only good on a hit-or-miss basis."

Clementine's eyes lit up. "Granny! That's it! We'll get cameras in the locker room after games. We'll have the jock-of-the-week, and we'll reveal everything about him. Everything!"

In execution, the idea had to be toned down a little. Ballplayers, while as graphic as the next man in their discussions of female anatomy, proved strangely shy about revealing all on national television. In fact, when Clementine came into the locker room for the first time after a brilliant 2–1 victory over Montreal, the speed with which everyone leapt to the nearest towel was twice as fast as they ever ran the baselines.

After overcoming the ballplayers' initial reluctance, the in-depth profiles, done by Carlos Edwards, proved very popular. They couldn't do one every week—there are only so many good-looking jocks, and they produce a limited number of heart-stopping plays. But every two or three weeks Clementine and Carlos Edwards would pick a player and produce an interview accompanied by candid photographs. Clementine's forthright, friendly manner got the men to reveal details about their lives that their wives and coaches didn't always know.

When Jimmy-Bob used his pressure at WXJ to keep the interviews off the air, the *Herald-Star* agreed to run the stories. The sports section included a poster-size picture of the player in uniform. The first thousand women to come to the ballpark on the next game day received a free copy of a candid glossy colour shot, and the player would meet twenty women for drinks on the first following non-game day. The women's names were selected by random drawing of their ticket stubs, so they had to come to the ballpark to participate.

The campaign proved so popular that other major-league teams soon started their own copycat programs. Lily was proud of her granddaughter's ingenuity. She secretly read the *Herald-Star* sports section on interview days. Teddy Wolitzer bragged openly, as did Leon DuVal.

The only person who wasn't happy was Jimmy-Bob Reedy. He already worried that fans preferred Carlos Edwards's reporting style. Carlos had been a Cy Young winning pitcher himself in a brilliant career with the Kansas City Royals. He not only understood the game well, but could talk about it.

Until the *Jock-Talk* program started, Jimmy-Bob got his pals in the Sockeye front office to keep Carlos's air time to a minimum. Now, however, the younger man was getting a lot of publicity. The *Herald-Star* articles proved so popular that the paper got their TV station, WSNP, to run tapes of Carlos's interviews. Jimmy-Bob tried blocking this in court, claiming it violated his exclusivity rights for Sockeye baseball coverage. He lost the suit and the newspapers made him look ridiculous.

Angry and humiliated, Jimmy-Bob started ridiculing Clementine on the air. His beady, lecherous eyes had taken in the fact that Carlos and Clementine were spending more and more time in restaurants and bars discussing *Jock-Talk*. He even happened to drive "casually" by Carlos's apartment one morning in time to see Clementine come out, laughing, arm-in-arm with Carlos.

The sight added to his rage, because his early amorous efforts with Clementine had been soundly rebuffed. No one ever knew exactly what happened between them in private, but the day after Jimmy-Bob had invited Clementine to stay late to work on publicity, he had taken time off to treat an abscessed tooth. When he finally returned to the studio, his jaw was badly swollen. "It might have been from dental work," one columnist said dubiously. The other sportswriters had a field day ("NCAA Pitching Ace Connects," the *Province* gleefully reported).

Jimmy-Bob hoped that Carlos might react wildly to his attacks on Clementine. Then he could get the Sockeyes to cancel his contract. Or his attacks might provoke a response from Clementine herself that would turn the Sockeye front office against her. So he carolled happily about her possible sex life, insinuating that all women athletes were lesbians, discussed her probable drug habits, and how she wouldn't have a job at all without Leon and Lily's influence. He was even foolhardy enough to allude to Wolitzer and Lily's forty-year-old romance.

Carlos controlled himself with an effort. He had played second fiddle to Jimmy-Bob for two years, maintaining a cheerful camaraderie on the air. He reminded himself of the three years he'd played for a manager who hated him and still won twenty games each season. Off the air, he contemplated lying in wait for Jimmy-Bob and mugging him, or fiddling with the brakes on his car so that he would plunge into Howe Sound when he next went fishing.

Leon DuVal put in his two cents with Teddy Wolitzer.

"Come'n, Teddy. That lump of lard is screwing my daughter on the air. Not to mention what he's saying about Lily, who doesn't take too kindly to insults."

Wolitzer lit a fresh cigar. "Just be glad he ain't screwing her in the press room, Leon. Come'n. This feud is sweet music to my ears. TV ratings have never been better. The fans are pouring into the ballpark. I ain't gonna put a plug in the guy's mouth. He may be crazy, but he's selling ad time for the network."

Word of Jimmy-Bob's attacks reached Lily quickly enough. Not from Clementine, who didn't pay much attention to him—she figured if he got too wild she'd just break the other side of his jaw— nor from Leon, who knew his mother's temper of old. But one or another of Lily's pals in the press corps came out for cocktails or dinner most days. And one of them, a drama critic, brought the word out to Fisherman's Cove.

Lily took the unprecedented step of turning on WXJ. In all the years Leon had played, when he batted .295 and won a Golden Glove three seasons running, Lily had never watched a Sockeye game. Now she spent all of one hot August week watching them in a road series with Chicago. Her eyes began to sparkle dangerously.

Clementine, dividing her evenings between Lily and Carlos— between tofu and hamburgers—came in one afternoon to find Lily pacing the length of the patio, green silk billowing around her as it sought to keep pace with the swift movement of her legs.

"That man is a menace," she pronounced majestically.

"What man, Granny? You don't mean Carlos, do you? I thought you liked him. And don't tell me I'm not old enough—"

Lily cut her short. "Don't be ridiculous. I'm delighted to see you having fun with a nice boy with good legs. I'm talking about that fat, slobbering ape on television."

Clementine's eyes opened wide. "Granny! Don't tell me you've been watching the games! You shouldn't, really. Jimmy-Bob is a jerk. Why, yesterday when Sergio Diaz was batting he called him Manford Yates, and when he took a curve that just clipped the inside of the plate, Jimmy-Bob started yelling that it was high and outside and should have been ball four!"

Lily snorted. "Don't talk like that in front of me, Clementine. You know I don't care for it. I have no interest in anything Jimmy-Bob might say about any ballgame. It is his personal comments that disturb me."

"You mean because he talks about me being a lesbian Communist? I don't care. If he bothers me too much, I'll just blacken both his eyes so he won't broadcast for a week."

Lily came to a halt in front of her granddaughter. "No doubt. I expect such a lack of subtlety from someone who eschewed the theatre for a baseball scholarship. And what are you going to do to stop his innuendos against me?" Her nostrils widened. "No, I'll think of a different way to cook his goose. Something he won't forget as fast as a black eye or two."

Clementine put an arm around her grandmother. "Whatever you say, Granny. Just don't be too rough with him—I think he's support-ing a couple of ex-wives and three or four children."

Lily decided her subtle silencing of Jimmy-Bob Reedy would take place in front of as many people as possible. She would invite the whole Sockeye front office, Jimmy-Bob, Carlos and the rest of the broadcast team, and of course the players, to a magnificent party out at Fisherman's Cove. A blanket invitation was given to reporters and TV personalities in the city.

Clementine told her the Sockeyes had a day off in a long home stand right after Labour Day, so Lily announced that as the party date. Only Carlos knew what she was planning, because she needed his help. He took to spending evenings at the mansion, huddled with Lily. Clementine found herself feeling jealous—after all, Lily had pretty nice legs herself. She might be seventy-five, but yoga and high spirits concealed the fact admirably.

Clementine tried to swallow her hurt feelings and took on her usual role at Lily's parties: managing all the practical details. All Lily would tell her granddaughter about the entertainment was that she wanted four five-foot televisions installed in the ballroom. Clementine sighed resignedly and called electronic shops: Granny only got worse if you acted as though you cared what she was doing.

Lily relaxed her strict vegetarian rules for the occasion, allowing Clementine to order fish and pâté to feed a guest list which grew with each passing day. Somehow a film producer just happened to be in town, the publisher of Lily's racy memoirs, the travel editor for the *New York Times*, and so it went. Sir Malcolm Darrough apparently had got wind of the affair and was jetting in on his company plane with a case or two of private label Glen Moray whiskey. And another old flame, head of a steel company, was flying in from Chicago.

For the bulk of the party Lily proposed champagne, so Clementine ordered thirteen cases of brut. Lily didn't waste her single-malt on the world at large. "It's not for silly ballplayers who want to get drunk as fast as possible. Only those who have the palate to appreciate it will be given a chance to drink it."

By the day of the party, the guest list had grown to three hundred. Since Lily always had everything her own way, even the weather cooperated: it was a sparkling September day, the leaves beginning to show hints of red and yellow, but the air kissed with the warmth of summer.

Guests began arriving in the early afternoon, laden with swimming suits for use at Lily's private beach. She managed to greet most people as they arrived. "Champagne and food on the patio and in the ballroom. Now you must be in the ballroom at six for the entertainment. It's really special."

Clementine herself served Glen Moray according to Lily's orders. Not even Teddy Wolitzer was allowed any—maybe, Clementine thought, all the tales about Lily and Teddy were so much smoke. Her grandmother's ex-lovers were always treated graciously, and the movie producer, Sir Malcolm, and the head of the Chicago steel company could be seen genially drinking and smoking in a corner together, with frequent visits from Lily herself.

By five P.M. it was clear that the party was one of Lily's major successes. Nine cases of champagne had already been disposed of, along with fifty pounds of shrimp, twenty of salmon, innumerable little cakes and giant bowls of fruit. While Lily, exotic in transparent silk and the emeralds which were world-famous, floated from one happy group to the other, it was Clementine who made the party tick. She kept a scrupulous eye on guests with a potential for battle, separating them dexterously into other groups, seeing that everyone was kept supplied with food and drink.

Jimmy-Bob, who had arrived early and was inclined to be aggressive, presented the biggest problem. Whenever Clementine tried to steer him from some prominent person whom he was offending, he would slip an arm tightly around her, squeeze her, and say, "I'm working to convert our little lesbian here. Me and Carlos are working on it together. Who's winning, babe?"

Because it was a public occasion, Clementine restrained herself from slugging him. She did once dig her pointed heels into his instep with a happy smile on her face. He winced in pain and loosened his grip so that she could break away from him and redirect the people he was talking to.

At six, Lily and Clementine herded the guests into the ballroom. Lily attached herself to Jimmy-Bob. "Now for my most special guest, a special place of honour." While three hundred people disposed themselves around four wide-screen TVs, Lily made sure that Jimmy-Bob had a front-row seat.

The lights went out and the screens came to life. To the strains of "Take Me Out to the Ballgame," the words, "Highlights of the Sockeyes' Man of the Hour" flashed on the screens. Then a close-up of Jimmy-Bob's face, red, veinous, slack-lipped. The crowd laughed. For the next fifteen minutes, they roared at a montage of Jimmy-Bob's greatest blunders, on and off the air.

Clementine watched silently. Lily had surely gone too far this time. Not to mention Carlos, who apparently had raided the WXJ tape library to pull the show together. Clementine wondered what she could do to stop it, and decided there wasn't a thing. She could only hope that Jimmy-Bob would feel too embarrassed to raise a legal stink, but knowing his temper, she didn't have much confidence in that. Carlos would lose his job; she'd probably lose hers, too. So maybe Lily could be persuaded to support the two of them. She was gloomily considering the possibility when a scream rose loud above the laughter, effectively shutting off the noise.

Clementine struggled to the wall where the lights were and turned them on. The ballroom was in total confusion. Some people were trying to leave, others to find what had caused the scream. As they pushed against each other, they created an immovable mass.

Clementine went behind the scenes where the A-V equipment was set up. She found Carlos doubled over with laughter.

"Enjoy yourself today, because tomorrow you're going to be out of work," she advised him shortly, hunting around in the equipment for a microphone.

She switched it on and spoke into it. Using her summer-camp counsellor voice, which effectively calmed screaming ten-year-olds, she asked for silence. When the room had quieted down, she explained where she was standing and requested anyone who knew of any problems to join her.

The ballroom promptly began buzzing again, but more quietly. She saw Leon work his way through the crowd to her.

"It's Jimmy-Bob," he explained when he reached her. "Someone stuck one of the carving knives for the salmon into him. I guess his blood seeped out to where one of the ladies from Los Angeles was sitting and she started to scream. I've already sent a waiter to call the police."

BY ELEVEN O'CLOCK the police had sorted through the bulk of the guests and had sent most of them home. The head of the investigating team, Lieutenant Oberlin, had asked Leon, Carlos, Lily and Clementine to wait for him in Lily's front drawing room. Teddy Wolitzer insisted on waiting, too, on the grounds that he needed to know any new developments which might affect the Sockeyes. A uniformed policeman stood guard, trying to control his awe at being with his childhood baseball heroes.

Every now and then, Lieutenant Oberlin sent in an additional suspect to wait. Jason Colby, the Sockeye starting pitcher, was among them. Sir Malcolm Darrough, although given permission to leave, hovered solicitously at Lily's emerald-laden shoulder. Lily herself, while losing none of her vivacity, had stopped trying to entertain her troubled guests.

When Lieutenant Oberlin finally joined them, his voice was hoarse from four hours of interrogations. He sent the uniformed man for a glass of water and settled back to talk to his chief suspects and their hostess.

"From what I have seen of the video, I'm surprised it was Mr. Reedy who was killed instead of you, Mr. Edwards, or—with respect—yourself, ma'am. I'd like to know what prompted you to show a libellous film like that to three hundred people with the subject watching."

Lily's painted eyebrows went up. "My good man—have you ever watched Jimmy-Bob Reedy's broadcasts of the Sockeyes? If you have, you know how he slandered everyone and anyone. I thought it was time to give him a dose of his own medicine."

She turned to Sir Malcolm, who was trying to silence her, and patted his hand. "Don't worry, Malcolm—I'm not telling the man anything he doesn't already know, I'm sure."

Lieutenant Oberlin swallowed some water and leaned back tiredly in his chair. "Now, I know Jimmy-Bob—Mr. Reedy—had been insulting you and Miss Clementine DuVal on the air: I heard him myself a few times. So the two of you were understandably angry with him. And Mr. Leon DuVal wanted Mr. Wolitzer here to take Reedy off the air. And Mr. Carlos Edwards, who's pretty friendly with Miss DuVal, was angry with the deceased for insulting her. So any of the four of you might have been angry enough to kill him.

"Mr. Reedy had also been insulting Jason Colby all year—saying that Clementine DuVal could out-pitch him and that he ought to be sent back to the minors. It's true Mr. Colby has had a bad season. I suppose any athlete should be used to being insulted by the press. But maybe you weren't, huh, Mr. Colby? I have statements from a couple of your team-mates who heard you threatening to kill the man a couple of times."

Colby turned a painful red under his sunburned skin. "I might've said something," he muttered. "You know, you get hot when you're not performing the way you think you should. But I didn't kill the guy."

"What about you, Mr. Edwards?"

Carlos looked embarrassed. "I agree the video wasn't in the best taste, Lieutenant. But it was such a sweet revenge on that jag-off—

better than murder. I sure didn't want to kill him this afternoon—I couldn't wait to see what he was going to do when the lights came up."

Oberlin nodded. "And I think the same could be said for Miss Lily DuVal. But you, Mr. DuVal—you were really angry about the attacks on your daughter's character. You were seen near Mr. Reedy before the lights went down. And as a trained athlete you certainly know enough about the human body to be able to stab a man to death. We're going to take you downtown for further questioning."

Clementine turned pale under her tan. "Wait a minute, Lieutenant. You're forgetting me: I'm a trained athlete, too, and it was me he was insulting. Besides, I live here—Leon doesn't—and I know all the silverware and stuff. I knew which knife to use."

Lily snorted. "Do stop the heroics, darling. Even if you haven't been in the theatre, a love of drama must be in your blood."

She turned to the policeman. "Lieutenant—could we use a little common sense? Let's talk about Mr. Reedy for a moment—however ugly a topic that is. Is there anyone in Vancouver who could stand listening to the man? He was disgusting. He apparently tried to rape every young lady who had to work with him—I've heard about pay-offs from Teddy Wolitzer to several women to keep their mouths shut. In addition, according to the boring stories my granddaughter brought home, he knew nothing about the game he was supposed to report on. The fans apparently preferred Mr. Edwards here, and it's not hard to understand why.

"Has it ever occurred to you to wonder why, in face of this concerted dislike, the Sockeyes let him announce their games?"

Lieutenant Oberlin looked at her intently. "Go on, ma'am."

Lily looked at Jason Colby. "I'm sorry to have to bring this up, Mr. Colby. But you have a daughter, don't you?"

Colby looked faint. "Alison," he said hoarsely. "She's eleven."

Lily nodded. "Teddy Wolitzer assaulted the child, didn't he? Last year?"

Jason only nodded without speaking.

"I've known Teddy for forty years now. Not a man who likes things going against him, are you, Teddy? I can guess what happened—he told you if you wanted to continue to pitch in the majors you wouldn't press charges."

Jason nodded again. "We sent her to live with her grandmother in California. But I can't get it out of my mind. My pitching's gone to hell. Then Jimmy-Bob made things worse, harping on and on about my playing. It was driving me off my head, but I didn't kill the guy. If I'd killed anyone, it would have been Wolitzer."

"Yes, dear," Lily said briskly. "Very upsetting. I don't blame you. But your daughter's story wasn't the well-kept secret Teddy might have hoped—Clementine brought home some garbled gossip about it earlier this summer. And presumably if Teddy did it once, there were other incidents with other little girls—right, Teddy? Did Jimmy-Bob find out about it? And use that information to force you to hire him and keep him in the lead announcing position?"

Leon nodded agreement. "Makes sense, Lily. You wouldn't know it, since you don't like baseball, but the commissioner would force him to sell the franchise if the word got out. Moral turpitude. They don't like the all-American game smirched by slime like child-abusers."

Lieutenant Oberlin got up and went over to Teddy. "We have people downtown looking through everyone's private papers for signs of blackmail or fraud involving Jimmy-Bob. So maybe we'll find something in your office, Mr. Wolitzer. Meanwhile, you have the right to remain silent, but if you give up that right, anything you say can be used as evidence against you ..."

After the police had left with Wolitzer, Lily leaned back in her chair. "Bring the Glen Moray, darling," she said to Clementine. "I think we all need a little drink."

Carlos followed Clementine from the room. "Listen, Clementine, don't be mad at me—I'm not in love with your grandmother—at least, I am, but not the way I am with you—I just wanted a chance to get revenge on that fat bastard. And you've got to admit—he died embarrassed."

They were gone for a long time. When they finally returned with the bottle, Lily raised her painted brows, but said only, "I thought you knew this house too well to get lost in it, darling."

She waited until everyone's glass had been filled before speaking again. "I spent several months with Teddy Wolitzer in 1946. I realized then what a vile man he was—which is why I never let him near my single-malt: that's for friends and whiskey lovers only." She raised her glass in a salute to them.

They lifted theirs to her.

"Lily," Sir Malcolm said, "you're incomparable."

String Music

by

GEORGE PELECANOS

WASHINGTON, D.C., 2001

TONIO HARRIS

Down around my way, when I'm not in school or lookin' out for my moms and little sister, I like to run ball. Pickup games mostly. That's not the only kind of basketball I do. I been playin' organized all my life, the Jelleff League and Urban Coalition, too. Matter of fact, I'm playin' for my school team right now, in the Interhigh. It's no boast to say that I can hold my own in most any kind of game. But pickup is where I really get amped.

In organized ball, they expect you to pass a whole bunch, take the percentage shot. Not too much showboatin', nothin' like that. In pickup, we ref our own games, and most of the hackin' and pushin' and stuff, except for the flagrant, it gets allowed. I can deal with that. But in pickup, see, you can pretty much freestyle, try everything out you been practising on your own. Like those Kobe and Vince Carter moves. What I'm sayin' is, out here on the asphalt you can really show your shit.

Where I come from, you've got to understand, most of the time it's rough. I don't have to describe it if you know the area of D.C. I'm talkin' about: the 4th District, down around Park View, in Northwest. I got problems at home, I got problems at school, I got problems walkin' down the street. I prob'ly got problems with my future, you want the plain truth. When I'm runnin' ball, though, I don't think on those problems at all. It's like all the chains are off, you understand what I'm sayin'? Maybe you grew up somewheres else, and if you did, it'd be hard for you to see. But I'm just tryin' to describe it, is all.

Here's an example: Earlier today I got into this beef with this boy James Wallace. We was runnin' ball over on the playground where I go to school, Roosevelt High, on 13th Street, just a little bit north of my neighbourhood. There's never any chains left on those outdoor buckets, but the rims up at Roosevelt are straight and the backboards are forgiving. That's like my home court. Those buckets they got, I been playin' them since I was a kid, and I can shoot the eyes out of those motherfuckers most any day of the week.

We had a four-on-four thing goin' on, a pretty good one, too. It was the second game we had played. Wallace and his boys, after we beat 'em the first game, they went over to Wallace's car, a black Maxima with a spoiler and pretty rims, and fired up a blunt. They were gettin' their heads up and listenin' to the new Nas comin' out the speakers from the open doors of the car. I don't like Nas's new shit much as I did *Illmatic*, but it sounded pretty good.

Wallace and them, they work for a dealer in my neighbourhood, so they always got good herb, too. I got no problem with that. I might even have hit some of that hydro with 'em if they'd asked. But they didn't ask.

Anyway, they came back pink-eyed, lookin' all cooked and shit, debatin' over which was better, Phillies or White Owls. We started the second game. Me and mines went up by three or four buckets pretty quick. Right about then I knew we was gonna win this one like we won the first, 'cause I had just caught a little fire.

Wallace decided to cover me. He had switched off with this other dude, Antuane, but Antuane couldn't run with me, not one bit. So Wallace switched, and right away he was all chest out, talkin' shit about how "now we gonna see" and all that. Whateva. I was on my inside game that day and I knew it. I mean, I was crossin' mother-fuckers *out*, just driving the paint at will. And Wallace, he was slow on me by, like, half a step. I had stopped passin' to the other fellas at that point, 'cause it was just too easy to take it in on him. I mean, he was givin' it to me, so why not?

'Bout the third time I drove the lane and kissed one in, Wallace bumped me while I was walkin' back up to the foul line to take the check. Then he said somethin' about my sneaks, somethin' that made his boys laugh. He was crackin' on me, is all, tryin' to shake me up. I got a nice pair of Jordans, the Air Max, and I keep 'em clean with Fantastik and shit, but they're from, like, last year. And James Wallace is always wearin' whatever's new, whatever it is they got sittin' up front at the Foot Locker, just came in. Plus Wallace didn't like me all that much. He had money from his druggin', I mean to tell you that boy had *every*thing, but he dropped out of school back in the tenth grade, and I had stayed put. My moms always says that some guys like Wallace resent guys like me who have hung in. Add that to the fact that he never did have my game. I think he was a little jealous of me, you want the truth.

I do know he was frustrated that day. I knew it, and I guess I shouldn't have done what I did. I should've passed off to one of my boys, but you know how it is. When you're proud about somethin', you got to show it, 'specially down here. And I was on. I took the check from him and drove to the bucket, just blew right past him as easy as I'd been doin' all afternoon. That's when Wallace called me a bitch right in front of everybody there.

There's a way to deal with this kinda shit. You learn it over time. I go six-two and I got some shoulders on me, so it wasn't like I feared Wallace physically or nothin' like that. I can go with my hands, too. But in this world we got out here, you don't want to be getting in any kinda beefs, not if you can help it. At the same time, you can't show no fear; you get a rep for weakness like that, it's like bein' a bird with a busted wing, sumshit like that. The other thing you can't do, though, you can't let that kind of comment pass. Someone tries to take you for bad like that, you got to respond. It's complicated, I know, but there it is.

"I ain't heard what you said," I said, all ice-cool and shit, seein' if he would go ahead and repeat it, lookin' to measure just how far he wanted to push it. Also, I was tryin' to buy a little time.

"Said you's a bitch," said Wallace, lickin' his lips and smilin' like he was a bitch his *own* self. He'd made a couple steps towards me and now he wasn't all that far away from my face.

I smiled back, halfway friendly. "You know I ain't no faggot," I said. "Shit, James, it hurts me to fart."

A couple of the fellas started laughin' then and pretty soon all of 'em was laughin'. I'd heard that line on one of my uncle's old-time comedy albums once, that old Signifyin' Monkey shit or maybe Pryor. But I guess these fellas hadn't heard it, and they laughed like a motherfucker when I said it. Wallace laughed, too. Maybe it was the hydro they'd smoked. Whatever it was, I had broken that shit down, turned it right back on him, you see what I'm sayin'? While they was still laughin', I said, "C'mon, check it up top, James, let's play."

I didn't play so proud after that. I passed off and only took a coupla shots myself the rest of the game. I think I even missed one on purpose towards the end. I ain't stupid. We still won, but not by much; I saw to it that it wasn't so one-sided, like it had been before.

When it was over, Wallace wanted to play another game, but the sun was dropping and I said I had to get on home. I needed to pick up my sister at aftercare, and my moms likes both of us to be inside our apartment when she gets home from work. Course, I didn't tell any of the fellas that. It wasn't somethin' they needed to know.

Wallace was goin' back my way, I knew, but he didn't offer to give me a ride. He just looked at me dead-eyed and smiled a little before him and his boys walked back to the Maxima parked along the curb. My stomach flipped some, I got to admit, seein' that flatline thing in his peeps. I knew from that empty look that it wasn't over between us, but what could I do?

I picked up my ball and headed over to Georgia Avenue. Walked south towards my mother's place as the first shadows of night were crawling onto the streets.

SERGEANT PETERS

It's five A.M. I'm sitting in my cruiser up near the station house, sipping a coffee. My first one of the night. Rolling my head around on these tired shoulders of mine. You get these aches when you're behind the wheel of a car six hours at a stretch. I oughta buy one of those things the African cabbies all sit on, looks like a rack of wooden balls. You know, for your back. I been doin' this for twenty-two years now, so I guess whatever damage I've done to my spine and all, it's too late.

I work midnights in the 4th District. 4D starts at the Maryland line and runs south to Harvard Street and Georgia. The western border is Rock Creek Park and the eastern line is North Capitol

Street. It's what the newspeople call a high-crime district. For a year or two I tried working 3D, keeping the streets safe for rich white people basically, but I got bored. I guess I'm one of those adrenaline junkies they're always talking about on those cop shows on TV, the shows got female cops who look more beautiful than any female cop I've ever seen. I guess that's what it is. It's not like I've ever examined myself or anything like that. My wife and I don't talk about it, that's for damn sure. A ton of cop marriages don't make it; I suppose mine has survived 'cause I never bring any of this shit home with me. Not that she knows about, anyway.

My shift runs from the stroke of twelve till dawn, though I usually get into the station early so I can nab the cruiser I like. I prefer the Crown Victoria. It's roomier, and once you flood the gas into the cylinders, it really moves. Also, I like to ride alone.

Last night, Friday, wasn't much different than any other. It's summer; more people are outside, trying to stay out of their unair-conditioned places as long as possible, so this time of year we put extra cars out on the streets. Also, like I reminded some of the younger guys at the station last night, this was the week welfare checks got mailed out, something they needed to know. Welfare checks mean more drunks, more domestic disturbances, more violence. One of the young cops I said it to, he said, "Thank you, Sergeant Dad," but he didn't do it in a bad way. I know those young guys appreciate it when I mention shit like that.

Soon as I drove south I saw that the avenue—Georgia Avenue, that is—was hot with activity. All those Jap tech bikes the young kids like to ride, curbed outside the all-night Wing n' Things. People spilling out of bars, hanging outside the Korean beer markets, scratching game cards, talking trash, ignoring the crackheads hitting them up for spare change. Drunks lying in the doorways of the closed-down shops, their heads resting against the riot gates. Kids, a lot of kids, standing on corners, grouped around tricked-out cars, rap music and that go-go crap coming from the open windows. The farther you go south, the worse all of this gets.

The bottom of the barrel is that area between Quebec Street and Irving. The newspapers lump it all in with a section of town called Petworth, but I'm talking about Park View. Poverty, drug activity, crime. They got that Section 8 housing back in there, the Park Morton complex. What we used to call the projects back when you could say it. Government-assisted hellholes. Gangs like the Park Street and Morton Street Crews. Open-air drug markets; I'm talking about blatant transactions right out there on Georgia Avenue. Drugs are Park View's industry; the dealers are the biggest employers in this part of town.

The dealers get the whole neighbourhood involved. They recruit kids to be lookouts for 'em. Give these kids beepers and cells to warn them off when the Five-O comes around. Entry-level positions. Some of the parents, when there *are* parents, participate, too. Let these drug dealers duck into their apartments when there's heat. Teach their kids not to talk to the Man. So you got kids being raised in a culture that says the drug dealers are the good guys and the cops are bad. I'm not lying. It's exactly how it is.

The trend now is to sell marijuana. Coke, crack and heroin, you can still get it, but the new thing is to deal pot. Here's why: In the District, possession or distribution of marijuana up to ten pounds— *ten pounds*—is a misdemeanour. Kid gets popped for selling grass, he knows he's gonna do no time. Even on a distribution beef, black juries won't send a black kid into the prison system for a marijuana charge, that's a proven fact. Prosecutors know this, so they usually no-paper the case. That means most of the time they don't even go to court with it. I'm not bullshitting. Makes you wonder why they even bother having drug laws to begin with. They legalize the stuff, they're gonna take the bottom right out the market, and the violent crimes in this city would go down to, like, nothing. Don't get me started. I know it sounds strange, a cop saying this. But you'd be surprised how many of us feel that way.

Okay, I got off the subject. I was talking about my night.

Early on I got a domestic call, over on Otis Place. When I got there, two cruisers were on the scene, four young guys, two of them with flashlights. A rookie named Buzzy talked to a woman at the front door of her row house, then came back and told me that the object of the complaint was behind the place, in the alley. I walked around back alone and into the alley and right off I recognized the man standing inside the fence of his tiny, brown-grass yard. Harry Lang, sixty-some years old. I'd been to this address a few times in the past ten years.

I said, "Hello, Harry," Harry said, "Officer," and I said, "Wait right here, okay?" Then I went through the open gate. Harry's wife was on her back porch, flanked by her two sons, big strapping guys, all of them standing under a triangle of harsh white light coming from a naked bulb. Mrs. Lang's face and body language told me that the situation had resolved itself. Generally, once we arrive, domestic conflicts tend to calm down on their own.

Mrs. Lang said that Harry had been verbally abusive that night, demanding money from her, even though he'd just got paid. I asked her if Harry had struck her, and her response was negative. But she had a job, too, she worked just as hard as him, why should she support his lifestyle and let him speak to her like that ... I was listening and not listening, if you know what I mean. I made my sincere face and nodded every few seconds or so.

I asked her if she wanted me to lock Harry up, and of course she said no. I asked what she did want, and she said she didn't want to see him "for the rest of the night." I told her I thought I could arrange that, and started back to have a talk with Harry. I felt the porch light go off behind me as I hit the bottom of the wooden stairs. Dogs had begun to bark in the neighbouring yards.

Harry was short and low-slung, a black black man, nearly feature-less in the dark. He wore a porkpie hat and his clothes were pressed and clean. He kept his eyes down as I spoke to him over the barks of the dogs. His reaction time was very slow when I asked for a response. I could see right away that he was on a nod.

Harry had been a controlled heroin junkie for the last thirty years. During that time, he'd always held a job, lived in this same house and been there, in one condition or another, for his kids. I'd wager he went to church on Sundays, too. But a junkie was what he was. Heroin was a slow ride down. Some folks could control it to some degree and never hit the bottom.

I asked Harry if he could find a place to sleep that night other than his house, and he told me that he "supposed" he could. I told him I didn't want to see him again any time soon, and he said, "It's mutual." I chuckled at that, giving him some of his pride back, which didn't cost me a thing. He walked down the alley, stopping once to cup his hands around a match as he put fire to a cigarette.

I drove back over to Georgia. A guy flagged me down just to talk. They see my car number and they know it's me. Sergeant Peters, the old white cop. You get a history with these people. Some of these kids, I know their parents. I've busted 'em from time to time. Busted their grandparents, too. Shows you how long I've been doing this.

Down around Morton I saw Tonio Harris, a neighbourhood kid, walking alone towards the Black Hole. Tonio was wearing those work boots and the baggy pants low, like all the other kids, although he's not like most of them. I took his mother in for drugs a long time ago, back when that *Love Boat* stuff was popular and making everyone crazy; his father—the one who impregnated his mother, I mean—he's doing a stretch for manslaughter, his third fall. Tonio's mother's clean now, at least I think she is; anyway, she's done a fairly good job with him. By that I mean he's got no juvenile priors, from what I know. A minor miracle down here, you ask me.

I rolled down my window. "Hey, Tonio, how's it going?" I slowed down to a crawl, took in the sweetish smell of reefer in the air. Tonio was still walking, not looking at me, but he mumbled something about "I'm maintainin'," or some shit like that. "You take care of yourself in there," I said, meaning in the Hole, "and get yourself home right after." He didn't respond verbally, just made a half-assed kind of acknowledgment with his chin.

I cruised around for the next couple of hours. Turned my spot on kids hanging in the shadows, told them to break it up and move along. Asked a guy in Columbia Heights why his little boy was out on the stoop, dribbling a basketball, at one in the morning. Raised my voice at a boy, a lookout for a dealer, who was sitting on top of a trash can, told him to get his ass on home. Most of the time, this is my night. We're just letting the critters know we're out here.

At around two I called in a few cruisers to handle the closing of the Black Hole. You never know what's going to happen at the end of the night there, what kind of beefs got born inside the club, who looked at who a little too hard for one second too long. Hard to believe that an ex-cop from Prince Georges County runs the place. That a cop would put all this trouble on us, bring it into our district. He's got D.C. cops moonlighting as bouncers in there, too, working the metal detectors at the door. I talked with one, a young white cop, earlier in the night. I noticed the brightness in his eyes and the sweat beaded across his forehead. He was scared, like I gave a shit. Asked us as a favour to show some kind of presence at closing time. Called me Sarge. Okay. I didn't answer him. I got no sympathy for the cops who work those go-go joints, especially not since Officer Brian Gibson was shot dead outside the Ibex Club a few years back. But if something goes down around the place, it's on me. So I do my job.

I called in a few cruisers and set up a couple of traffic barriers on Georgia, one at Lamont and one at Park. We diverted the cars like that, kept the kids from congregating on the street. It worked. Nothing too bad was happening that I could see. I was standing outside my cruiser, talking to another cop, Eric Young, who was having a smoke. That's when I saw Tonio Harris running east on Morton, heading for the housing complex. A late-model black import was behind him, and there were a couple of YBMs with their heads out the open windows, yelling shit out, laughing at the Harris kid, like that.

"You all right here?" I said to Young.

"Fine, Sarge," he said.

My cruiser was idling. I slid under the wheel and pulled down on the tree.

TONIO HARRIS

Just around midnight, when I was fixin' to go out, my moms walked into my room. I was sittin' on the edge of my bed, lacing up my Timbies, listening to PGC comin' from the box, Tigger doin' his shout-outs and then movin' right into the new Jay-Z, which is tight. The music was so loud that I didn't hear my mother walk in, but when I looked up, there she was, one arm crossed over the other like she does when she's tryin' to be hard, staring me down.

"Whassup, Mama?"

"What's up with *you*?"

I shrugged. "Back Yard is playin' tonight. Was thinkin' I'd head over to the Hole."

"Did you ask me if you could?"

"Do I *have* to?" I used that tone she hated, knew right away I'd made a mistake.

"You're living in my house, aren't you?"

"Uh-huh."

"You payin' rent now?"

"No, ma'am."

"Talkin' about *do I have to*."

"Can I go?"

Mama uncrossed her arms. "Thought you said you'd be studyin' up for that test this weekend."

"I will. Gonna do it tomorrow morning, first thing. Just wanted to go out and hear a little music tonight, is all."

I saw her eyes go soft on me then. "You gonna study for that exam, you hear?"

"I promise I will."

"Go on, then. Come right back after the show."

"Yes, ma'am."

I noticed as she was walkin' out the door her shoulders were getting stooped some. Bad posture and a hard life. She wasn't but thirty-six years old.

I spent a few more minutes listening to the radio and checking myself in the mirror. Pattin' my natural and shit. I got a nice modified cut, not too short, not too blown-out or nothin' like that. A lot of the fellas be wearin' cornrows now, tryin' to look like Iverson. But I don't think it would look right on me. And I know what the girls like. They look at me, they like what they see. I can tell.

Moms has been ridin' me about my college entrance exam. I fucked up the first one I took. I went out and got high on some fierce chronic the night before it, and my head was filled up with cobwebs the next morning when I sat down in the school cafeteria to take that test. I'm gonna take it again, though, and do better next time.

I'm not one of those guys who's got, what do you call that, illusions about my future. No hoop dreams about the NBA, nothin' like that. I'm not good enough or tall enough, I know it. I'm sixth man on my high school team, that ought to tell you somethin' right there. My uncle Gaylen, he's been real good to me, and straight-up with me, too. Told me to have fun with ball and all that, but not to depend on it. To stick with the books. I know I fucked up that test, but next time I'm gonna do better, you can believe that.

I was thinkin', though, I could get me a partial scholarship playin' for one of those small schools in Virginia or Maryland, William and Mary or maybe Goucher up in Baltimore. Hold up—Goucher's for women only, I think. Maybe I'm wrong. Have to ask my guidance counsellor, soon as I can find one. Ha, ha.

The other thing I should do, for real, is find me a part-time job. I'm tired of havin' no money in my pockets. My mother works up at the Dollar Store in the Silver Spring mall, and she told me she could hook me up there. But I don't wanna work with my mother. And I don't want to be workin' at no *Mac*Donald's or sumshit like that. Have the neighbourhood slangers come in and make fun of me and shit, standin' there in my minimum-wage uniform. But I do need some money. I'd like to buy me a nice car soon. I'm not talkin' about some hooptie, neither.

I did have an interview for this restaurant downtown, bussin' tables. White boy who interviewed kept sayin' shit like, "Do you think you can make it into work on time?" and do you think this and do you think that? Might as well gone ahead and called me a nigger right to my face. The more he talked, the more attitude I gave him with my eyes. After all that, he smiled and sat up straight, like he was gonna make some big announcement, and said he was gonna give me a try. I told him I changed my mind and walked right out of there. Uncle Gaylen said I should've taken that job and showed him he was wrong, for all of us. But I couldn't. I can't stand how white people talk to you sometimes. Like they're just there to make their own selves feel better. I hired a Negro today, and like that.

I *am* gonna take that test over, though.

I changed my shirt and went out through the living room. My sister was watchin' the BET videos on TV, her mouth around a straw, sippin' on one of those big sodas. She's startin' to get some titties on her. Some of the slick young niggas in the neighbourhood been commentin' on it, too. Late for her to be awake, but it was Friday night. She didn't look up as I passed. I yelled good-bye to my moms and heard her say my name from the kitchen. I knew she was back up in there 'cause I smelled the smoke comin' off her cigarette. There was a ten-dollar bill sittin' in a bowl by the door. I folded it up and slipped it inside my jeans. My mother had left it there for me. I'm tellin' you, she is cool people.

Outside the complex, I stepped across this little road and the dark courtyard real quick. We been livin' here a long time, and I know most everyone by sight. But in this place here, that don't mean shit.

The Black Hole had a line goin' outside the door when I got there. I went through the metal detector and let a white rent-a-cop pat me down while I said hey to a friend going into the hall. I could feel the bass from way out in the lobby.

The hall was crowded and the place was bumpin'. I could smell sweat in the damp air. Also chronic, and it was nice. Back Yard was doin' "Freestyle," off *Hood Related*, that double CD they got. I kind of made my way towards the stage, careful not to bump nobody, nodding to the ones I did. I knew a lot of young brothers there. Some of 'em run in gangs, some not. I try to know a little bit of everybody, you see what I'm sayin'? Spread your friends out in case you run into some trouble. I was smilin' at some of the girls, too.

Up near the front I got into the groove. Someone passed me somethin' that smelled good, and I hit it. Back Yard was turnin' that shit out. I been knowin' their music for like ten years now. They had the whole joint up there that night, I'm talkin' about a horn section and everything else. I must have been up there close to the stage for about, I don't know, an hour, sumshit like that, just dancing. It seemed like all of us was all movin' together. On "Do That Stuff," they went into this extended drum thing, shout-outs for the hoodies and the crews; I was sweatin' clean through my shirt, right about then.

I had to pee like a motherfucker, but I didn't want to use the bathroom in that place. All the hard motherfuckers be congregatin' in there, too. That's where trouble can start, just 'cause you gave someone some wrong kinda look.

When the set broke, I started to talkin' to this girl who'd been dancin' near me, smilin' my way. I'd seen her around. Matter of fact, I ran ball sometimes with her older brother. So we had somethin' to talk about straight off. She had that Brandy thing goin' on with her hair, and a nice smile.

While we was talkin', someone bumped me from behind. I turned around and it was Antuane, that kid who ran with James Wallace. Wallace was with him, and so were a coupla Wallace's boys. I nodded at Antuane, tryin' to communicate to him, like, "Ain't no thing, you bumpin' me like that." But Wallace stepped in and said somethin' to me. I couldn't even really hear it with all the crowd noise, but I could see by his face that he was tryin' to step *to* me. I mean, he was right up in my face.

We stared at each other for a few. I shoulda just walked away, right, but I couldn't let him punk me out like that in front of the girl.

Wallace's hand shot up. Looked like a bird flutterin' out of nowhere or somethin'. Maybe he was just makin' a point with that hand, like some do. But it rattled me, I guess, and I reacted. Didn't even think about it, though I should've. My palms went to his chest and I shoved him back. He stumbled. I saw his eyes flare with anger, but there was that other thing, too, worse than me puttin' my hands on him: I had stripped him of his pride.

There was some yellin' then from his boys. I just turned and bucked. I saw the bouncers started to move, talkin' into their head-sets and shit, but I didn't wait. I bucked. I was out on the street pretty quick, runnin' towards my place. I didn't know what else to do.

I heard Wallace and them behind me, comin' out the Hole. They said my name. I didn't look back. I ran to Morton and turned right. Heard car doors opening and slammin' shut. The engine of the car turnin' over. Then the cry of tires on the street and Wallace's boys laughin', yellin' shit out. I kept runnin' towards Park Morton. My heart felt like it was snappin' on a rubber string.

There were some younguns out in the complex. They were sittin' up on top of a low brick wall like they do, and they watched me run by. It's always dark here, ain't never no good kinda light. They got some dim yellow bulbs back in the stairwells, where the old-school types drink gin and shoot craps. They was back up in there, too, hunched down in the shadows. There was some kind of fog or haze out that night, too, it was kind of rollin' around by that old playground equipment, all rusted and shit, they got in the courtyard. I was runnin' through there, tryin' to get to my place.

I had to cross the little road in the back of the complex to get to my mother's apartment. I stepped into it and that's when I saw the black Maxima swing around the corner. Coupla Wallace's boys jumped out while the car was still movin'. I stopped runnin'. They knew where I lived. If they didn't, all they had to do was ask one of those younguns on the wall. I wasn't gonna bring none of this home to my moms.

Wallace was out of the driver's side quick, walkin' towards me. He was smilin' and my stomach shifted. Antuane had walked back by the playground. I knew where he was goin'. Wallace and them keep a gun, a nine with a fifteen-round mag, buried in a shoe box back there.

"Junior," said Wallace, "you done fucked up big." He was still smilin'.

I didn't move. My knees were shakin' some. I figured this was it. I was thinkin' about my mother and tryin' not to cry. Thinkin' about how if I did cry, that's all anyone would remember about me. That I went out like a bitch before I died. Funny me thinkin' about stupid shit like that while I was waitin' for Antuane to come back with that gun.

I saw Antuane's figure walkin' back out through that fog.

And then I saw the spotlight movin' across the courtyard, and where it came from. An MPD Crown Vic was comin' up the street, kinda slow. The driver turned on the overheads, throwing colours all around. Antuane backpedalled and then he was gone.

The cruiser stopped and the driver's door opened. The white cop I'd seen earlier in the night got out. Sergeant Peters. My moms had told me his name. Told me he was all right.

Peters was puttin' on his hat as he stepped out. He had pulled his nightstick, and his other hand just brushed the Glock on his right hip. Like he was just lettin' us all know he had it.

"Evening, gentlemen," he said easylike. "We got a problem here?"

"Nope," said Wallace, kinda in a white-boy's voice, still smiling.

"Somethin' funny?" said Peters.

Wallace didn't say nothin'. Peters looked at me and then back at Wallace.

"You all together?" said Peters.

"We just out here havin' a conversation," said Wallace.

Sergeant Peters gave Wallace a look then, like he was disgusted with him, and then he sighed.

"You," said Peters, turnin' to me. I was prayin' he wasn't gonna say my name, like me and him was friends and shit.

"Yeah?" I said, not too friendly but not, like, impolite.

"You live around here?" He *knew* I did.

I said, "Uh-huh."

"Get on home."

I turned around and walked. Slow but not too slow. I heard the white cop talkin' to Wallace and the others, and the crackle of his radio comin' from the car. Red and blue was strobin' across the bricks of the complex. Under my breath I was sayin', Thanks, God.

In my apartment everyone was asleep. I turned off the TV set and covered my sister, who was lyin' on the couch. Then I went back to my room and turned the box on so I could listen to my music low. I sat on the edge of the bed. My hand was shaking. I put it together with my other hand and laced my fingers tight.

SERGEANT PETERS

After the Park Morton incident, I answered a domestic call over on First and Kennedy. A young gentleman, built like a fullback, had beat his girl up pretty bad. Her face was already swelling when I arrived and there was blood and spittle bubbling on the side of her mouth. The first cops on the scene had cuffed the perp and had him bent over the hood of their cruiser. At this point the girlfriend, she was screaming at the cops. Some of the neighbourhood types, hanging outside of a windowless bar on Kennedy, had begun screaming at the cops, too. I figured they were drunk and high on who knew what, so I radioed in for a few more cars.

We made a couple of additional arrests. Like they say in the TV news, the situation had escalated. Not a full-blown riot, but trouble nonetheless. Someone yelled out at me, called me a "cracker-ass motherfucker." I didn't even blink. The county cops don't take an ounce of that kinda shit, but we take it every night. Sticks and stones, like that. Then someone started whistling the theme from the old *Andy Griffith Show*, you know, the one where he played a small-town sheriff, and everyone started to laugh. Least they didn't call me Barney Fife. The thing was, when the residents start with the comedy, you know it's over, that things have gotten under control. So I didn't mind. Actually, the guy who was whistling, he was pretty good.

When that was over with, I pulled a car over on 5th and Princeton, back by the Old Soldier's Home, that matched a description of a shooter's car from earlier in the night. I waited for backup, standing behind the left rear quarter panel of the car, my holster unsnapped, the light from my Mag pointed at the rear window.

When my backup came, we searched the car and frisked the four

YBMs. They had those little-tree deodorizers hangin' from the rearview, and one of those plastic, king-crown deodorizers sitting on the back panel, too. A crown. Like they're royalty, right? God, sometimes these people make me laugh. Anyhow, they were clean with no live warrants, and we let them go.

I drove around, and it was quiet. Between three A.M. and dawn, the city gets real still. Beautiful in a way, even for down here.

The last thing I did, I helped some Spanish guy try to get back into his place in Petworth. Said his key didn't work, and it didn't. Someone, his landlord or his woman, had changed the locks on him, I figured. Liquor stench was pouring out of him. Also, he smelled like he hadn't taken a shower for days. When I left him he was standing on the sidewalk, sort of rocking back and forth, staring at the front of the row house, like if he looked at it long enough the door was gonna open on its own.

So now I'm parked here near the station, sipping coffee. It's my ritual, like. The sky is beginning to lighten. This here is my favourite time of night.

I'm thinking that on my next shift, or the one after, I'll swing by and see Tonio Harris's mother. I haven't talked to her in years, anyway. See how she's been doing. Suggest to her, without acting like I'm telling her what to do, that maybe she ought to have her son lie low some. Stay in the next few weekend nights. Let that beef he's got with those others, whatever it is, die down. Course, I know those kinds of beefs don't go away. I'll make her aware of it, just the same.

The Harris kid, he's lucky he's got someone like his mother, lookin' after him. I drive back in there at the housing complex, and I see those young kids sitting on that wall at two in the morning, looking at me with hate in their eyes, and all I can think of is, where are the parents? Yeah, I know, there's a new curfew in effect for minors. Some joke. Like we've got the manpower and facilities to enforce it. Like we're supposed to raise these kids, too.

Anyway, it's not my job to think too hard about that. I'm just lettin' these people know that we're out here, watching them. I mean, what else can you do?

My back hurts. I got to get me one of those things you sit on, with the wood balls. Like those African cabdrivers do.

TONIO HARRIS

This morning I studied some in my room until my eyes got sleepy. It was hard to keep my mind on the book 'cause I was playin' some Method Man on the box, and it was fuckin' with my concentration. That cut he does with Redman, called "Tear It Off"? That joint is tight.

I figured I was done for the day, and there wasn't no one around to tell me different. My mother was at work at the Dollar Store, and my sister was over at a friend's. I put my sneaks on and grabbed my ball and headed up to Roosevelt.

I walked up Georgia, dribblin' the sidewalk when I could, usin' my left and keeping my right behind my back, like my coach told me to do. I cut down Upshur and walked up 13th, past my school, to the court. The court is on the small side and its backboards are square, with bumper stickers and shit stuck on the boards. It's beside a tennis court and all of it is fenced in. There's a baseball field behind it; birds always be sittin' on that field.

There was a four-on-four full-court thing happenin' when I got there. I called next with another guy, Dimitrius Johnson, who I knew could play. I could see who was gonna win this game, 'cause the one team had this boy named Peter Hawk who could do it all. We'd pick up two off the losers' squad. I watched the game and after a minute I'd already had those two picked out.

The game started kind of slow. I was feelin' out my players and those on the other side. Someone had set up a box courtside and they had that live Roots thing playin'. It was one of those pretty days with the sun out and high clouds, the kind look like pillows, and the weather and that upbeat music comin' from the box set the tone. I felt loose and good.

Me and Hawk was coverin' each other. He was one of those who could go left or right, dribble or shoot with either hand. He took me to the hole once or twice. Then I noticed he always eye-faked in the opposite direction he was gonna go before he made his move. So it gave me the advantage, knowin' which side he was gonna jump to, and I gained position on him like that.

I couldn't shut Hawk down, not all the way, but I forced him to change his game. I made a couple of nice assists on offence and drained one my own self from way downtown. One of Hawk's players tried to claim a charge, doin' that Reggie Miller punk shit, his arms windmillin' as he went back. That shit don't go in pickup, and even his own people didn't back him. My team went up by one.

We stopped the game for a minute or so, so one of mines could tie up his sneaks. I was lookin' across the ball field at the seagulls and crows, catchin' my wind. That's when I saw James Wallace's black Maxima, cruisin' slow down Allison, that street that runs alongside the court.

We put the ball back into play. Hawk drove right by me, hit a runner. I fumbled a pass goin' back upcourt, and on the turnover they scored again. The Maxima was going south on 13th, just barely moving along. I saw Wallace in the driver's seat, his window down, lookin' my way with that smile of his and his dead-ass eyes.

"You playin', Tone?" asked Dimitrius, the kid on my team.

I guess I had lost my concentration and it showed. "I'm playin'," I said. "Let's ball."

Dimitrius bricked his next shot. Hawk got the 'bound and brought the ball up. I watched him do that eye-fake thing again and I stole the ball off him in the lane before he could make his move. I went bucket-to-bucket with it and leaped. I jammed the motherfucker and swung on the rim, comin' down and doin' one of those Patrick Ewing silent growls at Hawk and the rest of them before shootin' downcourt to get back on D. I was all fired up. I felt like we could turn the shit around.

Hawk hit his next shot, a jumper from the top of the key. Dimitrius brought it down, and I motioned for him to dish me the pill. He led me just right. In my side sight I saw a black car rollin' down Allison, but I didn't stop to check it out. I drove off a pick, pulled up in front of Hawk, made a head move and watched him bite. Then I went up. I was way out there but I could tell from how the ball rolled off my fingers that it was gonna go. Ain't no chains on those rims, but I could see the links dance as that rock dropped through. I'm sayin' that I could see them dance in my mind.

We was runnin' now. The game was full-on and it was fierce. I grabbed one off the rim and made an outlet pass, then beat the defenders myself on the break. I saw black movin' slow on 13th but I didn't even think about it. I was higher than a motherfucker then, my feet and the court and the ball were all one thing. I felt like I could drain it from anywhere, and Hawk, I could see it in his eyes, he knew it, too.

I took the ball and dribbled it up. I knew what I was gonna do, knew exactly where I was gonna go with it, knew wasn't nobody out there could stop me. I wasn't thinkin' about Wallace or the stoop of my moms's shoulders or which nigga was gonna be lookin' to fuck my baby sister, and I wasn't thinkin' on no job or college test or my future or nothin' like that.

I was concentratin' on droppin' that pill through the hole. Watching myself doin' it before I did. Out here in the sunshine, every dark thing far away. Runnin' ball like I do. Thinkin' that if I kept runnin', that black Maxima and everything else, it would just go away.

Concrete Evidence

by

IAN RANKIN

"IT'S AMAZING WHAT YOU FIND in these old buildings," said the contractor, a middle-aged man in safety helmet and overalls. Beneath the overalls lurked a shirt and tie, the marks of his station. He was the chief, the gaffer. Nothing surprised him any more, not even unearthing a skeleton.

"Do you know," he went on, "in my time, I've found everything from ancient coins to a pocket-watch. How old do you reckon he is then?"

"We're not even sure it *is* a he, not yet. Give us a chance, Mr. Beesford."

"Well, when can we start work again?"

"Later on today."

"Must be gey old though, eh?"

"How do you make that out?"

"Well, it's got no clothes on, has it? They've perished. Takes time for that to happen, plenty of time ..."

Rebus had to concede, the man had a point. Yet the concrete floor beneath which the bones had been found ... *it* didn't look so old, did it? Rebus cast an eye over the cellar again. It was situated a storey or so beneath road-level, in the basement of an old building off the Cowgate. Rebus was often in the Cowgate; the mortuary was just up the road. He knew that the older buildings here were a veritable warren, long narrow tunnels ran here, there and, it seemed, everywhere, semi-cylindrical in shape and just about high enough to stand up in. This present building was being given the full works—gutted, new drainage system, rewiring. They were taking out the floor in the cellar to lay new drains and also because there seemed to be damp—certainly there was a fousty smell to the place—and its cause needed to be found.

They were expecting to find old drains, open drains perhaps. Maybe even a trickle of a stream, something which would lead to damp. Instead, their pneumatic drills found what remained of a corpse, perhaps hundreds of years old. Except, of course, for that concrete floor. It couldn't be more than fifty or sixty years old, could it? Would clothing deteriorate to a visible nothing in so short a time? Perhaps the damp could do that. Rebus found the cellar oppressive. The smell, the shadowy lighting provided by portable lamps, the dust.

But the photographers were finished, and so was the pathologist, Dr. Curt. He didn't have too much to report at this stage, except to comment that he preferred it when skeletons were kept in cupboards, not confined to the cellar. They'd take the bones away, along with samples of the earth and rubble around the find, and they'd see what they would see.

"Archaeology's not really my line," the doctor added. "It may take me some time to bone up on it." And he smiled his usual smile.

IT TOOK SEVERAL DAYS for the telephone call to come. Rebus picked up the receiver.

"Hello?"

"Inspector Rebus? Dr. Curt here. About our emaciated friend."

"Yes?"

"Male, five feet ten inches tall, probably been down there between thirty and thirty-five years. His left leg was broken at some time, long before he died. It healed nicely. But the little finger on his left hand had been dislocated and it did *not* heal so well. I'd say it was crooked all his adult life. Perfect for afternoon tea in Morningside."

"Yes?" Rebus knew damned well Curt was leading up to something. He knew, too, that Curt was not a man to be hurried.

"Tests on the soil and gravel around the skeleton show traces of human tissue, but no fibres or anything which might have been clothing. No shoes, socks, underpants, nothing. Altogether, I'd say he was buried there in the altogether."

"But did he die there?"

"Can't say."

"All right, what did he die *of?*"

There was an almost palpable smile in Curt's voice. "Inspector, I thought you'd never ask. Blow to the skull, a blow of considerable force to the back of the head. Murder, I'd say. Yes, definitely murder."

THERE WERE, OF COURSE, ways of tracing the dead, of coming to a near-infallible identification. But the older the crime, the less likely this outcome became. Dental records, for example. They just weren't *kept* in the 50s and 60s the way they are today. A dentist practising then would most probably be playing near–full-time golf by now. And the record of a patient who hadn't been in for his check-up since 1960? Discarded, most probably. Besides, as Dr. Curt pointed out, the man's teeth had seen little serious work, a few fillings, a single extraction.

The same went for medical records, which didn't stop Rebus from checking. A broken left leg, a dislocated left pinkie. Maybe some aged doctor would recall? But then again, maybe not. Almost certainly not. The local papers and radio were interested, which was a bonus. They were given what information the police had, but no memories seemed to be jogged as a result.

Curt had said he was no archaeologist; well, Rebus was no historian either. He knew other cases—contemporary cases—were yammering for his attention. The files stacked up on his desk were evidence enough of that. He'd give this one a few days, a few hours of his time. When the dead ends started to cluster around him, he'd drop it and head back for the here and now.

Who owned the building back in the 1950s? That was easy enough to discover: a wine importer and merchant. Pretty much a one-man operation, Hillbeith Vintners had held the premises from 1948 until 1967. And yes, there was a Mr. Hillbeith, retired from the trade and living over in Burntisland, with a house gazing out across silver sands to the grey North Sea.

He still had a cellar, and insisted that Rebus have a "wee taste" from it. Rebus got the idea that Mr. Hillbeith liked visitors—a socially acceptable excuse for a drink. He took his time in the cellar (there must have been over 500 bottles in there) and emerged with cobwebs hanging from his cardigan, holding a dusty bottle of something nice. This he opened and sat on the mantelpiece. It would be half an hour or so yet at the very least before they could usefully have a glass.

Mr. Hillbeith was, he told Rebus, seventy-four. He'd been in the wine trade for nearly half a century and had "never regretted a day, not a day, nor even an hour." Lucky you, Rebus thought to himself.

"Do you remember having that new floor laid in the cellar, Mr. Hillbeith?"

"Oh, yes. That particular cellar was going to be for best claret. It was just the right temperature, you see, and there was no vibration from passing buses and the like. But it was damp, had been ever since I'd moved in. So I got a building firm to take a look. They suggested a new floor and some other alterations. It all seemed fairly straightforward and their charges seemed reasonable, so I told them to go ahead."

"And when was this, sir?"

"1960. The spring of that year. There you are, I've got a great memory where business matters are concerned." His small eyes beamed at Rebus through the thick lenses of their glasses. "I can even tell you how much the work cost me ... and it was a pretty penny at the time. All for nothing, as it turned out. The cellar was still damp, and there was always that *smell* in it, a very unwholesome smell. I couldn't take a chance with the claret, so it became the general stockroom, empty bottles and glasses, packing-cases, that sort of thing."

"Do you happen to recall, Mr. Hillbeith, was the smell there *before* the new floor was put in?"

"Well, certainly there was *a* smell there before the floor was laid, but the smell afterwards was different somehow." He rose and fetched two crystal glasses from the china cabinet, inspecting them for dust. "There's a lot of nonsense talked about wine, Inspector. About decanting, the type of glasses you must use and so on. Decanting can help, of course, but I prefer the feel of the bottle. The bottle, after all, is part of the wine, isn't it?" He handed an empty glass to Rebus. "We'll wait a few minutes yet."

Rebus swallowed drily. It had been a long drive. "Do you recall the name of the firm, sir, the one that did the work?"

Hillbeith laughed. "How could I forget? Abbot & Ford, they were called. I mean, you just don't forget a name like that, do you? Abbot & Ford. You see, it sounds like Abbotsford, doesn't it? A small firm they were, mind. But you may know one of them, Alexander Abbot."

"Of Abbot Building?"

"The same. He went on to make quite a name for himself, didn't he? Quite a fortune. Built up quite a company, too, but he started out small like most of us do."

"How small, would you say?"

"Oh, small, small. Just a few men." He rose and stretched an arm towards the mantelpiece. "I think this should be ready to taste, Inspector. If you'll hold out your glass—"

Hillbeith poured slowly, deliberately, checking that no lees escaped into the glass. He poured another slow, generous measure for himself. The wine was reddish-brown. "Robe and disc not too promising," he muttered to himself. He gave his glass a shake and studied it. "Legs not promising either." He sighed. "Oh dear." Finally, Hillbeith sniffed the glass anxiously, then took a swig.

"Cheers," said Rebus, indulging in a mouthful. A mouthful of vinegar. He managed to swallow, then saw Hillbeith spit back into the glass.

"Oxidization," the old man said, sounding cruelly tricked. "It happens. I'd best check a few more bottles to assess the damage. Will you stay, Inspector?" Hillbeith sounded keen.

"Sorry, sir," said Rebus, ready with his get-out clause. "I'm still on duty."

ALEXANDER ABBOT, aged fifty-five, still saw himself as the force behind the Abbot Building Company. There might be a dozen executives working furiously beneath him, but the company had grown from *his* energy and from *his* fury. He was Chairman, and a busy man too. He made this plain to Rebus at their meeting in the executive offices of ABC. The office spoke of business confidence, but then in Rebus's experience this meant little in itself. Often, the more dire straits a company was in, the healthier it tried to look. Still, Alexander Abbot seemed happy enough with life.

"In a recession," he explained, lighting an overlong cigar, "you trim your workforce pronto. You stick with regular clients, good payers, and don't take on too much work from clients you don't know. They're the ones who're likely to welch on you or go bust, leaving nothing but bills. Young businesses … they're always hit hardest in a recession, no back-up you see. Then, when the recession's over for another few years, you dust yourself off and go touting for business again, re-hiring the men you laid off. That's where we've always had the edge over Jack Kirkwall."

Kirkwall Construction was ABC's main competitor in the Lowlands, when it came to medium-sized contracts. Doubtless Kirkwall was the larger company. It, too, was run by a "self-made" man, Jack Kirkwall. A larger-than-life figure. There was, Rebus quickly realized, little love lost between the two rivals.

The very mention of Kirkwall's name seemed to have dampened Alexander Abbot's spirits. He chewed on his cigar like it was a debtor's finger.

"You started small though, didn't you, sir?"

"Oh aye, they don't come much smaller. We were a pimple on the bum of the construction industry at one time." He gestured to the walls of his office. "Not that you'd guess it, eh?"

Rebus nodded. "You were still a small firm back in 1960, weren't you?"

"1960. Let's think. We were just starting out. It wasn't ABC then, of course. Let's see. I think I got a loan from my dad in 1957, went into partnership with a chap called Hugh Ford, another self-employed builder. Yes, that's right. 1960, it was Abbot & Ford. Of course it was."

"Do you happen to remember working at a wine merchant's in the Cowgate?"

"When?"

"The spring of 1960."

"A wine merchant's?" Abbot furrowed his brow. "Should be able to remember that. Long time ago, mind. A wine merchant's?"

"You were laying a new floor in one of his cellars, amongst other work. Hillbeith Vintners."

"Oh, aye, Hillbeith, it's coming back now. I remember him. Little funny chap with glasses. Gave us a case of wine when the job was finished. Nice of him, but the wine was a bit off as I remember."

"How many men were working on the job?"

Abbot exhaled noisily. "Now you're asking. It was over thirty years ago, Inspector."

"I appreciate that, sir. Would there be any records?"

Abbot shook his head. "There might have been up to about ten years ago, but when we moved into this place a lot of the older stuff got chucked out. I regret it now. It'd be nice to have a display of stuff from the old days, something we could set up in the reception. But no, all the Abbot & Ford stuff got dumped."

"So you don't remember how many men were on that particular job? Is there anyone else I could talk to, someone who might—"

"We were small back then, I can tell you that. Mostly using casual labour and part-timers. A job that size, I wouldn't think we'd be using more than three or four men, if that."

"You don't recall anyone going missing? Not turning up for work, that sort of thing?"

Abbot bristled. "I'm a stickler for time-keeping, Inspector. If anyone had done a bunk, I'd remember, I'm pretty sure of that. Besides, we were careful about who we took on. No lazy buggers, nobody who'd do a runner halfway through a job."

Rebus sighed. Here was one of the dead ends. He rose to his feet. "Well, thanks anyway, Mr. Abbot. It was good of you to find time to see me." The two men shook hands, Abbot rising to his feet.

"Not at all, Inspector. Wish I could help you with your little mystery. I like a good detective story myself." They were almost at the door now.

"Oh," said Rebus, "just one last thing. Where could I find your old partner Mr. Ford?"

Abbot's face lost its animation. His voice was suddenly that of an old man. "Hugh died, Inspector. A boating accident. He was drowned. Hell of a thing to happen. Hell of a thing."

Two dead ends.

MR. HILLBEITH'S TELEPHONE CALL came later that day, while Rebus was ploughing through the transcript of an interview with a rapist. His head felt full of foul-smelling glue, his stomach acid with caffeine.

"Is that Inspector Rebus?"

"Yes, hello, Mr. Hillbeith. What can I do for you?" Rebus pinched the bridge of his nose and screwed shut his eyes.

"I was thinking all last night about that skeleton."

"Yes?" In between bottles of wine, Rebus didn't doubt.

"Well, I was trying to think back to when the work was being done. It might not be much, but I definitely recall that there were four people involved. Mr. Abbot and Mr. Ford worked on it pretty much full-time, and there were two other men, one of them a teenager, the other in his forties. They worked on a more casual basis."

"You don't recall their names?"

"No, only that the teenager had a nickname. Everyone called him by that. I don't think I ever knew his real name."

"Well, thanks anyway, Mr. Hillbeith. I'll get back to Mr. Abbot and see if what you've told me jogs his memory."

"Oh, you've spoken to him then?"

"This morning. No progress to report. I didn't realize Mr. Ford had died."

"Ah, well, that's the other thing."

"What is?"

"Poor Mr. Ford. Sailing accident, wasn't it?"

"That's right."

"Only I remember that, too. You see, that accident happened just after they'd finished the job. They kept talking about how they were going to take a few days off and go fishing. Mr. Abbot said it would be their first holiday in years."

Rebus's eyes were open now. "How soon was this after they'd finished your floor?"

"Well, directly after, I suppose."

"Do you remember Mr. Ford?"

"Well, he was very quiet. Mr. Abbot did all the talking, really. A very quiet man. A hard worker though, I got that impression."

"Did you notice anything about his hands? A misshapen pinkie?"

"Sorry, Inspector, it *was* a long time ago."

Rebus appreciated that. "Of course it was, Mr. Hillbeith. You've been a great help. Thank you."

He put down the receiver. A long time ago, yes, but still murder, still calculated and cold-blooded murder. Well, a path had opened in front of him. Not much of a path perhaps, a bit overgrown and treacherous. Nevertheless ... Best foot forward, John. Best foot forward.

OF COURSE, he kept telling himself, he was still ruling possibilities out rather than ruling them in, which was why he wanted to know a little more about the boating accident. He didn't want to get the information from Alexander Abbot.

Instead, the morning after Hillbeith's phone-call, Rebus went to the National Library of Scotland on George IV Bridge. The doorman let him through the turnstile and he climbed an imposing staircase to the reading room. The woman on the desk filled in a one-day reader's card for him, and showed him how to use the computer. There were two banks of computers, being used by people to find the books they needed. Rebus had to go into the reading room and find an empty chair, note its number and put this on his slip when he'd decided which volume he required. Then he went to his chair and sat, waiting.

There were two floors to the reading room, both enveloped by shelves of reference books. The people working at the long desks downstairs seemed bleary. Just another morning's graft for them; but Rebus found it all fascinating. One person worked with a card index in front of him, to which he referred frequently. Another seemed asleep, head resting on arms. Pens scratched across countless sheets of paper. A few souls, lost for inspiration, merely chewed on their pens and stared at the others around them, as Rebus was doing.

Eventually, his volume was brought to him. It was a bound edition of the *Scotsman*, containing every issue for the months from January to June, 1960. Two thick leather buckles kept the volume closed. Rebus unbuckled these and began to turn the pages.

He knew what he was looking for, and pretty well where to find it, but that didn't stop him browsing through football reports and front page headlines. 1960. He'd been busy trying to lose his virginity and supporting Hearts. Yes, a long time ago.

The story hadn't quite made the front page. Instead, there were two paragraphs on page three. "Drowning Off Lower Largo." The victim, Mr. Hugh Ford, was described as being twenty-six years of age (a year older than the survivor, Mr. Alex Abbot) and a resident of Duddingston, Edinburgh. The men, on a short fishing-holiday, had taken a boat out early in the morning, a boat hired from a local man, Mr. John Thomson. There was a squall, and the boat capsized. Mr. Abbot, a fair swimmer, had made it back to the shore. Mr. Ford, a poor swimmer, had not. Mr. Ford was further described as a "bachelor, a quiet man, shy according to Mr. Abbot, who was still under observation at the Victoria Hospital, Kirkcaldy." There was a little more, but not much. Apparently, Ford's parents were dead, but he had a sister, Mrs. Isabel Hammond, somewhere out in Australia.

Why hadn't Abbot mentioned any of this? Maybe he wanted to forget. Maybe it still gave him the occasional bad dream. And of course he would have forgotten all about the Hillbeith contract precisely because this tragedy happened so soon afterwards. So soon. Just the one line of print really bothered Rebus; just that one sentence niggled.

"Mr. Ford's body has still not been recovered."

RECORDS MIGHT GET LOST in time, but not by Fife Police. They sent on what they had, much of it written in fading ink on fragile paper, some of it typed—badly. The two friends and colleagues, Abbot and Ford, had set out on Friday evening to the Fishing-Net Hotel in Largo, arriving late. As arranged, they'd set out early next morning on a boat they'd hired from a local man, John Thomson. The accident had taken place only an hour or so after setting out. The boat was recovered. It had been overturned, but of Ford there was no sign. Inquiries were made. Mr. Ford's belongings were taken back to Edinburgh by Mr. Abbot, after the latter was released from hospital, having sustained a bump to the head when the boat went over. He was also suffering from shock and exhaustion. Mr. Ford's sister, Mrs. Isabel Hammond, was never traced.

They had investigated a little further. The business run jointly by Messrs. Abbot and Ford now became Mr. Abbot's. The case-notes contained a good amount of information and suspicion—between the lines, as it were. Oh yes, they'd investigated Alexander Abbot, but there had been no evidence. They'd searched for the body, had found none. Without a body, they were left with only their suspicions and their nagging doubts.

"Yes," Rebus said quietly to himself, "but what if you were looking for the body in the wrong place?" The wrong place at the wrong time. The work on the cellar had ended on Friday afternoon and by Saturday morning Hugh Ford had ceased to exist.

The path Rebus was on had become less overgrown, but it was still rock-strewn and dangerous, still a potential dead-end.

THE FISHING-NET HOTEL was still in existence, though apparently much changed from its 1960 incarnation. The present owners told Rebus to arrive in time for lunch if he could and it would be on the house. Largo was north of Burntisland but on the same coastline. Alexander Selkirk, the original of Defoe's Robinson Crusoe, had a connection with the fishing village. There was a small statue of him somewhere which Rebus had been shown as a boy (but only after much hunting, he recalled). Largo was picturesque, but then so were most, if not all, of the coastal villages in Fife's "East Neuk." But it was not yet quite the height of the tourist season and the customers taking lunch at the Fishing-Net Hotel were businessmen and locals.

It was a good lunch, as picturesque as its surroundings but with a bit more flavour. And afterwards, the owner, an Englishman for whom life in Largo was a long-held dream come true, offered to show Rebus round, including "the very room your Mr. Ford stayed in the night before he died."

"How can you be sure?"

"I looked in the register."

Rebus managed not to look too surprised. The hotel had changed hands so often since 1960, he despaired of finding anyone who would remember the events of that weekend.

"The register?"

"Yes, we were left a lot of old stuff when we bought this place. The store-rooms were chockablock. Old ledgers and what have you going back to the 1920s and 30s. It was easy enough to find 1960."

Rebus stopped in his tracks. "Never mind showing me Mr. Ford's room, would you mind letting me see that register?"

He sat at a desk in the manager's office with the register open in front of him, while Mr. Summerson's finger stabbed the line. "There you are, Inspector, H. Ford. Signed in at 11.50 p.m., address given as Duddingston. Room number seven."

It wasn't so much a signature as a blurred scrawl and above it, on a separate line, was Alexander Abbot's own more flowing signature.

"Bit late to arrive, wasn't it?" commented Rebus.

"Agreed."

"I don't suppose there's anyone working here nowadays who worked in the hotel back then?"

Summerson laughed quietly. "People do retire in this country, Inspector."

"Of course, I just wondered." He remembered the newspaper story. "What about John Thomson? Does the name mean anything to you?"

"Old Jock? Jock Thomson? The fisherman?"

"Probably."

"Oh, yes, he's still about. You'll almost certainly find him down by the dockside or else in the Harbour Tavern."

"Thanks. I'd like to take this register with me if I may?"

JOCK THOMSON sucked on his pipe and nodded. He looked the archetype of the "old salt," from his baggy cord trousers to his chiselled face and silvery beard. The only departure from the norm was, perhaps, the Perrier water in front of him on a table in the Harbour Tavern.

"I like the fizz," he explained after ordering it, "and besides, my doctor's told me to keep off the alcohol. Total abstinence, he said, total abstinence. Either the booze goes, Jock, or the pipe does. No contest."

And he sucked greedily on the pipe. Then complained when his drink arrived without "the wee slice of lemon." Rebus returned to the bar to fulfill his mission.

"Oh aye," said Thomson, "remember it like it was yesterday. Only there's not much to remember, is there?"

"Why do you say that?"

"Two inexperienced laddies go out in a boat. Boat tips. End of story."

"Was the weather going to be bad that morning?"

"Not particularly. But there *was* a squall blew up. Blew up and blew out in a matter of minutes. Long enough though."

"How did the two men seem?"

"How do you mean?"

"Well, were they looking forward to the trip?"

"Don't know, I never saw them. The younger one, Abbot was it? He phoned to book a boat from me, said they'd be going out early, six or thereabouts. I told him he was daft, but he said there was no need for me to be on the dockside, if I'd just have the boat ready and tell him which one it was. And that's what I did. By the time I woke up that morning, he was swimming for the shore and his pal was food for the fish."

"So you never actually saw Mr. Ford?"

"No, and I only saw the lad Abbot afterwards, when the ambulance was taking him away."

It was fitting into place almost too easily now. And Rebus thought, sometimes these things are only visible with hindsight, from a space of years. "I don't suppose," he ventured, "you know anyone who worked at the hotel back then?"

"Owner's moved on," said Thomson, "who knows where to. It might be that Janice Dryman worked there then. Can't recall if she did."

"Where could I find her?"

Thomson peered at the clock behind the bar. "Hang around here ten minutes or so, you'll bump into her. She usually comes in of an afternoon. Meantime, I'll have another of these if you're buying."

Thomson pushed his empty glass over to Rebus. Rebus, most definitely, was buying.

MISS DRYMAN—"never married, never really saw the point"—was in her early fifties. She worked in a gift-shop in town and after her stint finished usually nipped into the Tavern for a soft drink and "a bit of gossip." Rebus asked what she would like to drink.

"Lemonade, please," she said, "with a drop of whisky in it." And she laughed with Jock Thomson, as though this were an old and cherished joke between them. Rebus, not used to playing the part of straight-man, headed yet again for the bar.

"Oh yes," she said, her lips poised above the glass. "I was working there at the time all right. Chambermaid and general dogsbody, that was me."

"You wouldn't see them arrive though?"

Miss Dryman looked as though she had some secret to impart. "*Nobody* saw them arrive, I know that for a fact. Mrs. Dennis who ran the place back then, she said she'd be buggered if she'd wait up half the night for a couple of fishermen. They knew what rooms they were in and their keys were left at reception."

"What about the front door?"

"Left unlocked, I suppose. The world was a safer place back then."

"Aye, you're right there," added Jock Thomson, sucking on his sliver of lemon.

"And Mr. Abbot and Mr. Ford knew this was the arrangement?"

"I suppose so. Otherwise it wouldn't have worked, would it?"

So Abbot knew there'd be nobody around at the hotel, not if he left it late enough before arriving.

"And what about in the morning?"

"Mrs. Dennis said they were up and out before she knew anything about it. She was annoyed because she'd already cooked the kippers for their breakfast before she realized."

So nobody saw them in the morning either. In fact …

"In fact," said Rebus, "nobody saw Mr. Ford at all. Nobody at the hotel, not you, Mr. Thomson, nobody." Both drinkers conceded this.

"I saw his stuff though," said Miss Dryman.

"What stuff?"

"In his room, his clothes and stuff. That morning. I didn't know anything about the accident and I went in to clean."

"The bed had been slept in?"

"Looked like it. Sheets all rumpled. And his suitcase was on the floor, only half unpacked. Not that there was much *to* unpack."

"Oh?"

"A single change of clothes, I'd say. I remember them because they seemed mucky, you know, not fresh. Not the sort of stuff *I'd* take on holiday with me."

"What? Like he'd been working in them?"

She considered this. "Maybe."

"No point wearing clean clothes for fishing," Thomson added. But Rebus wasn't listening.

Ford's clothes, the clothes he had been working in while laying the floor. It made sense. Abbot bludgeoned him, stripped him and covered his body in fresh cement. He'd taken the clothes away with him and put them in a case, opening it in the hotel room, ruffling the sheets. Simple, but effective. Effective these past thirty years. The motive? A falling out perhaps, or simple greed. It was a small company, but growing, and perhaps Abbot hadn't wanted to share. Rebus placed a five-pound note on the table.

"To cover the next couple of rounds," he said, getting to his feet. "I'd better be off. Some of us are still on duty."

THERE WERE THINGS to be done. He had to speak to his superior, Chief Inspector Lauderdale. And that was for starters. Maybe Ford's Australian sister could be traced this time round. There had to be someone out there who could acknowledge that Ford had suffered from a broken leg in youth, and that he had a crooked finger. So far, Rebus could think of only one person—Alexander Abbot.

Somehow, he didn't think Abbot could be relied on to tell the truth, the whole truth.

Then there was the hotel register. The forensics lab could ply their cunning trade on it. Perhaps they'd be able to say for certain that Ford's signature was merely a bad rendition of Abbot's. But again, he needed a sample of Ford's handwriting in order to substantiate that the signature was not genuine. Who did he know who might possess such a document? Only Alexander Abbot. Or Mr. Hillbeith, but Mr. Hillbeith had not been able to help.

"No, Inspector, as I told you, it was Mr. Abbot who handled all the paperwork, all that side of things. If there is an invoice or a receipt, it will be in his hand, not Mr. Ford's. I don't recall ever seeing Mr. Ford writing anything."

No through road.

Chief Inspector Lauderdale was not wholly sympathetic. So far all Rebus had to offer were more suppositions to add to those of the Fife Police at the time. There was no proof that Alexander Abbot had killed his partner. No proof that the skeleton was Hugh Ford. Moreover, there wasn't even much in the way of circumstantial evidence. They could bring in Abbot for questioning, but all he had to do was plead innocence. He could afford a good lawyer; and even bad lawyers weren't stupid enough to let the police probe too deeply.

"We need proof, John," said Lauderdale, "concrete evidence. The simplest proof would be that hotel signature. If we prove it's not Ford's, then we have Abbot at that hotel, Abbot in the boat and Abbot shouting that his friend has drowned, *all* without Ford having been there. That's what we need. The rest of it, as it stands, is rubbish. You know that."

Yes, Rebus knew. He didn't doubt that, given an hour alone with Abbot in a darkened alley, he'd have his confession. But it didn't work like that. It worked through the law. Besides, Abbot's heart might not

be too healthy. BUSINESSMAN, 55, DIES UNDER QUESTION-
ING. No, it had to be done some other way.

The problem was, there *was* no other way. Alexander Abbot was
getting away with murder. Or was he? Why did his story have to be
false? Why did the body have to be Hugh Ford's? The answer was:
because the whole thing seemed to fit. Only, the last piece of the
jigsaw had been lost under some sofa or chair a long time ago, so long
ago now that it might remain missing forever.

HE DIDN'T KNOW why he did it. If in doubt, retrace your steps ...
something like that. Maybe he just liked the atmosphere. Whatever,
Rebus found himself back in the National Library, waiting at his desk
for the servitor to bring him his bound volume of old news. He
mouthed the words of "Yesterday's Papers" to himself as he waited.
Then, when the volume appeared, he unbuckled it with ease and
pulled open the pages. He read past the April editions, read through
into May and June. Football results, headlines—and what was this? A
snippet of business news, barely a filler at the bottom right-hand
corner of a page. About how the Kirkwall Construction Company was
swallowing up a couple of smaller competitors in Fife and Midlothian.

"The 1960s will be a decade of revolution in the building industry," said Managing Director Mr. Jack Kirkwall, "and Kirkwall
Construction aims to meet that challenge through growth and
quality. The bigger we are, the better we are. These acquisitions
strengthen the company, and they're good news for the workforce,
too."

It was the kind of sentiment which had lasted into the 1980s. Jack
Kirkwall, Alexander Abbot's bitter rival. Now there was a man Rebus
ought to meet ...

THE MEETING, however, had to be postponed until the following
week. Kirkwall was in hospital for a minor operation.

"I'm at that age, Inspector," he told Rebus when they finally met, "when things go wrong and need treatment or replacing. Just like any bit of well-used machinery."

And he laughed, though the laughter, to Rebus's ears, had a hollow centre. Kirkwall looked older than his sixty-two years, his skin saggy, complexion wan. They were in his living-room, from where, these days, he did most of his work.

"Since I turned sixty, I've only really wandered into the company headquarters for the occasional meeting. I leave the daily chores to my son, Peter. He seems to be managing." The laughter this time was self-mocking.

Rebus had suggested a further postponement of the meeting, but when Jack Kirkwall knew that the subject was to be Alexander Abbot, he was adamant that they should go ahead.

"Is he in trouble then?"

"He might be," Rebus admitted. Some of the colour seemed to reappear in Kirkwall's cheeks and he relaxed a little further into his reclining leather chair. Rebus didn't want to give Kirkwall the story. Kirkwall and Abbot were still business rivals, after all. Still, it seemed, enemies. Given the story, Kirkwall might try some underhand tactic, some rumour in the media, and if it got out that the story originally came from a police inspector, well. Hello, being sued and goodbye, pension.

No, Rebus didn't want that. Yet he did want to know whether Kirkwall knew anything, knew of any reason why Abbot might wish, might *need* to kill Ford.

"Go on, Inspector."

"It goes back quite a way, sir. 1960, to be precise. Your firm was at that time in the process of expansion."

"Correct."

"What did you know about Abbot & Ford?"

Kirkwall brushed the palm of one hand over the knuckles of the other. "Just that they were growing, too. Of course, they were younger than us, much smaller than us. ABC still is much smaller than us. But they were cocky, they were winning some contracts ahead of us. I had my eye on them."

"Did you know Mr. Ford at all?"

"Oh yes. Really, he was the cleverer of the two men. I've never had much respect for Abbot. But Hugh Ford was quiet, hardworking. Abbot was the one who did the shouting and got the firm noticed."

"Did Mr. Ford have a crooked finger?"

Kirkwall seemed bemused by the question. "I've no idea," he said at last. "I never actually met the man, I merely knew *about* him. Why? Is it important?"

Rebus felt at last that his meandering, narrowing path had come to the lip of a chasm. Nothing for it but to turn back.

"Well," he said, "it would have clarified something."

"You know, Inspector, my company *was* interested in taking Abbot & Ford under our wing."

"Oh?"

"But then with the accident, that tragic accident. Well, Abbot took control and he wasn't at all interested in any offer we had to make. Downright rude, in fact. Yes, I've always thought that it was such a *lucky* accident so far as Abbot was concerned."

"How do you mean, sir?"

"I mean, Inspector, that Hugh Ford was on our side. He wanted to sell up. But Abbot was against it."

So, Rebus had his motive. Well, what did it matter? He was still lacking that concrete evidence Lauderdale demanded.

"... Would it show up from his handwriting?"

Rebus had missed what Kirkwall had been saying. "I'm sorry, sir, I didn't catch that."

"I said, Inspector, if Hugh Ford had a crooked finger, would it show from his handwriting?"

"Handwriting?"

"Because I had his agreement to the takeover. He'd written to me personally to tell me. Had gone behind Abbot's back, I suppose. I bet Alex Abbot was mad as hell when he found out about that." Kirkwall's smile was vibrant now. "I always thought that accident was a bit too lucky where Abbot was concerned. A bit too neat. No proof though. There was never any proof."

"Do you still have the letter?"

"What?"

"The letter from Mr. Ford, do you still have it?"

Rebus was tingling now, and Kirkwall caught his excitement. "I never throw anything away, Inspector. Oh yes, I've got it. It'll be upstairs."

"Can I see it? I mean, can I see it now?"

"If you like," Kirkwall made to stand up, but paused. "*Is* Alex Abbot in trouble, Inspector?"

"If you've still got that letter from Hugh Ford, then, yes, sir, I'd say Mr. Abbot could be in very grave trouble indeed."

"Inspector, you've made an old man very happy."

IT WAS THE LETTER against Alex Abbot's word, of course, and he denied everything. But there was enough now for a trial. The entry in the hotel, while it was *possibly* the work of Alexander Abbot was *certainly* not the work of the man who had written the letter to Jack Kirkwall. A search warrant gave the police the powers to look through Abbot's home and the ABC headquarters. A contract, drawn up between Abbot and Ford when the two men had gone into partnership, was discovered to be held in a solicitor's safe. The signature matched that on the letter to Jack Kirkwall. Kirkwall himself appeared in court to give evidence. He seemed to Rebus a different man altogether from the person he'd met previously: sprightly, keening, enjoying life to the full.

From the dock, Alexander Abbot looked on almost reproachfully, as if this were just one more business trick in a life full of them. Life, too, was the sentence of the judge.

April in Paris

by

PETER ROBINSON

THE GIRL SITTING OUTSIDE the café reminds me of April. She has the same long, hennaed hair, which she winds around her index finger in the same abstracted way. She is waiting for someone, clearly—a lover, perhaps—and as she waits she smokes, holding her cigarette in the same way, taking the same short, hurried puffs as April used to do. With her free hand, she alternates between taking sips of milky pastis and tapping her cigarette packet on the table. She is smoking Marlborough, as everyone in Paris seems to do these days. Back then, it was all Gitanes, Gauloise, and Disque Bleu.

Still, it wasn't smoking that killed April; it was love.

IT IS LATE SEPTEMBER, and though the weather is mild, it is still too cold outside for an old man like me, with blood as thin and as lacking in nutrients as workhouse gruel. Instead, I sit inside the little café on the Boulevard St. Germain over a *pichet* of red wine, just watching the people come and go. The young people. I have spent most of my life surrounded by the young, and though I grow inexorably older every year, they always seem to stay young. *Immortal youth*. Like Tithonus, I am "a white-haired shadow roaming like a dream." But unlike Tennyson's luckless narrator, who gained eternal life but not eternal youth, I am not immortal.

Six months, perhaps less, the doctors say. Something is growing inside me; my cells are mutating. As yet, I feel little pain, though my appetite has diminished, and I often suffer from extreme weariness.

Dying, I find, lends an edge to living, gives a clarity and a special, golden hue to the quotidian scenes parading before me: a swarthy man with a briefcase, glancing at his watch, speeding up, late for an important appointment; a woman chastising her little girl at the corner, wagging her finger, the girl crying and stamping her foot; a distracted priest stumbling briefly as he walks up the steps to the church across the boulevard.

Dying accentuates the beauty of the young, sets their energy in relief, enhances the smooth glow of their unwrinkled skin. But dying does not make me bitter. I am resigned to my fate; I have come to the end of my three-score and ten; I have seen enough. If you wish to travel, my doctors told me, do it now, while you're still strong enough. So here I am, revisiting the scene of my one and only great amour.

April. She always pronounced it *Ap-reel.* When I think of her, I still hear Thelonious Monk playing "April in Paris," hesitant at first, feeling his way into the song, reluctant to define the theme, then worrying away at it, and once finding it, altering it so much that the music becomes his own, only to be abandoned finally.

Of course, April didn't give a tinker's for Thelonious Monk. She listened to him dutifully, as they all did, for they were the heirs of Kerouac, Ginsberg, and Burroughs, to whom Monk, Bird, Trane,

Miles, and Mingus were gods, sacred and cool. But April's generation had its own gods—The Doors, Cream, Jimi Hendrix, Bob Dylan—gods of words and images as well as of music, and it was they who provided the sound track to which I lived during my year as a visiting lecturer in American literature at the Sorbonne in 1968.

This café hasn't changed much. A lick of paint, perhaps, if that. It probably hasn't changed much since Hemingway and Fitzgerald used to hang out around here. Even the waiters are probably the same. It was here I first met April, of course (why else would I come here?), one fine evening toward the end of March that year, when I was still young enough to bear the slight chill of a clear spring evening.

THAT APRIL WAS BEAUTIFUL almost goes without saying. I remember her high cheekbones, smooth, olive complexion, dark, watchful eyes, and rich, moist lips, downturned at the edges, often making her look sulky or petulant when she was far from it. I remember also how she used to move with grace and confidence when she remembered, but how the gaucheness of late adolescence turned her movements into a country girl's gait when she was at her most un-self-conscious. She was tall, slim, and long-legged, and her breasts were small, round, and high. The breasts of a Cranach nude.

We met, as I say, one late March evening in 1968 at this café, the Café de la Lune, where I was then sitting with the usual group: Henri, Nadine, Brad, Brigitte, Alain, and Paul. This was only days after Daniel Cohn-Bendit and seven other students had occupied the dean's office at Nanterre to protest the recent arrest of six members of the National Vietnam Committee, an event that was to have cataclysmic effects on us all not long afterward. Much of the time in those days we spoke of revolution, but that evening we were discussing, I remember quite clearly, F. Scott Fitzgerald's *Tender Is the Night*, when in she walked, wearing a woolly jumper and close-fitting, bell-bottomed jeans with flowers embroidered around the bells. She was carrying a bulky leather shoulder bag, looking radiant and slightly lost, glancing around for someone she knew.

It turned out that she knew Brad, an American backpacker who had attached himself to our group. People like Brad had a sort of fringe, outlaw attraction for the students. They seemed, with their freedom to roam and their contempt for rules and authority, to embody the very principles that the students themselves, with their heavy workloads, exams, and future careers, could only imagine or live vicariously. There were always one or two Brads around. Some dealt in drugs to make a living; Brad, though he spoke a good revolution, lived on a generous allowance wired regularly by his wealthy Boston parents via Western Union.

April went up to Brad and kissed him on both cheeks, a formal French gesture he seemed to accept with thinly veiled amusement. In his turn, Brad introduced her to the rest of us. That done, we resumed our discussion over another bottle of wine, the tang of Gauloise and café noir infusing the chill night air, and April surprised me by demonstrating that she not only had read *Tender Is the Night*, but had thought about it, too, even though she was a student of history, not of literature.

"Don't you think those poor young girls are terribly *used?*" she said. "I mean, Nicole is Dick's *patient*. He should be healing her, not sleeping with her. And the way Rosemary is manipulated by her mother … I'd go so far as to say that the mother seems to be *pimping* for her. Those films she made"—and here April gave her characteristic shrug, no more than a little shiver rippling across her shoulders—"they were no doubt made to appeal to older men." She didn't look at me as she said this, but my cheeks burned nonetheless.

"Have you read *Day of the Locust*?" Henri, one of the other students, chimed in. "If you want to know about how Hollywood warps people, that's your place to start. There's a mother in there who makes Rosemary's look like a saint."

"Huxley?" asked Nadine, not our brightest.

"No," said April. "That was *After Many a Summer*. *Day of the Locust* was Nathanael West, I think. Yes?"

Here, she looked directly at me, the professor, for the first time, turned on me the full blaze of her beauty. She knew she was right, of course, but she still deferred to me out of politeness.

"That's right," I said, smiling, feeling my heart lurch and my soul tingle inside its chains of flesh. "Nathanael West wrote *Day of the Locust*."

And from that moment on, I was smitten.

I TOLD MYSELF not to be a fool, that April was far too young for me, and that a beautiful woman like her couldn't possibly be interested in a portly, forty-year-old lecturer, even if he did wear faded denim jeans, had a goatee, and grew what wisps of hair remained a little longer than some of his colleagues thought acceptable. But after that first meeting, I found myself thinking about April a lot. In fact, I couldn't get her out of my mind. It wasn't mere lust—though Lord knows it was that, too—but I loved the sound of her voice, loved the way she twisted strands of hair around her finger as she spoke, the way she smoked her cigarette, loved the passion of her arguments, the sparkle of her laughter, the subtle jasmine of her perfume.

Love.

That night, she had left the café after about an hour, arm in arm with Brad—young, handsome, rich, footloose and fancy-free Brad—and I had lain awake tormented by images of their passionate love-making. I had never felt like that before, never felt so consumed by desire for someone and so wracked by pain at the thought of someone else having her. It was as if an alien organism had invaded my body, my very soul, and wrought such changes there that I could hardly cope with the more mundane matters, such as teaching and writing, eating and sleeping.

The second time I met her it was raining. I was walking along the *quai* across from Notre Dame, staring distractedly at the rain pitting the river's steely surface, thinking of her, when she suddenly ducked under my umbrella and took my arm.

I must have gasped out loud.

"Professor Dodgson," she said. Not a question. She *knew* who I was. "Sorry I startled you."

But that wasn't why I gasped, I wanted to tell her. It was the sudden apparition of this beautiful creature I had been dreaming about for days. I looked at her. The driving rain had soaked her hair and face. Like Dick in *Tender Is the Night*, I wanted to drink the rain that ran from her cheeks. "How did you recognize me under this?" I asked her.

She gave that little shrug that was no more than a ripple and smiled up at me. "Easy. You're carrying the same old briefcase you had last week. It's got your initials on it."

"How sharp of you," I said. "You should become a detective."

"Oh, I could never become a fascist pig." She said this with a completely straight face. People said things like that back then.

"Just a joke," I said. "Where are you going?"

"Nowhere special."

"Coffee?"

She looked at me again, chewing on her lower lip for a moment as she weighed up my invitation. "All right," she said finally. "I know a place." And her gentle pressure on my arm caused me to change direction and enter the narrow alleys that spread like veins throughout the Latin Quarter. "Your French is very good," she said as we walked. "Where did you learn?"

"School, mostly. Then university. I seem to have a facility for it. We used to come here when I was a child, too, before the war. Brittany. My father fought in the first war, you see, and he developed this love for France. I think the fighting gave him a sort of stake in things."

"Do you, too, have this stake in France?"

"I don't know."

She found the café she was looking for on the Rue St. Severin, and we ducked inside. "Can you feel what's happening?" she asked me, once we were warm and dry, sitting at the zinc counter with hot, strong coffees before us. She lit a Gauloise and touched my arm. "Isn't it exciting?"

I couldn't believe what I was hearing. *She* thought something was happening between us. I could hardly disguise my joy. But I was also so tongue-tied that I couldn't think of anything wise or witty to say. I probably sat there, my mouth opening and closing like a guppy's before saying, "Yes. *Yes*, it is exciting."

"There'll be a revolution before spring's over, you mark my words. We'll be rid of de Gaulle and ready to start building a new France."

Ah, yes. *The revolution*. I should have known. It was the topic on everyone's mind at the time. Except mine, that is. I tried not to show my disappointment. Not that I wasn't interested—you couldn't be in Paris in the spring of 1968 and *not* be interested in the revolution one way or another—but I had been distracted from politics by my thoughts of April. Besides, as radical as I might have appeared to some people, I was still a foreign national, and I had to do my best to keep a low political profile, difficult as it was. One false step and I'd not only be out of a job but out of the country, and far away from April, forever. And I had answered her question honestly; I didn't know whether I had a stake in France or not.

"What does Brad think?" I asked.

"Brad?" She seemed surprised by my question. "Brad is an anarchist."

"And you?"

She twisted her hair around her finger. "I'm not sure. I know I want change. I think I'm an anarchist, too, though I'm not sure I'd want to be completely without any sort of government at all. But we want the same things. Peace. A new, more equal society. He is an American, but they have had many demonstrations there, too, you know. Vietnam."

"Ah, yes. I remember some of them."

We passed a while talking about my experiences in California, which seemed to fascinate April, though I must admit I was far more interested in tracing the contours of her face and drinking in the beauty of her eyes and skin than I was in discussing the war in Vietnam.

In the end she looked at her watch and said she had to go to a lecture but would probably see me later at the café. I said I hoped so and watched her walk away.

YOU WILL HAVE GATHERED that I loved April to distraction, but did she love me? I think not. She liked me well enough. I amused her, entertained her, and she was perhaps even flattered by my attentions; but ultimately, brash youth wins out over suave age. It was Brad she loved. Brad, whose status in my mind quickly changed from that of a mildly entertaining, reasonably intelligent hanger-on to the bane of my existence.

He always seemed to be around, and I could never get April to myself. Whether this was deliberate—whether he was aware of my interest and made jealous by it—I do not know. All I know is that I had very few chances to be alone with her. When we were together, usually at a café or walking in the street, we talked—talked of what was happening in France, of the future of the university, of literature, of the anarchists, Maoists, Trotskyites, and Communists, talked about all these, but not, alas, of love.

Perhaps this was my fault. I never pushed myself on her, never tried to make advances, never tried to touch her, even though my cells ached to reach out and mingle with hers, and even though the most casual physical contact, a touch on the arm, for example, set me aflame with desire. After our first few meetings, she would greet me with kisses on each cheek, the way she greeted all her friends, and my cheeks would burn for hours afterward. One day she left a silk scarf at the café, and I took it home and held it to my face like a lovesick schoolboy, inhaling April's perfume as I tried to sleep that night.

But I did not dare make a pass; I feared her rejection and her laughter far more than anything else. While we do not have the capacity to choose our feelings in the first place, we certainly have the ability to choose not to act on them, and that was what I was trying to do, admittedly more for my own sake than for hers.

WHEN I DID SEE APRIL alone again, it was late in the morning of the third of May, and I was still in bed. I had been up late the night before trying to concentrate on a Faulkner paper I had to present at a conference in Brussels that weekend, and as I had no actual classes on Fridays, I had slept in.

The soft but insistent tapping at my door woke me from a dream about my father in the trenches (why is it we never seem to dream at night about those we dream about all day?), and I rubbed the sleep out of my eyes.

I must explain that at the time, like the poor French workers, I wasn't paid very much; consequently, I lived in a small pension in a cobbled alley off the Boulevard St. Michel, between the university and the Luxembourg Gardens. As I could easily walk from the pension to my office at the Sorbonne, usually ate at the university or at a cheap local bistro, and spent most of my social hours in the various bars and cafés of the Latin Quarter, I didn't really need much more than a place to lay my head at night.

I stretched, threw on my dressing gown, and opened the door. I'm sure you can imagine my shock on finding April standing there. Alone. She had been to the room only once previously, along with

Brad and a couple of others for a nightcap of cognac after a Nina Simone concert, but she clearly remembered where I lived.

"Oh, I'm sorry, Richard—" She had started calling me by my first name, at my insistence, though of course she pronounced it in the French manner, and it sounded absolutely delightful to me every time she spoke it. "I didn't know …"

"Come in," I said, standing back. She paused a moment in the doorway, smiled shyly, then entered. I lay back on the bed, mostly because there was hardly enough room for two of us to sit together.

"Shall I make coffee?" she asked.

"There's only instant."

She made a typical April moue at the idea of instant coffee, as any true French person would, but I directed her to the tiny kitchenette behind the curtain, and she busied herself with the kettle, calling out over her shoulder as she filled it and turned on the gas.

"There's trouble at the university," she said. "That's what I came to tell you. It's happening at last. Everything's boiling over."

I remembered that there was supposed to be a meeting about the Nanterre Eight, who were about to face disciplinary charges the following Monday, and I assumed that was what she meant.

"What's happening?" I asked, still not quite awake.

April came back into the bedroom and sat demurely on the edge of my only chair, trying not to look at me lying on the bed. "The revolution," she said. "There's already a big crowd there. Students and lecturers together. They're talking about calling the police. Closing down the university."

This woke me up a little more. "They're what?"

"It's true," April went on. "Somebody told me that the university authorities said they'd call in the police if the crowds didn't disperse. But they're not dispersing; they're getting bigger." She lit a Gauloise and looked around for an ashtray. I passed her one I'd stolen from the Café de la Lune. She smiled when she saw it and took those short little puffs at her cigarette, hardly giving herself time to inhale and enjoy the tobacco before blowing it out and puffing again. "Brad's already there," she added.

"Then he'd better be careful," I said, getting out of bed. "He's neither a student nor a French citizen."

"But don't you see? This is everybody's struggle!"

"Try telling that to the police."

"You can be so cynical sometimes."

"I'm sorry, April," I said, not wanting to offend her. "I'm just concerned for him, that's all." Of course I was lying. Nothing would have pleased me better than to see Brad beaten to a pulp by the police or, better still, deported, but I could hardly tell April that. The kettle boiled and she gave me a smile of forgiveness and went to make the coffee. She only made one cup—for me—and as I sipped it, she talked on about what had happened that morning and how she could feel change in the air. Her animation and passion excited me, and I had to arrange my position carefully to avoid showing any obvious evidence of my arousal.

Even in the silences, she seemed inclined to linger, and in the end I had to ask her to leave while I got dressed, as there was nowhere for her to retain her modesty, and the thought of her standing so close to me, facing the wall, as I took off my dressing gown was too excruciating for me to bear. She pouted and left, saying she'd wait for me outside. When I rejoined her, we walked to the Sorbonne together, and I saw that she was right about the crowds. There was defiance in the air.

We found Brad standing with a group of anarchists, and April went over to take his arm. I spoke with him briefly for a while, alarmed at some of the things he told me. I found some colleagues from the literature department, and they said the police had been sent for. By four o'clock in the afternoon, the university was surrounded by the Campagnies Républicaines de Sécurité—the CRS, riot police—and a number of students and lecturers had been arrested. Before long, even more students arrived and started fighting with the CRS to free those who had been arrested. Nobody was backing down this time.

The revolution had begun.

I TOOK THE TRAIN to Brussels on Saturday morning and didn't come back until late on Tuesday, and though I had heard news of events in Paris, I was stunned at what awaited me on my return. The city was a war zone. The university was closed, and nobody knew when, or in what form, it would reopen. Even the familiar smell of the city—its coffee, cheese, and something-slightly-overripe aroma—had changed, and it now smelled of fire, burnt plastic, and rubber. I could taste ashes in my mouth.

I wandered the Latin Quarter in a dream, remnants of the previous day's tear gas stinging my eyes, barricades improvised from torn-up paving stones all over the place. Everywhere I went I saw the CRS, looking like invaders from space in their gleaming black helmets, with chin straps and visors, thick black uniforms, jackboots, and heavy truncheons. They turned up out of nowhere in coaches with windows covered in wire mesh, clambered out, and blocked off whole streets, apparently at random. Everywhere they could, people gathered and talked politics. The mood was swinging; you could taste it in the air along with the gas and ashes. This wasn't just another student demonstration, another Communist or anarchist protest; this was civil war. Even the bourgeoisie were appalled at the violence of the police attacks. There were reports of pregnant women being beaten, of young men being tortured, their genitals shredded.

This was the aftermath of what later came to be known as Bloody Monday, when the Nanterre Eight had appeared at the Sorbonne, triumphantly singing the "Internationale," and sparked off riots.

I had missed April terribly while I was in Brussels, and now I was worried that she might have been hurt or arrested. I immediately tried to seek her out, but it wasn't easy. She wasn't at her student residence nor at Brad's hotel. I tried the Café de la Lune and various other watering holes in the area, but to no avail. Eventually, I ran into someone I knew, who was able to tell me that he thought she was helping one of the student groups produce posters, but he didn't know where. I gave up and went back to my room, unable to sleep, expecting her gentle rap on the door at any moment. It never came.

I saw her again on Thursday, putting up posters on the Rue St. Jacques.

"I was worried about you," I told her.

She smiled and touched my arm. For a moment I let myself believe that my concern actually mattered to her. I could understand her dedication to what was happening; after all, she was young, and it was her country. I knew that all normal social activities were on hold, that the politics of revolution had little time or space for the personal, for such bourgeois indulgences as love, but still I selfishly wanted her, wanted to be with her.

My chance came on the weekend, when the shit really hit the fan.

ALL WEEK, negotiations had been going back and forth between the government and the students. The university stayed closed, and the students threatened to "liberate" it. De Gaulle huffed and puffed. The Latin Quarter remained an occupied zone. On Friday, the workers threw in their lot with the students and called for a general strike the following Monday. The whole country was on its knees in a way it hadn't been since the German occupation.

Thus far, I had been avoiding the demonstrations, not out of cowardice or lack of commitment, but because I was a British subject, not a French one. By the weekend, that no longer mattered. It had become a world struggle: us against them. We were fighting for a new world order. I was in. I had a stake. Besides, the university was closed, so I didn't even have a job to protect anymore. And perhaps, somewhere deep down, I hoped that heroic deeds on the barricades might win the heart of a fair lady.

So confusing was everything, so long-running and spread-out the battle, that I can't remember now whether it was Friday or Saturday. Odd that, the most important night of my life, and I can't remember what night it was. No matter.

It all started with a march toward the Panthéon, red and black flags everywhere, the "Internationale" bolstering our courage. I had found April and Brad earlier, along with Henri, Alain, and Brigitte, in the university quadrangle looking at the improvised bookstalls, and we went to the march together. April had her arm linked through mine on one side, and Alain's on the other.

It was about half-past nine when things started to happen. I'm not sure what came first, the sharp explosions of the gas grenades or the flash of a Molotov cocktail, but all of a sudden, pandemonium broke out, and there was no longer an organized march, only a number of battle fronts.

In the melee, April and I split off, losing Brad and the rest, and we found ourselves among those defending the front on the Boulevard St. Michel. Unfortunate drivers, caught in the chaos, pressed down hard on their accelerators, honked their horns and drove through red lights to get away, knocking pedestrians aside as they went. The explosions were all around us now, and a blazing CRS van silhouetted figures throwing petrol bombs and pulling up paving stones for the barricades. The restaurants and cafés were all closing hurriedly, waiters ushering clients out into the street and putting up the shutters.

The CRS advanced on us, firing gas grenades continuously. One landed at my feet, and I kicked it back at them. I saw one student fall to them, about ten burly police kicking him as he lay and beating him mercilessly with their truncheons. There was nothing we could do.

Clouds of gas drifted from the canisters, obscuring our view. We could see distant flames, hear the explosions and the cries, see vague shadows bending to pick up stones to throw at the darkness. The CRS charged. Some of us had come armed with Molotov cocktails and stones, but neither April nor I had any weapons, any means to defend ourselves, so we ran.

We were both scared. This was the worst the fighting had been so far. The demonstrators weren't just taking what the CRS dished out, they were fighting back, and that made the police even more vicious. They would show no quarter, neither with a woman nor a foreign national. We could hardly see for the tears streaming from our eyes as we tried to get away from the advancing CRS, who seemed to have every side street blocked off.

"Come on," I said, taking April's hand in mine. "This way."

We jumped the fence and edged through the pitch-dark Luxembourg Gardens, looking for an unguarded exit. When we found one, we dashed out and across to the street opposite. A group of CRS saw us and turned. Fortunately, the street was too narrow and the buildings were too high for the gas guns. The police fired high in the air and most of the canisters fell harmlessly onto the roofs above us. Nobody gave chase.

Hand in hand, we made our way through the dark back streets to my pension, which, though close to the fighting, seemed so far unscathed. We ran up to my tiny room and locked the door behind us. Our eyes were streaming, and both of us felt a little dizzy and sick from the tear gas, but we also felt elated from the night's battle. We could still hear the distant explosions and see flashes and flames, like Guy Fawkes Night back in England. Adrenaline buzzed in our veins.

Just as I can't say exactly what night it was, I can't say exactly who made the first move. All I remember is that suddenly the room seemed too small for the two of us, our bodies were pressed together and I was tasting those moist, pink lips for the first time, savouring her small, furtive tongue in my mouth. My legs were like jelly.

"You know when I came here the other morning and you were in bed?" April said as she unbuttoned my shirt.

"Yes," I said, tugging at her jeans.

She slipped my shirt off my shoulders. "I wanted to get into bed with you."

I unhooked her bra. "Why didn't you?"

"I didn't think you wanted me."

We managed to get mostly undressed before falling onto the bed. I kissed her breasts and ran my hands down her naked thighs. I thought I would explode with ecstasy when she touched me. Then she was under me, and I buried myself in her, heard her sharp gasp of pleasure.

At last, April was mine.

I LIVED ON THE MEMORY of April's body, naked beside me, the two of us joined in love, while the country went insane. I didn't see her for three days, and even then we were part of a group; we couldn't talk intimately. That was what things were like then; there was little place for the individual. Everything was chaos. Normal life was on hold, perhaps never to be resumed again.

The university was closed, the campus hardly recognizable. The pillars in the square were plastered with posters of Marx, Lenin, Trotsky, and Che Guevara. There was a general strike. Everything ground to a halt: Metro, buses, coal production, railways. Everywhere I walked I saw burned-out vans and cars, gutted news kiosks, piles of paving stones, groups of truncheon-swinging CRS. People eating in the cafés had tears streaming down their faces from the remnants of tear gas in the morning-after air.

And every morning was a morning after.

I spotted Brad alone in a side street one night not long after dark, and as I had been wanting to talk to him about April, I thought I might never get a better opportunity. He was on his way to a meeting, he said, but could spare a few minutes. We took the steps down to the Seine by the side of the Pont St. Michel, where we were less likely to get hassled by the CRS. It was dark and quiet by the river, though we could hear the crack of gas guns and explosions of Molotovs not so far away.

"Have you talked to April recently?" I asked him.

"Yes," he said. "Why?"

"I was wondering if ... you know ... she'd told you ... ?"

"Told me what?"

"Well ..." I swallowed. "About us."

He stopped for a moment, then looked at me and laughed. "Oh, yes," he said. "Yes, she did, as a matter of fact."

I was puzzled by his attitude. "Well?" I said. "Is that all you have to say?"

"What do you want me to say?"

"Aren't you angry?"

"Why should I be angry? It didn't mean anything."

I felt an icy fear grip me. "What do you mean, *it didn't mean anything?*"

"You know. It was just a quickie, a bit of a laugh. She said she got excited by the street fighting and you happened to be the nearest man. It's not the first time, you know. I don't expect April to be faithful or any of that bourgeois crap. She's her own woman."

"What did you say?"

"I said it didn't mean anything. You don't think she could be serious about someone like you, do you? Come off it, Richard, with your tatty jeans and your little goatee beard. You think you're a real hip intellectual, but you're nothing but a joke. That's all you were to her. A quickie. A laugh. A joke. She came straight to me afterward for a real—"

The blow came from deep inside me, and my fist caught him on the side of his jaw. I heard a sharp crack, distinct from the sound of a distant gas gun, and he keeled over into the Seine. We were under a bridge, and it was very dark. I stopped, listened, and looked around, but I could see no one, hear only the sounds of battle in the distance. Quickly, my blood turning to ice, I climbed the nearest stairs and reentered the fray.

I HAD NEVER IMAGINED that love could turn to hatred so quickly. Though I had fantasized about getting rid of Brad many times, I had never really intended to harm him, and certainly not in the way, or for the reason, that I did. I had never thought of myself as someone capable of killing another human being.

They pulled his body out of the Seine two days later, and the anarchists claimed that he had been singled out and murdered by the CRS. Most of the students were inclined to believe this, and another bloody riot ensued.

As for me, I'd had it. Had it with April, had it with the revolution, and had it with Paris. If I could have, I would have left for London immediately, but the cross-channel ferries weren't operating, and Skyways had no vacancies for some days. What few tourists remained trapped in Paris were queuing for buses to Brussels, Amsterdam, or Geneva, anywhere as long as they got out of France.

Mostly, I felt numb in the aftermath of killing Brad, though this was perhaps more to do with what he had told me about April than about the act itself, which had been an accident, and for which I didn't blame myself.

April. How could she deceive me so? How could she be so cold, so cruel, so callous? I meant nothing to her, just the nearest man to scratch her itch.

A quickie. A joke.

I saw her only once more, near the Luxembourg Gardens, the same gardens we jumped into that marvellous night a million years ago, and as she made to come toward me, I took off into a side street. I didn't want to talk to her again, didn't even want to see her. And it wasn't only April. I stayed away from all of them: Henri, Alain, Brigitte, Nadine, the lot of them. To me they had all become inextricably linked with April's humiliation of me, and I couldn't bear to be with them.

One day, Henri managed to get me aside and told me that April had committed suicide. He seemed angry rather than sad. I stared at him in disbelief. When he started to say something more, I cut him off and fled. I don't think anyone knew that I had killed Brad, but clearly April lamented his loss so much she no longer felt her life worth living. *He wasn't worth it,* I wanted to say, remembering the things he had told me under the bridge that night. If anyone was the killer, it was Brad, not me. He had killed my love for April, and now he had killed April.

I refused to allow myself to feel anything for her.

The people at Skyways said I might have some luck if I came out to the airport and waited for a vacancy on standby, which I did. Before I left, I glanced around my room one last time and saw nothing I wanted to take with me, not even April's silk scarf, which I had kept. So, in the clothes I was wearing, with the five hundred francs that was all the Bank of France allowed me to withdraw, I left the country and never went back.

UNTIL NOW.

I think it must be the memory of tear gas that makes my eyes water so. I wipe them with the back of my hand, and the waiter comes to ask me if I am all right. I tell him I am and order another *pichet*. I have nowhere else to go except the grave; I might as well stay here and drink myself to death. What is the point of another miserable six months on earth anyway?

The girl who reminds me of April crushes out her cigarette and twists a strand of hair. Her lover is late. I dream of consoling her, but what have I to offer?

"Professor Dodgson? Richard? Is that you?"

I look up slowly at the couple standing over me. The man is grey-haired, distinguished-looking, and there is something about him....
His wife, or companion, is rather stout with grey eyes and short salt-and-pepper hair. Both are well-dressed, healthy-looking, the epitome of the Parisian bourgeoisie.

"Yes," I say. "I'm afraid you have me at a disadvantage."

"Henri Boulanger," he says. "I was once your student. My wife, Brigitte, was also a student."

"Henri? Brigitte?" I stand to shake his hand. "Is it really you?"

He smiles. "Yes. I wasn't sure about you at first. You haven't changed all that much in the face, the eyes, but you ... perhaps you have lost weight?"

"I'm ill, Henri. Dying, in fact. But please sit down. Be my guests. Let's share some wine. Waiter."

Henri looks at Brigitte, who nods, and they sit. She seems a little embarrassed, uncomfortable, though I can't for the life of me imagine why. Perhaps it is because I told them I am dying. No doubt many people would feel uncomfortable sitting at a café drinking wine with death.

"Funnily enough," I tell them, "I was just thinking about you. What are you doing here?"

Henri beams. "Now *I'm* the professor," he says with great pride. "I teach literature at the Sorbonne."

"Good for you, Henri. I always believed you'd go far."

"It's a pity you couldn't have stayed around."

"They were difficult times, Henri. Interesting, as the Chinese say."

"Still ... It was a sad business about that girl. What was her name?"

"April?" I say, and I feel an echo of my old love as I say her name. *Ap-reel.*

"April. Yes. That was around the time you went away."

"My time here was over," I tell him. "I had no job, the country was in a state of civil war. It wasn't my future."

Henri frowns. "Yes, I know. Nobody blames you for getting out … it's not that …"

"Blames me for what, Henri?"

He glances at Brigitte, who looks deep into her glass of wine. "You remember," he says. "The suicide? I told you about it."

"I remember. She killed herself over an American boy the CRS beat to death."

"Brad? But that wasn't … I mean …" He stares at me, wide-eyed. "You mean you don't *know?*"

"Don't know what?"

"I tried to tell you at the time, but you turned away."

"Tell me what?"

Brigitte looks up slowly from her wine and speaks. "Why did you desert her? Why did you turn your back on her?"

"What do you mean?"

"You rejected her. You broke her heart. The silly girl was in love with you, and you spurned her. *That's* why she killed herself."

"That's ridiculous. She killed herself because of the American."

Brigitte shakes her head. "No. Believe me, it was you. She told me. She could talk only about you in the days before …"

"But … Brad?"

"Brad was jealous. Don't you understand? She was never more than a casual girlfriend to him. He wanted more, but she fell for you."

I shake my head slowly. I can't believe this. Can't *allow* myself to believe this. The world starts to become indistinct, all shadows and echoes. I can't breathe. My skin tingles with pins and needles. I feel a touch on my shoulder.

"Are you all right? Richard? Are you all right?"

It is Henri. I hear him call for a brandy, and someone places a cool glass in my hand. I sip. It burns and seems to dispel the mist a little. Brigitte rests her hand on my arm and leans forward. "You mean you really didn't know?"

I shake my head.

"Henri tried to tell you."

"Brad," I whisper. "Brad told me she just used me, that she thought I was a joke. I believed him."

Henri and Brigitte look at one another, then back at me, concern and pity in their eyes. A little more than that in Henri's, too: suspicion. Maybe everybody wasn't convinced that the CRS had killed Brad after all.

"He was jealous," Brigitte repeats. "He lied."

Suddenly, I start to laugh, which horrifies them. But I can't help myself. People turn and look at us. Henri and Brigitte are embarrassed. When the laughter subsides, I am left feeling hollow. I sip more brandy. Henri has placed his cigarettes on the table. Gauloise, I notice.

"May I?" I ask, reaching for the packet, even though I haven't smoked in twenty years.

He nods.

I light a Gauloise. Cough a little. What does it matter if I get lung cancer now? I'm already as good as dead. After a few puffs, the cigarette even starts to taste good, brings back, as tastes and smells do so well, even more memories of the cafés and nights of 1968. I begin to wonder whatever happened to that silk scarf I left in the drawer at my pension. I wish I could smell her jasmine scent again.

Outside, the girl's lover arrives. He is young and handsome and he waves his arms as he apologizes for being late. She is sulky at first, but she brightens and kisses him. He runs his hand down her smooth, olive cheek, and I can smell tear gas again.

Biding Time

by

ROBERT J. SAWYER

ERNIE GARGALIAN WAS FAT—"Gargantuan Gargalian," some called him. Fortunately, like me, he lived on Mars; it was a lot easier to carry extra weight here. He must have massed a hundred and fifty kilos, but it felt like a third of what it would have on Earth.

Ironically, Gargalian was one of the few people on Mars wealthy enough to fly back to Earth as often as he wanted to, but he never did; I don't think he planned to ever set foot on the mother planet again, even though it was where all his rich clients were. Gargalian was a dealer in Martian fossils: he brokered the transactions between those lucky prospectors who found good specimens and wealthy collectors back on Earth, taking the same oversize slice of the financial pie as he would have of a real one.

His shop was in the innermost circle—appropriately; he knew

everyone. The main door was transparent alloquartz with his business name and trading hours laser-etched into it; not quite carved in stone, but still a degree of permanence suitable to a dealer in prehistoric relics. The business name was Ye Olde Fossil Shoppe—as if there were any other kind.

The shoppe's ye olde door slid aside as I approached—somewhat noisily, I thought. Well, Martian dust gets everywhere, even inside our protective dome; some of it was probably gumming up the works.

Gargalian, seated by a long worktable covered with hunks of rock, was in the middle of a transaction. A prospector—grizzled, with a deeply lined face; he could have been sent over from Central Casting—was standing next to Gargantuan (okay, I was one of those who called him that, too). Both of them were looking at a monitor, showing a close-up of a rhizomorph fossil.

"*Aresthera weingartenii*," Gargalian said, with satisfaction; he had a clipped Lebanese accent and a deep, booming voice. "A juvenile, too—we don't see many at this particular stage of development. And see that rainbow sheen? Lovely. It's been permineralized with silicates. This will fetch a nice price—a nice price indeed."

The prospector's voice was rough. Those of us who passed most of our time under the dome had enough troubles with dry air; those who spent half their lives in surface suits, breathing bottled atmosphere, sounded particularly raspy. "How nice?" he said, his eyes narrowing.

Gargantuan frowned while he considered. "I can sell this quickly for perhaps eleven million ... or, if you give me longer, I can probably get thirteen. I have some clients who specialize in *A. weingartenii* who will pay top coin, but they are slow in making up their minds."

"I want the money fast," said the prospector. "This old body of mine might not hold out much longer."

Gargalian turned his gaze from the monitor to appraise the prospector, and he caught sight of me as he did so. He nodded in my direction, and raised a single finger—the finger that indicated "one minute," not the other finger, although I got that often enough when I entered places, too. He nodded at the prospector, apparently agreeing that the guy wasn't long for this or any other world, and said, "A speedy resolution, then. Let me give you a receipt for the fossil …"

I waited for Gargalian to finish his business, and then he came over to where I was standing. "Hey, Ernie," I said.

"Mr. Double-X himself!" declared Gargalian, bushy eyebrows rising above his round, flabby face. He liked to call me that because both my first and last names—Alex Lomax—ended in that letter.

I pulled my datapad out of my pocket and showed him a picture of a seventy-year-old woman, with grey hair cut in sensible bangs above a crabapple visage. "Recognize her?"

Gargantuan nodded, and his jowls shook as he did so. "Sure. Megan Delacourt, Delany, something like that, right?"

"Delahunt," I said.

"Right. What's up? She your client?"

"She's *nobody's* client," I said. "The old dear is pushing up daisies."

I saw Gargalian narrow his eyes for a second. Knowing him, he was trying to calculate whether he'd owed her money or she'd owed him money. "Sorry to hear that," he said with the kind of regret that was merely polite, presumably meaning that at least he hadn't lost anything. "She was pretty old."

"'Was' is the operative word," I said. "She'd transferred."

He nodded, not surprised. "Just like that old guy wants to." He indicated the door the prospector had exited through. It was a common-enough scenario. People come to Mars in their youth, looking to make their fortunes by finding fossils here. The lucky ones stumble across a valuable specimen early on; the unlucky ones keep on searching and searching, getting older in the process. If they ever do find a decent specimen, first thing they do is transfer before it's too late. "So, what is it?" asked Gargalian. "A product-liability case? Next of kin suing NewYou?"

I shook my head. "Nah, the transfer went fine. But somebody killed the uploaded version shortly after the transfer was completed."

Gargalian's bushy eyebrows went up. "Can you do that? I thought transfers were immortal."

I knew from bitter recent experience that a transfer could be killed with equipment specifically designed for that purpose, but the only broadband disrupter here on Mars was safely in the hands of the New Klondike constabulary. Still, I'd seen the most amazing suicide a while ago, committed by a transfer.

But this time the death had been simple. "She was lured down to the shipyards, or so it appears, and ended up standing between the engine cone of a big rocket ship, which was lying on its belly, and a brick wall. Someone fired the engine, and she did a Margaret Hamilton."

Gargalian shared my fondness for old films; he got the reference and winced. "Still, there's your answer, no? It must have been one of the rocket's crew—someone who had access to the engine controls."

I shook my head. "No. The cockpit was broken into."

Ernie frowned. "Well, maybe it was one of the crew, trying to make it look like it *wasn't* one of the crew."

God save me from amateur detectives. "I checked. They all had alibis—and none of them had a motive, of course."

Gargantuan made a harrumphing sound. "What about the original version of Megan?" he asked.

"Already gone. They normally euthanize the biological original immediately after making the copy; can't have two versions of the same person running around, after all."

"Why would anyone kill someone after they transferred?" asked Gargalian. "I mean, if you wanted the person dead, it's got to be easier to off them when they're still biological, no?"

"I imagine so."

"And it's still murder, killing a transfer, right? I mean, I can't recall it ever happening, but that's the way the law reads, isn't it?"

"Yeah, it's still murder," I said. "The penalty is life imprisonment—down on Earth, of course." With any sentence longer than two mears—two Mars years—it was cheaper to ship the criminal down to Earth, where air is free, than to incarcerate him or her here.

Gargantuan shook his head, and his jowls, again. "She seemed like a nice old lady," he said. "Can't imagine why someone would want her dead."

"The 'why' is bugging me, too," I said. "I know she came in here a couple of weeks ago with some fossil specimens to sell; I found a receipt recorded in her datapad."

Gargalian motioned toward his desktop computer, and we walked over to it. He spoke to the machine, and some pictures of fossils appeared on the same monitor he'd been looking at earlier. "She brought me three pentapeds. One was junk, but the other two were very nice specimens."

"You sold them?"

"That's what I do."

"And gave her her share of the proceeds?"

"Yes."

"How much did it come to?"

He spoke to the computer again, and pointed at the displayed figure. "Total, nine million solars."

I frowned. "NewYou charges 7.5 million for their basic service. There can't have been enough cash left over after she transferred to be worth killing her for, unless …" I peered at the images of the fossils she'd brought in, but I was hardly a great judge of quality. "You said two of the specimens were really nice." "Nice" was Gargantuan's favourite adjective; he'd apparently never taken a creative-writing course.

He nodded.

"*How* nice?"

He laughed, getting my point at once. "You think she'd found the alpha?"

I lifted my shoulders a bit. "Why not? If she knew where it was, that'd be worth killing her for."

The alpha deposit was where Simon Weingarten and Denny O'Reilly—the two private explorers who first found fossils on Mars—had collected their original specimens. That discovery had brought all the other fortune seekers from Earth. Weingarten and O'Reilly had died twenty mears ago—their heat shield had torn off while reentering Earth's atmosphere after their third trip here—and the location of the alpha died with them. All anyone knew was that it was somewhere here in the Isidis Planitia basin; whoever found it would be rich beyond even Gargantuan Gargalian's dreams.

"I told you, one of the specimens was junk," said Ernie. "No way it came from the alpha. The rocks of the alpha are extremely fine-grained—the preservation quality is as good as that from Earth's Burgess Shale."

"And the other two?" I said.

He frowned, then replied almost grudgingly, "They were good."

"Alpha good?"

His eyes narrowed. "Maybe."

"She could have thrown in the junk piece just to disguise where the others had come from," I said.

"Well, even junk fossils are hard to come by."

That much was true. In my own desultory collecting days, I'd never found so much as a fragment. Still, there had to be a reason why someone would kill an old woman just after she'd transferred her consciousness into an artificial body.

And if I could find that reason, I'd be able to find her killer.

My CLIENT was Megan Delahunt's ex-husband—and he'd been ex for a dozen mears, not just since Megan had died. Jersey Delahunt had come into my little office at about half past ten that morning. He was shrunken with age, but looked as though he'd been broad-shouldered in his day. A few wisps of white hair were all that was left on his liver-spotted head. "Megan struck it rich," he'd told me.

I'd regarded him from my swivel chair, hands interlocked behind my head, feet up on my battered desk. "And you couldn't be happier for her."

"You're being sarcastic, Mr. Lomax," he said, but his tone wasn't bitter. "I don't blame you. Sure, I'd been hunting fossils for thirty-six Earth years, too. Megan and me, we'd come here to Mars together, right at the beginning of the rush, hoping to make our fortunes. It hadn't lasted though—our marriage, I mean; the dream of getting rich lasted, of course."

"Of course," I said. "Are you still named in her will?"

Jersey's old, rheumy eyes regarded me. "Suspicious, too, aren't you?"

"That's what they pay me the medium-sized bucks for."

He had a small mouth, surrounded by wrinkles; it did the best it could to work up a smile. "The answer is no, I'm not in her will. She left everything to our son Ralph. Not that there was much left over after she spent the money to upload, but whatever there was, he got—or will get, once her will is probated."

"And how old is Ralph?"

"Thirty-four." Age was always expressed in Earth years.

"So he was born after you came to Mars? Does he still live here?"

"Yes. Always has."

"Is he a prospector, too?"

"No. He's an engineer. Works for the water-recycling authority."

I nodded. Not rich, then. "And Megan's money is still there, in her bank account?"

"So says the lawyer, yes."

"If all the money is going to Ralph, what's your interest in the matter?"

"My interest, Mr. Lomax, is that I once loved this woman very much. I left Earth to come here to Mars because it's what she wanted to do. We lived together for ten mears, had children together, and—"

"Children," I repeated. "But you said all the money was left to your *child*, singular, this Ralph."

"My daughter is dead," Jersey said, his voice soft.

It was hard to sound contrite in my current posture—I was still leaning back with feet up on the desk. But I tried. "Oh. Um. I'm … ah …"

"You're sorry, Mr. Lomax. Everybody is. I've heard it a million times. But it wasn't your fault. It wasn't anyone's fault, although …"

"Yes?"

"Although Megan blamed herself, of course. What mother wouldn't?"

"I'm not following."

"Our daughter JoBeth died thirty years ago, when she was two months old." Jersey was staring out my office's single window, at one of the arches supporting the habitat dome. "She smothered in her sleep." He turned to look at me, and his eyes were red as Martian sand. "The doctor said that sort of thing happens sometimes—not often, but from time to time." His face was almost unbearably sad. "Right up till the end, Megan would cry whenever she thought of JoBeth. It was heartbreaking. She couldn't get over it."

I nodded, because that was all I could think of to do. Jersey didn't seem inclined to say anything else, so, after a moment, I went on. "Surely the police have investigated your ex-wife's death."

"Yes, of course," Jersey replied. "But I'm not satisfied that they tried hard enough."

This was a story I'd heard often. I nodded again, and he continued to speak: "I mean, the detective I talked to said the killer was probably off-planet now, headed to Earth."

"That *is* possible, you know," I replied. "Well, at least it is if a ship has left here in the interim."

"Two have," said Jersey, "or so the detective told me."

"Including the one whose firing engine, ah, did the deed?"

"No, that one's still there. *Lennick's Folly*, it's called. It was supposed to head back to Earth, but it's been impounded."

"Because of Megan's death?"

"No. Something to do with unpaid taxes."

I nodded. With NewYou's consciousness-uploading technology, not even death was certain anymore—but taxes were. "Which detective were you dealing with?"

"Some Scottish guy."

"Dougal McCrae," I said. Mac wasn't the laziest man I'd ever met—and he'd saved my life recently when another case had gone bad, so I tried not to think uncharitable thoughts about him. But if there was a poster boy for complacent policing, well, Mac wouldn't be it; he wouldn't bother to get out from behind his desk to show up for the photo shoot. "All right," I said. "I'll take the case."

"Thank you," said Jersey. "I brought along Megan's datapad; the police gave it back to me after copying its contents." He handed me the little tablet. "It's got her appointment schedule and her address book. I thought maybe it would help you find the killer."

I motioned for him to put the device on my desk. "It probably will, at that. Now, about my fee ..."

SINCE MARS NO LONGER HAD SEAS, it was all one landmass: you could literally walk anywhere on the planet. Still, on this whole rotten globe, there was only one settlement—our domed city of New Klondike, three kilometres in diameter. The city had a circular layout: nine concentric rings of buildings, cut into blocks by twelve radial roadways. The NewYou franchise—the only place you could go for uploading on Mars—was just off Third Avenue in the fifth ring. According to her datapad, Megan Delahunt's last appointment at NewYou had been three days ago, when her transfer had actually been done. I headed there after leaving Ye Olde Fossil Shoppe.

The NewYou franchise was under new management since the last time I'd visited. The rather tacky showroom was at ground level; the brain-scanning equipment was on the second floor. The basement—quite rare on Mars, since the permafrost was so hard to dig through—was mostly used for storage.

"Mr. Lomax!" declared Horatio Fernandez, an employee held over from the previous ownership. Fernandez was a beefy guy—arms as big around as Gargalian's, but his bulk was all muscle.

"Hello," I said. "Sorry to bother you, but—"

"Let me guess," said Fernandez. "The Megan Delahunt murder."

"Bingo."

He shook his head. "She was really pleasant."

"So people keep telling me."

"It's true. She was a real lady, that one. Cultured, you know? Lots of people here, spending their lives splitting rocks, they get a rough edge. But not her; she was all 'please' and 'thank you.' Of course, she was pretty long in the tooth …"

"Did she have any special transfer requests?" I asked.

"Nah. Just wanted her new body to look the way she had fifty Earth years ago, when she was twenty—which was easy enough."

"What about mods for outside work?" Lots of transfers had special equipment installed in their new bodies so that they could operate more easily on the surface of Mars.

"Nah, nothing. She said her fossil-hunting days were over. She was looking forward to a nice long future, reading all the great books she never had time for before."

If she'd found the alpha, she'd probably have wanted to work it herself, at least for a while—if you're planning on living forever, and you had a way to become super-rich, you'd take advantage of it. "Hmmph," I said. "Did she mention any titles?"

"Yeah," said Fernandez. "She said she was going to start with *Remembrance of Things Past*."

I nodded, impressed at her ambition. "Anybody else come by to ask about her since she was killed?"

"Well, Detective McCrae called."

"Mac came here?"

"No, he *called*. On the phone."

I smiled. "That's Mac."

I HEADED OVER to Gully's Gym, since it was on the way to my next stop, and did my daily workout—treadmill, bench press, and so on. I worked up quite a sweat, but a sonic shower cleaned me up. Then it was off to the shipyards. Mostly, this dingy area between the eighth and ninth circles was a grave for abandoned ships, left over from the early fossil-rush days when people were coming to Mars in droves. Now only a small amount of maintenance work was done here. My last visit to the shipyards had been quite unpleasant—but I suppose it hadn't been as bad as Megan Delahunt's last visit.

I found *Lennick's Folly* easily enough. It was a tapered spindle, maybe a hundred metres long, lying on its side. The bow had a couple of square windows, and the stern had a giant engine cone attached. There was a gap of only a few metres between the cone and a brick firewall, which was now covered with soot. Whatever had been left of Megan's shiny new body had already been removed.

The lock on the cockpit door hadn't been repaired, so I had no trouble getting in. Once inside the cramped space, I got to work.

There were times when a private detective could accomplish things a public one couldn't. Mac had to worry about privacy laws, which were as tight here on Mars as they were back down on Earth—and a good thing, too, for those, like me, who had come here to escape our pasts. Oh, Mac doubtless had collected DNA samples here—gathering them at a crime scene was legal—but he couldn't take DNA from a suspect to match against specimens from here without a court order, and to get that, he'd have to show good reason up front for why the suspect might be guilty—which, of course, was a catch-22. Fortunately, the only catch-22 I had to deal with was the safety on my trusty old Smith & Wesson .22.

I used a GeneSeq 109, about the size of a hockey puck. It collected even small fragments of DNA in a nanotrap, and could easily compare sequences from any number of sources. I did a particularly thorough collecting job on the control panel that operated the engine. Of course, I looked for fingerprints, too, but there weren't any recent ones, and the older ones had been smudged either by someone operating the controls with gloved hands, which is what I suspected, or, I suppose, by artificial hands—a transfer offing a transfer; that'd be a first.

Of course, Mac knew as well as I did that family members commit most murders. I'd surreptitiously taken a sample from Jersey Delahunt when he'd visited my office; I sample everyone who comes there. But my GeneSeq reported that the DNA collected here didn't match Jersey's. That wasn't too surprising: I'd been hired by guilty parties before, but it was hardly the norm—or, at least, the kind of people who hired me usually weren't guilty of the particular crime they wanted me to investigate.

And so I headed off to find the one surviving child of Megan and Jersey Delahunt.

JERSEY HAD SAID his son Ralph had been born shortly after he and Megan had come to Mars thirty-six Earth years ago. Ralph certainly showed all the signs of having been born here: he was 210 centi-metres if he was an inch; growing up in Mars's low gravity had that effect. And he was a skinny thing, with rubbery, tubular limbs—Gumby in an olive-green business suit. Most of us here had been born on Earth, and it still showed in our musculature, but Ralph was Martian, through and through.

His office at the water works was much bigger than mine, but then, he didn't personally pay the rent on it. I had a DNA collector in my palm when I shook his hand, and while he was getting us both coffee from a maker on his credenza, I transferred the sample to the GeneSeq, and set it to comparing his genetic code to the samples from the rocket's cockpit.

"I want to thank you, Mr. Lomax," Ralph said, handing me a steaming mug. "My father called to say he'd hired you. I'm delighted. Absolutely delighted." He had a thin, reedy voice, matching his thin, reedy body. "How anyone could do such a thing to my mother ..."

I smiled, sat down, and took a sip. "I understand she was a sweet old lady."

"That she was," said Ralph, taking his own seat on the other side of a glass-and-steel desk. "That she was."

The GeneSeq bleeped softly three times, each bleep higher pitched than the one before—the signal for a match. "Then why did you kill her?" I said.

He had his coffee cup halfway to his lips, but suddenly he slammed it down, splashing double-double, which fell to the glass desktop in Martian slo-mo. "Mr. Lomax, if that's your idea of a joke, it's in very poor taste. The funeral service for my mother is tomorrow, and—"

"And you'll be there, putting on an act, just like the one you're putting on now."

"Have you no decency, sir? My mother ..."

"Was killed. By someone she trusted—someone who she would follow to the shipyards, someone who told her to wait in a specific spot while he—what? Nipped off to have a private word with a ship's pilot? Went into the shadows to take a leak? Of course, a professional engineer could get the manual for a spaceship's controls easily enough, and understand it well enough to figure out how to fire the engine."

Ralph's flimsy form was quaking with rage, or a good simulation of it. "Get out. Get out now. I think I speak for my father when I say you're fired."

I didn't get up. "It was damn-near a perfect crime," I said, my voice rock steady. "*Lennick's Folly* should have headed back to Earth, taking any evidence of who'd been in its cockpit with her; indeed, you probably hoped it'd be gone long before the melted lump that once was your mother was found. But you can't fire engines under the dome without consuming a lot of oxygen—and somebody has to pay for that. It doesn't grow on trees, you know—well, down on Earth it does, sort of. But not here. And so the ship is hanging around, like the telltale heart, like an albatross, like—" I sought a third allusion, just for style's sake, and one came to me: "like the sword of Damocles."

Ralph looked left and right. There was no way out, of course; I was seated between him and the door, and my Smith & Wesson was now in my hand. He might have done a sloppy job, but I never do. "I ... I don't know what you're talking about," he said.

I made what I hoped was an ironic smile. "Guess that's another advantage of uploading, no? No more DNA being left behind. It's almost impossible to tell if a specific transfer has been in a specific room, but it's child's play to determine what biologicals have gone in and out of somewhere. Did you know that cells slough off the alveoli of your lungs and are exhaled with each breath? Oh, only two or three—but today's scanners have no trouble finding them, and reading the DNA in them. No, it's open-and-shut that you were the murderer: you were in the cockpit of *Lennick's Folly*, you touched the engine controls. Yeah, you were bright enough to wear gloves—but not bright enough to hold your breath."

He got to his feet, and started to come around from behind his funky desk. I undid the safety on my gun, and he froze.

"I frown on murder," I said, "but I'm all for killing in self-defence—so I'd advise you to stand perfectly still." I waited to make sure he was doing just that, then went on. "I know *that* you did it, but I still don't know why. And I'm an old-fashioned guy—grew up reading Agatha Christie and Peter Robinson. In the good old days, before DNA and all that, detectives wanted three things to make a case: method, motive, and opportunity. The method is obvious, and you clearly had opportunity. But I'm still in the dark on the motive, and, for my own interest, I'd like to know what it was."

"You can't prove any of this," sneered Ralph. "Even if you have a DNA match, it's inadmissible."

"Dougal McCrae is lazy, but he's not stupid. If I tip him off that you definitely did it, he'll find a way to get the warrant. Your only chance now is to tell me *why* you did it. Hell, I'm a reasonable man. If your justification was good enough, well, I've turned a blind eye before. So, tell me: why wait until your mother uploaded to kill her? If you had some beef with her, why didn't you off her earlier?" I narrowed my eyes. "Or had she done something recently? She'd struck it rich, and that sometimes changes people—but ..." I paused, and after a few moments, I found myself nodding. "Ah, of course. She struck it rich, and she was old. You'd thought, hey, she's going to drop off soon, and you'll inherit her new-found fortune. But when she squandered it on herself, spending most of it on uploading, you were furious." I shook my head in disgust. "Greed. Oldest motivation there is."

"You really are a smug bastard, Lomax," said Ralph. "And you don't know *anything* about me. Do you think I care about money?" He snorted. "I've never wanted money—as long as I've got enough to pay my life-support tax, I'm content."

"People who are indifferent to thousands often change their ways when millions are at stake."

"Oh, now you're a philosopher, too, eh? I was born here on Mars, Lomax. My whole life I've been surrounded by people who spend all their time looking for paleontological pay dirt. My parents both did that. It was bad enough that I had to compete with things that have been dead for hundreds of millions of years, but …"

I narrowed my eyes. "But what?"

He shook his head. "Nothing. You wouldn't understand."

"No? Why not?"

He paused, then: "You got brothers? Sisters?"

"A sister," I said. "Back on Earth."

"Older or younger?"

"Older, by two years."

"No," he said. "You couldn't possibly understand."

"Why not? What's that got—" And then it hit me. I'd encountered lots of scum in my life: crooks, swindlers, people who'd killed for a twenty-solar coin. But nothing like this. That Ralph had a scarecrow's form was obvious, but, unlike the one from Oz, he clearly *did* have a brain. And although his mother had been the tin man, so to speak, after she'd uploaded, I now knew it was Ralph who'd been lacking a heart.

"JoBeth," I said softly.

Ralph staggered backward as if I'd hit him. His eyes, defiant till now, could no longer meet my own. "Christ," I said. "How could you? How could anyone …"

"It's not like that," he said, spreading his arms like a praying mantis. "I was four years old, for God's sake. I—I didn't mean—"

"You killed your own baby sister."

He looked at the carpeted office floor. "My parents had little enough time for me as it was, what with spending twelve hours a day looking for the god-damned alpha."

I nodded. "And when JoBeth came along, suddenly you were getting no attention at all. And so you smothered her in her sleep."

"You can't prove that. Nobody can."

"Maybe. Maybe not."

"She was cremated, and her ashes were scattered outside the dome thirty years ago. The doctor said she died of natural causes, and you can't prove otherwise."

I shook my head, still trying to fathom it all. "You didn't count on how much it would hurt your mother—or that the hurt would go on and on, mear after mear."

He said nothing, and that was as damning as any words could be.

"She couldn't get over it, of course," I said. "But you thought, you know, eventually ..."

He nodded, almost imperceptibly—perhaps he wasn't even aware that he'd done so. I went on, "You thought eventually she would die, and then you wouldn't have to face her anymore. At some point, she'd be gone, and her pain would be over, and you could finally be free of the guilt. You were biding your time, waiting for her to pass on."

He was still looking at the carpet, so I couldn't see his face. But his narrow shoulders were quivering. I continued. "You're still young—thirty-four, isn't it? Oh, sure, your mother might have been good for another ten or twenty years, but *eventually* ..."

Acid was crawling its way up my throat. I swallowed hard, fighting it down. "Eventually," I continued, "you would be free—or so you thought. But then your mother struck it rich, and uploaded her consciousness, and was going to live for centuries if not forever, and you couldn't take that, could you? You couldn't take her always being around, always crying over something that you had done so long ago." I lifted my eyebrows, and made no effort to keep the contempt out of my voice. "Well, they say the first murder is the hardest."

"You can't prove any of this. Even if you have DNA specimens from the cockpit, the police still don't have any probable cause to justify taking a specimen from me."

"They'll find it. Dougal McCrae is lazy—but he's also a father, with a baby girl of his own. He'll dig into this like a bulldog, and won't let go until he's got what he needs to nail you, you—"

I stopped. I wanted to call him a son of a bitch—but he wasn't; he was the son of a gentle, loving woman who had deserved so much better. "One way or another, you're going down," I said. And then it hit me, and I started to feel that maybe there was a little justice in the universe after all. "And that's exactly right: you're going down, to Earth."

Ralph at last did look up, and his thin face was ashen. *"What?"*

"That's what they do with anyone whose jail sentence is longer than two mears. It's too expensive in terms of life-support costs to house criminals here for years on end."

"I—I can't go to Earth."

"You won't have any choice."

"But—but I was *born* here. I'm Martian, born and raised. On Earth, I'd weigh ... what? Twice what I'm used to ..."

"Three times, actually. A stick-insect like you, you'll hardly be able to walk there. You should have been doing what I do. Every morning, I work out at Gully's Gym, over by the shipyards. But you ..."

"My ... my heart ..."

"Yeah, it'll be quite a strain, won't it? Too bad ..."

His voice was soft and small. "It'll kill me, all that gravity."

"It might at that," I said, smiling mirthlessly. "At the very least, you'll be bedridden until the end of your sorry days—helpless as a baby in a crib."

Avenging Miriam

by

PETER SELLERS

"'I JUST WANT TO PUT IT BEHIND ME and get on with my life.' That's what one of them said." He handed the paper to Kieran, who read the first few paragraphs of the article and saw the quote for himself.

"I must confess, I find the cold-bloodedness of that even more incomprehensible now than when I first read it," Sebastian said. "Imagine. Saying something like that, as if she had failed a math test or dented her father's car, instead of kicking another fourteen-year-old girl to death."

To Kieran, it did seem a cynical attitude. "What's this to do with me?" He handed back the clipping.

"The killers are all young offenders," Sebastian said. "They'll do three years at most. They'll be out in time to apply for their first driver's licences or attend their high school graduations. That doesn't seem fair. So I want to hire you."

"To kill that girl?" He pointed at the article.

"To kill them all."

There were nine in the group of children who had beaten a schoolmate to death one evening after dinner, while other kids were taking piano lessons or hanging at the mall.

"I'm sorry to disappoint you," Kieran said, "but I don't kill children for money."

Sebastian shook his head. "Don't be fooled by acne and braces and innocent looks. Children don't slaughter their peers. Chronologically they may be fourteen or fifteen, but they're not children, I assure you. They're monsters."

"That may be, but I won't execute them for you." Kieran sipped his coffee. "What's your interest? You the father? Uncle? What?"

"I'm not related to Miriam. I'm just a concerned citizen who can see when a gross injustice is being committed and who has the wherewithal to do something about it."

"You're more noble than I am."

As if he hadn't heard, Sebastian took a folded sheet of paper from an inside jacket pocket and held it out. "Here are their names and addresses."

Kieran didn't take the paper, but Sebastian did not withdraw it. Eventually Kieran reached out but he did not unfold it. "You shouldn't have this," he said. "Nobody's supposed to know who they are."

"Legally, true. But we're both men of the world. You know as well as I do, every time there's a case such as this, people in the community know. It's not hard to learn who the culprits are."

Curiosity got the better of Kieran. He unfolded the sheet. Miriam's name was at the top, then the identities of her killers. Each name and address was on a single line, in simple Helvetica. There was nothing in the way the words looked to give any hint of what the people they stood for had done: Adam, Rebecca, Tiffany, one common or artificial name after another.

Kieran scanned the list quickly. He read it again slowly, and then more slowly still. His sadness must have shown.

"It's an awful thing, but some crimes are too great to be ignored. When you have the power to make a difference and don't, aren't you an accessory? I always felt so. Do you have children?"

Kieran did not discuss his personal life with clients, but this situation felt different. "I have two daughters." He had not seen the girls in years, his occupation driving a wedge between him and their mother.

"Unpalatable as this might be, before you make a decision, think about one of your daughters in that situation."

Kieran tried to imagine what it must have been like for the murdered girl. The incomprehension when the gang turned on her. They were all people she thought of as friends, who she so wanted to be like and to impress. Why were they doing this? The question must have loomed so large in her mind that she didn't feel the blows at first. Their existence would have numbed her to the pain they caused.

Then terror must have set in. Surrounded, driven to the ground, blows from fists and open hands turning to dehumanizing kicks. The expensive cross trainers and the Docs and the trendy hiking shoes slamming into her body as she squirmed, trying to find escape. But there were nine of them, so it was easy to surround her. No matter where she put her hands to ward off the blows, most of her body was left unprotected. For every kick deflected, eight others found their marks. She cried and begged, but mercy was not forthcoming. At some point, one of them, her leg growing tired, picked up a stick and used that to beat the victim on the head and neck.

Did they talk to her, Kieran wondered, as they were killing her? Did they explain to her why? Did they call her names and abuse her with their mouths as well? Did they hurl accusations and condemn her family? Did they laugh?

Then, for a moment, they had stopped. All nine of them had stepped back and let Miriam rise painfully to her feet. They were letting her go. She was bleeding and stunned and every step was painful but they let her stagger away. How did she feel then, as hope soared inside her? Did she thank them? Did she thank God for making them stop? Or did she just move as quickly as she could, urging on her unsteady limbs, wondering what she would tell her parents and how she would explain to her teachers why her homework was not done.

In the end, none of that mattered. Miriam hadn't gone fifty yards before they set on her again. That, to Kieran, was the cruellest part—letting hope build and then grinding it out. They beat her and kicked her and finally left her lying on the bank of a small creek where she died.

Kieran shook his head. It was senseless. He couldn't conceive of either of his daughters in such a circumstance. He folded the list and placed the paper against his pursed lips, shut his eyes and considered for some time.

"All right," he said at length.

Sebastian smiled. "I know this is a huge undertaking. Thank you for doing the right thing."

"It's business," Kieran said.

"I don't imagine there's a volume discount."

Kieran shook his head. "In fact, there's a volume premium. Nine random people, you'd get a break. But nine kids all linked to the same event, the cops are going to know what's up from the word Go. That adds a whole whack of danger pay. You okay with that?"

"This has to be done, and it has to be done right. As my grandfather used to say, 'The craftsman is worthy of his hire.'"

"Yes," Kieran said. "I'm worthy all right."

KIERAN EXPLAINED that Sebastian would have to be patient. The first of the killers would die quickly. The rest would be on guard then so Kieran would have to wait for them to relax again, and begin to forget that there was someone there in the dark, waiting.

"The wheels of justice grind slow," Sebastian said. "But they grind fine. I'm confident that the job will be done to my satisfaction. Time is not of the essence." He handed Kieran a manila envelope. "Photos of the monsters," he said.

KIERAN DROVE TO VANCOUVER. He was tired when he arrived but, instead of going to his hotel, he went to the airport and left his car in long-term parking. People tended to notice out-of-province plates. He took a bus downtown, checked in and had a nap.

He killed the first three the next night. This had not been his plan. He'd anticipated spending a few days scouting the situation and working out the most efficient and least risky way of picking them off one by one. But then, as he cruised past the home of one of the female killers, the door opened and she stepped outside. Kieran followed her discreetly. It wasn't difficult. The car he'd rented was in no way distinctive and the quarry, like so many teenagers, was oblivious to everything that was not of direct concern to her.

She made two stops, meeting young men who Kieran recognized as other members of the group of nine. It was better than he had hoped. They were together, in clear violation of their probation. Better yet, they headed straight for the centre of Stanley Park to toke up. Kieran followed and they were all dead before the joint went around once. He dragged their bodies into the bushes. They might be discovered in the morning by a jogger, or they could lie undisturbed for days. Kieran hoped for the latter, but he planned on the former.

Driving back over the Burrard Street Bridge, Kieran thought about what had happened. He hadn't said a word to the kids. He'd just dropped them as cleanly and as quickly as possible. In the instant between life and death he doubted if they made any connection with what was happening to them and what they had done to Miriam by the side of a rubbish-choked creek. He'd heard that, at the point of dying, your life flashes before your eyes. If that were true, did the lives of those three young killers freeze-frame on their viciousness and cause the truth to ignite a spontaneous chorus of, "Oh, so *this* is why we're being killed. I guess there is justice after all"? Kieran doubted it. He decided then that the rest of the condemned, like prisoners mounting the gallows, would know why.

KIERAN REQUESTED A SMOKING ROOM in the hotel. Once inside, he took out the photos of the dead and burned them. They were high school yearbook photos, with their bland artlessness and frozen smiles. He wondered what the old scientists who felt you could distinguish a criminal by his face would have made of these images. He held each photo in turn over an ashtray and watched as the flames melted the photographic paper, twisting the faces grotesquely, making them truly monstrous. He watched until the flames licked his fingers. When all three were done, he emptied the ashtray in the toilet and flushed.

THE NEXT MORNING, there was nothing in the *Vancouver Sun* or the *Province* about three bodies found in Stanley Park. Nor was there anything about three missing teens. Maybe they were frequently out all night, so no one was concerned yet.

Whatever the reason, Kieran had a chance to get further ahead than he had envisaged. He went over the list while sitting at an outdoor cafe and chose a boy named Christopher. He found it difficult to work up as much enthusiasm for executing the girls.

Christopher's family had moved away from the neighbourhood where most of the others still lived. They had settled in the suburb of Burnaby. Perhaps they thought they could escape the notoriety, the stares and the whispers. But Burnaby was not so far. And the reality, as Kieran knew, was that you can't leave the past behind. Try as you might, it will find you, and stop your heart.

Kieran found the new address and scouted the area thoroughly. Then he went to a nearby mall and waited in the food court. He ate tandoori, drank coffee and watched the kids who gathered there, any of them capable of anything.

He scrutinized the faces and realized in surprise that Christopher was there, laughing with a new gang of friends.

An hour later the boy left in the company of a few companions. Kieran wondered if they would head straight home or stop in a desolate spot and slaughter one of their number.

They set off in a four-by-four. Kieran followed as the driver let passengers off along the route. When Christopher got out at the top of a flight of steps that led into a ravine, Kieran knew that the boy would have to follow the path that led across a small footbridge, then climb the hill to the street where his family's house stood.

Kieran drove as quickly as the speed limit allowed and parked near the exit of the ravine. He walked in, pistol in his jacket pocket, and reached the footbridge ahead of Christopher. Kieran had just crossed the bridge when he recognized the figure coming towards him. Christopher must have seen Kieran at the same moment, for he took two more faltering steps and stopped. Kieran kept walking forward. Christopher took a step back, but he was still gazing into the gloom, trying to figure out if he should stand his ground or flee.

Kieran said, "Hi, Chris," in a friendly voice.

The familiarity froze Christopher momentarily. Who was this who knew his name but who he was sure he did not recognize? The same soft voice said, "Miriam says hello." Then Christopher knew the only smart thing to do was run.

Christopher was lean and his legs were long. Under other circumstances, he could far outpace a middle-aged man. But he was wearing his jeans pulled low around his hips, showing the tops of boxer shorts. As he ran his pants slipped down his legs. He stumbled and tried to wrestle his pants higher while still fleeing as fast as he could. His pants seemed reluctant to move but the boy was unwilling to stop and do the job properly. He kept on his erratic pace, turning his head frequently to watch in wide-eyed panic the man who followed him. Then he tripped on a root, perhaps, or an unevenness of ground. He fell abruptly and hard. He made one abortive attempt to get up, an attempt that his consuming need caused to fail. Then he began crawling, scrambling along the dirt path, weeping and sniffling. Kieran easily caught up with him. He looked down at the boy half-curled on the ground, his hands about his head, making incomprehensible noises of pleading.

It would have been easy to have shot him and left immediately. But Kieran remembered the first three dying in ignorance. This boy was going to know, just as his family was going to know, as soon as his three dead friends were found. They'd know that their son had not died in a random act of violence. Not the way Miriam died, but *because* Miriam died. That made Kieran wonder what Christopher's mother thought of her son when she looked at him across the breakfast table, knowing about him what she knew.

Kieran crouched next to the prone youth. "Sit up," he said. "We're going to have a little chat." Tentatively, the boy shifted one arm from over his eyes and peered at Kieran. Uncertain at first, and then with growing hope, he rose to his knees, sniffled and wiped his eyes with his sleeve. His lip quivered. "Don't kill me," he said. "Please."

Kieran indicated a tree with the barrel of his gun. "Sit," he said.

The boy leaned against the tree and stared at the gun. "Please," he said again.

"Is that what she said as you were killing her? How many times, I wonder? After the first couple, it must have been easier to ignore."

The boy started to cry again. Kieran waited until the weeping subsided. "Why did you do it?"

The boy shook his head. "I don't know. I don't know why."

"Because other people were doing it? Or did you start it? Was it planned out in advance? Or was it something that just happened?"

"I don't know. I was just there."

Kieran wondered what the truth was. Had there been a phone tree? "Hi, it's Tracy. Whatcha doin' tonight? You wanna get together? We're gonna, like, go grab a latte, check out this new club and, then, like, beat Miriam to death. Yeah, I think it sounds cool. Call Mike and tell him and ask him to phone Lindsay. Oh and you know that new zit cream? Does it, like, work any good?" He hoped it hadn't been like that, but with kids these days you never knew.

"Wearing your pants like that makes it tough to run, doesn't it? You know why you wear your pants like that? I bet you don't have a clue. It's a gang thing from L.A. The gangs started wearing their pants baggy in the crotch so they could hide weapons. If you'd had a weapon hidden in there you might not be in the predicament you're currently facing."

The boy sobbed harder. Kieran began to feel uneasy. He didn't want to stay too long. "Listen," he said, "I'm going to teach you another valuable lesson. You know why this is happening, right?"

The kid looked panicky and blank and shook his head, wiping his nose on his sleeve. "Miriam," Kieran said. Christopher started to wail more loudly.

Kieran decided there was little point in dragging things out. "Here's the lesson. Most teenage kids think they're invincible, that they're going to live forever. If they understood and embraced their own mortality, they'd be better off I think. They'd be more empathetic. Make more constructive use of their time. So I'm helping you realize your mortality right now. This is a valuable life lesson, one of the secrets of the universe. You're lucky. Not many young people get to die with such clarity of mind." Then Kieran put the pistol away. Christopher stared in disbelief, as if he could smell mercy. Until, considering the surrounding neighbourhood, Kieran reached into another pocket and took out a guitar string.

KIERAN STAYED in Vancouver a few more days. By then all four bodies had been found. Nothing was mentioned in the papers about the connection between them. But the cops would have linked them instantly and the rest of the targets would drop out of sight. There'd be no more opportunity in the immediate future. There was, however, one stop Kieran could make on the way home.

Just like Christopher's parents, Rachel's mother thought she could run away from trouble. She had taken her daughter to stay with relatives in Calgary. Further than Burnaby, but still not far enough.

Sebastian had supplied him with the new address, the names of the people with whom Rachel and her mother were staying, the phone number. He'd even provided Kieran with a new photograph of the girl, who had cut and dyed her hair. The photo was taken on the street, showing the girl in company with an older woman. Kieran studied Rachel briefly and then focused on the mother. She was perhaps forty and attractive, with lines that gave her face character and depth. He looked at the face for a considerable time.

Kieran went to the airport and got his car. The rate they charged for parking was usurious, but he reckoned Sebastian could afford it.

IN CALGARY, Kieran drove to Rachel's cousin's place. It was a typical subdivision house, rather ugly, squatting behind a bloated two-car garage. There was a minivan in the driveway and a sprinkler on the lawn. There was no sign of life. He came back that evening and watched for a brief time. Lights burned in the windows and he saw silhouetted figures moving behind sheer curtains, but no one came out.

He drove past the local schools until he found the high school he suspected Rachel would be attending. Then he went downtown for dinner.

Since he was in Alberta, he had a steak while he tried to think of a plan to kill Rachel, but his thoughts kept drifting. He was distracted by snatches of conversation from other tables. He found himself watching female patrons and waitresses as they breezed past. The image of Rachel's mother kept crowding into his head. It wasn't just that the mother was attractive. It was seeing them together, mother and daughter so much alike, in a photo where they looked happy and ordinary. But when he looked at them, together and smiling, he wondered what she thought about her daughter now. How did she rationalize the enormity of the crime? He wanted to ask her. He knew it was time to go home. All the way, across a thousand miles of prairie and through the vast northern woods, thoughts of Rachel's mother kept him company.

"WE'RE CERTAINLY OFF to a flying start," Sebastian said. "Five down, four to go."

Kieran hadn't been paying much attention. It took a while before the words sank in. Three in the park. One in the ravine. Four, no matter how you add it up. "Five?" he asked.

Sebastian nodded. "I guess you haven't read this yet." He handed Kieran a newspaper clipping from the *Calgary Herald*, dated the day after Kieran left town. Rachel's body had been found in her room. She had taken an overdose of sleeping pills.

"Her mother's pills?" Kieran asked.

Sebastian shook his head. "They were her own. She'd been having trouble sleeping, apparently. Nightmares."

No mention was made of bad dreams in the article, nor of what might have caused them. Nothing in the brief piece indicated that this was anything other than another sad teenage suicide.

Sebastian said, "She was also having trouble at her new school. She didn't fit in and I understand she was picked on. What goes around, comes around, I suppose."

Kieran handed him back the cutting. "I don't suppose there's a rebate for this one?" Sebastian said.

"You can ask," Kieran said.

Sebastian chuckled. "Well, hearing about the deaths of her friends must have helped nudge her along. So I guess you can take partial credit anyway."

KIERAN MONITORED THE VANCOUVER MEDIA, and when the four killings of the previous autumn had not been mentioned for three months, it was time to go back. He took the train, booking a stopover in Calgary.

It was not difficult to find Rachel's mother. She no longer lived in the house he had observed in the fall. Instead, she had recently purchased a modest condominium in a residential area near the downtown core.

As he watched her for several days, the pattern of Rachel's mother's habits became obvious. Her routine was consistent, including having lunch most days in one of the same three restaurants with the same individual co-workers or the same small knot of people. He was struck by the ordinariness of it and marvelled at the tenacity that kept people going in such tedious circumstances.

He also discovered that, after work, she rarely went out with anyone. She either stayed in, or walked by herself to a small pub near her home. Once in the pub, she would sit at a table for two against the back wall. There was a wall sconce beside the table in which two flame-shaped bulbs burned dimly. By this light, she would read a book while slowly nursing a glass of red wine. She never had more than one glass and she never stayed longer than an hour.

Rachel's mother read slowly and occasionally flipped back a page, presumably to pick up a line or a thought that she had missed. Kieran watched her surreptitiously for the first few nights. He sat in a different spot each evening. One night he watched a hockey game on the

TV behind the bar. One night he did the crossword in the *Globe &
Mail*. One night he read a book of his own.

After almost two weeks, Kieran approached her. She had just sat
down and the waitress had not yet come to take her order. "Excuse
me," he said. "I was wondering if I could buy you a drink."

She looked up at him intently and did not respond right away.

"I'm not trying to pick you up or anything," he said. "I just admire
anyone who reads Dickens." He indicated the copy of *Oliver Twist*
that lay on the table and then held up *Bleak House*, which he had
been pretending to read for the last few evenings.

He ordered each of them a glass of red wine and sat opposite her.
"Do you live near here?" she asked.

"No. I'm just in town on business. My hotel's close by."

"Which one?"

"Journey's End."

She nodded. "Where are you from?"

"Toronto now," he said. "But I'm from Vancouver originally."

Her face brightened. "Really? That's where I'm from."

"No kidding. What a coincidence! How long you been here?"

What she told him was mostly the truth, based on what he knew
of her life, and she willingly accepted the carefully constructed story
he presented as reality.

"I don't want you to get the wrong impression," he said, "but I've
been in here a few nights and I couldn't help but notice you."

She looked at him as if expecting the advance to come now.

"You must like it here," was all he said.

She smiled. "It gets me out of the house."

"Lots of things do that. You could take up yoga or join a book
club. You like to read."

"I don't feel very social a lot of the time."

"It's none of my business, but you look kind of sad. Anything you'd
care to discuss with a stranger you're never going to see again?"

"How can you be sure of that?"

"I'm forty-two years old and I've never been to Calgary before in my life. It's a fluke I'm here now. I had to cover for somebody who got sick. The odds of our meeting again are extremely long. So, is there anything you want to talk about?"

She shook her head. "Not really. Do you have any kids?"

"Two," Kieran said. "Daughters. They live with their mother. How about you?"

"I had a daughter, too."

"Had?"

Rachel's mother shook her head. "She died last spring."

"I'm terribly sorry. I didn't mean to stir up bad memories."

"It's all right. Everything stirs up bad memories. You didn't know."

They sat in silence, Kieran studying the woman's face while she watched the reminiscences unspool in her head. "What work do you do?" he asked her softly.

She looked in his eyes and smiled. "You don't have to change the subject," she said. "I don't mind talking about it."

"I figured, because you just said …"

"I lied. I want to talk about it but I try to keep myself under control. That's why I come to this place. Nobody here talks to me about anything. I think my friends are tired of hearing about it—not that I have that many friends here—so I try to hide. But it doesn't always work. Rachel killed herself."

Kieran let out his breath slowly. "I can't imagine what that must be like," he said. "Losing a child that way."

"You know, it's been almost a year and I still can't imagine it either."

"Was there something specific that happened? Had there been any signs?"

Rachel's mother looked down at the table again. Her hands played with the stem of her glass and then began riffling the pages of her book. "No," she said. "There'd been some trouble back in Vancouver. She got involved with some bad kids. I tried to tell her, but how many fourteen-year-olds listen to their mothers? I brought her here thinking we could leave the trouble behind."

"I guess trouble has a way of following you around."

"Sad but true," Rachel's mother said with an unhappy smile.

"Things didn't change when you got here?"

"For a bit. A few weeks. A month. Just until she got settled in a little and found the kids here who were just like the kids at home. And then it was like nothing was any different."

"How did she behave?"

"I don't know. She'd do things out of spite. She used to hitchhike to school. This started just before she turned thirteen. I'd tell her not to do it, but then she'd leave the house in the morning and I'd leave for work a few minutes later and I'd see her a block or so away, standing by the side of the road with her thumb out. She'd stare right at me, like a challenge. There must have been things I could have done better, but for the life of me I don't know what they are."

She sipped her wine and Kieran remained silent. She had more to say yet, and she wasn't after his opinion.

"When I used to see kids on the street, I thought that they all left home because they were beaten or abused. I realize now how naive I was. Some of those kids were just like Rachel. There was nothing awful going on at home. Nothing unusual, anyway. They just left. They skipped school. They ran away. She used to tell me that she was spending the night at this friend's house, or that one. Those other kids must have told their parents the same thing, I suppose. But they never spent the night at anyone's house. Sometimes they'd sleep in apartment building stairwells. Why? What was the reason?"

"It must have been difficult for you."

She shrugged. "It had its moments. You know what the hardest thing is? I have so many questions for her that nobody will ever be able to answer. Even if they could, I don't imagine I'd accept them because I don't think I could understand."

"It sounds like she was pretty lost."

"Yes. That's what hurts. I never saw the amount of pain she must have been in." Rachel's mother raised her face and held her chin forward bravely. "She was a good girl. Really she was."

Kieran imagined one of the pictures of Miriam, murdered, her head in the creek, face down, hair matted. Her body indelibly marked by the ferocity of her attackers. He resisted the urge to tell Rachel's mother that, despite what she might claim, good girls didn't do that to other children. "I'm sure she was a good girl. I guess it's just that everybody's got conflicts. Everybody's confused at least some of the time."

Rachel's mother was silent for a while. "I'm sorry," Kieran said finally. He was tired of talking about it, even if she wasn't. "This is a bit of a downer. I really didn't mean to dredge up so much."

She made a dismissive gesture. "Most days, it doesn't take much dredging."

"Would you like to get something to eat?" he asked.

KIERAN TOOK THE TRAIN to Vancouver the next afternoon. Much of the way, he thought about his time with Rachel's mother. It hadn't been entirely satisfying. He'd never felt the moment was quite right to ask many of the questions he had. He hadn't been able to divine the answers he was looking for through less direct means. But he had a job to do. He forced the disappointment aside and tried to focus.

He dispatched the first three of the four remaining killers over two nights. The third one was dead before the first two bodies had been found, before panic among the families could erupt, before the police could go on alert. His waiting had proven wise. The targets were careless and obviously considered themselves beyond the reach of vengeance.

They all cried. One of them announced that it wasn't his fault, that the other kids forced him to do it. One claimed he hadn't done anything at all, just watched. Kieran explained how, if that were true, it was worse than taking part. The third one pleaded for mercy because he was only fifteen. "Well," Kieran told him, "look on the bright side. You got one more year than Miriam did."

THERE WAS ONE LEFT. Kieran's opportunity came two days later. She was walking home from a movie when Kieran pulled up beside her, got out and opened the passenger door. "Get in," he said.

He wasn't sure that she wouldn't scream and run, but she didn't. She stood and looked at him. He waited by the open door, saying nothing, making no move. He could almost feel her thinking. Then she started toward the car. He wondered, as she climbed in and he shut the door, if she used to hitchhike like Rachel did and was used to getting into strange vehicles.

When he was settled behind the wheel, he said, "For a minute there, I wasn't sure what you were going to do."

She shrugged. "I thought about taking off. I wasn't sure at first. But you'd have chased after me, right?"

"Yes, I'd have come after you."

"I've always known that eventually you would," she said.

"So you know why I'm here."

"Yeah. I've just been wondering *when* you'd show up."

"I spent some time with Rachel's mother." He felt a need to explain, as if the delay had inconvenienced the girl.

She looked surprised. "Why? How do you know Rachel's mom? Rachel killed herself."

He nodded, answering her first question, ignoring the second. "I wanted to try to find out why she did it, and find out how her mother felt about it." He pulled away from the curb.

"I'll tell you why she did it. Because there was this bogeyman out there, coming around at night to splatter her brains on the ground, just like he did to all her friends."

"That may be part of it." He felt calm. "Do you suppose it might have been because she felt badly about what she'd done?"

She opened her purse and pulled out a pack of cigarettes. The rental car was non-smoking but it seemed to Kieran that it would be petty to stop her. She lit up and blew out a great plume. "I was getting scared waiting for you."

"Oh?"

"I was afraid you wouldn't come."

"There was no need to fear that," he said.

They drove in silence for several minutes before she asked, "Why do you think this has been happening?" There was a plaintive note in her voice. "Why has someone killed all my friends? What did they do to deserve that?"

"Maybe it wasn't what they did but how they did it, and why."

"What the hell does that mean?"

"What did Miriam do to deserve to die?"

She crossed her arms and turned to face out the side window. "You wouldn't understand."

"You could try me."

"Does everybody die for good reasons? Do you ever really know why you're doing it?"

"Sometimes," he said.

"Yeah, right. I don't want to talk about this anymore."

He ignored her. "It should have been quick," he said. "Abrupt, sudden, painless. Not dragged out. I bet she didn't even know why it was happening."

"So you've never done that? You've never prolonged the agony?"

He thought carefully about how to answer. "No. I've never done it," he said at length, "unless it was to make sure that the person understood clearly why they were dying. Did Miriam have that understanding, do you suppose?"

The girl shrugged. "She probably knew she was going to die because nobody liked her. Would that be enough reason for you?"

He didn't answer. He had driven to an isolated industrial area of warehouses and small manufacturing facilities. He stopped the car.

She looked at the surroundings, then at him. "I must be stupid," she said. "I was relieved to see you." Kieran figured the details had fallen into place. "You knew about Rachel. You know about everything that's been going on. You're not here to protect me."

"I'm afraid not," he said. He took out the pistol and brought it to bear. It was not as steady as it had been each time before.

She looked at her cigarette and laughed bitterly. "My last smoke and I didn't even take the time to appreciate it." She ground the butt out on the dashboard with sharp, angry motions. "Do I get any last words?"

He released the safety on the pistol.

She said, "You're kidding yourself, you know, if you think you don't do what we did. You've tortured us for months. We couldn't sleep. Afraid to go out. Waiting for you to show up. How many of us got the value of your wisdom before you blew our fucking brains out?"

"Are you finished?" he asked. It took all his energy to focus on the pistol, to keep it steady and aimed true.

"That's up to you, isn't it?" It was warm and close in the confined space. "So," she said, turning in the seat to face him, "what are you going to do now, Dad?"

Necessary Women

by

KARIN SLAUGHTER

I WAS FOURTEEN YEARS OLD when I watched my mama die. Her pale skin turned white as she clutched her throat, blood seeping through her fingers like she was squeezing a sponge instead of trying to hold onto her life. She was barely thirty years old when she passed, but my daddy had put age on her. Streaks of silver shot through her dark hair like lines on a blackboard, and there was a hardness about her eyes that made you look away fast, before you could be drawn into the sadness.

I try not to think of Mama this way now. When I close my eyes, I think of Saturday nights sitting on the floor in the living room, Mama in the chair behind me, brushing my hair so it would look good for Sunday services. Mama wasn't particularly religious herself, but we lived in a small border town, smack on the line between

Georgia and Alabama, and people would have talked. I'm glad we had nights like this, because now that she is gone, I can think back on it, sometimes even feel the bristles of the brush going through my hair and the soft touch of Mama's hand on my shoulder. It comforts me.

We lived in a three-room house made of cement block, which kept heat in like a kiln. Thankfully, pecan trees shaded the roof so most days we didn't get the full intensity of the sun. In a county that routinely saw hundred-plus temperatures, this made a difference. Come summertime, we would pick the pecans, salt them and sell them to vacationers on their way to the Florida Panhandle. Sometimes Daddy brought in peanuts, and Mama would boil them. I can still see her standing in front of the cauldron, stirring the peanuts with a long two-by-four, her shins bright red from the open flame beneath the pot.

Our life had a settled routine to it and while I can't say that we were happy, we made do with what we had. At night, sometimes we would hear people beeping their horns as they crossed into Alabama, and Mama would get a wistful look on her face. She never said anything, but I remember the first time I saw that look I got a pain in my gut as I realized that maybe Mama wasn't happy, that maybe she didn't want to be here with me and Daddy. Like most things, this passed, and soon we learned to ignore the honking vacationers. Around about the middle of summer, every supper would go something like, "Pass the—" Honk-honk. Or, "Can I have some—" Toot-toot.

Daddy was a long hauler, driving semis across the nation for this company or that, and he would be gone for weeks, sometimes months, at a time. Mostly when he was home I slept on the couch, but when he was gone, I would sleep with Mama in their bed. We would stay up at night, talking about him, both missing him. I think these are the happiest memories I have of my mother. At night with the lights off there was no work to do: no floors to scrub, meals to fix, shirts to iron. Mama had two jobs then: one cleaning the rest rooms at the welcome centre on the Alabama side, the other working nights at the laundry. When I would lay with her, I could smell an odd mixture of Clorox bleach and dry-cleaning solvent. I often think if that knife had not killed her, the chemicals she used would have sent her to an early grave.

About a week before she died, Mama had a talk with me. We had turned in early, just as the sun was dipping into the horizon, because Mama was due at work around four the next morning. A hard rain was sweeping across the tin roof, making shushing noises to lull us to sleep. I was just about to nod off when Mama rolled over in bed, nudging me awake.

"We need to talk," she said.

"Shh-shh-shh," the rain warned, none too softly.

Mama spoke over the hush, her voice firm. "We need to have that talk."

I knew what she meant. There was a boy at school, Rod Henry, who had started to pay attention to me. With no encouragement from me, he had gotten off the bus at my stop instead of his, which was three miles down. I had no particular interest in Rod Henry other than in the fact that he was an older boy, about sixteen. He had what could on a generous day be called a mustache along his upper lip and his hair was long enough to pull back into a ponytail. When he pulled me behind the pecan shack in our front yard, I did not stop him. Out of curiosity, I let him kiss me. Out of curiosity, I let him touch me.

"That Rod Henry," Mama said. "He's no good."

"He has a tattoo," I told her, because I had seen it. "I don't like him much."

"I didn't like your daddy much when I met him, either," Mama said. "But things happen."

I knew that I was the thing that happened to her, the thing that took her out of school at the age of fifteen, the thing that put her in the welcome centre cleaning toilets instead of working at the Belk over in Mobile like she had planned to do when she got out of school. Her sister Ida worked there as a manager, and it had been lined up for years that Mama would go over and help Ida out as soon as she finished school. She would live in Ida's apartment and they would save their money and one day they would meet nice, respectable boys and settle down. The plan was perfect until Daddy came along.

To hear Mama tell it, there was no romance in the way Daddy got her. It was a night of firsts that changed her life. Her first cigarette, her first beer, her first kiss, her first time having sex.

"That's all it takes, baby," Mama said, her fingers digging into my arm, her stubby nails like slivers of hot metal. "Just one time is all it takes."

I closed my eyes, crying for no reason, thinking about what it must have been like for Mama, just a few years older than me, to feel my daddy on top of her for the first time. He was not a gentle man, and he was large, six four at least with a wide chest and arms so big around he had to cut the sleeves of his T-shirts just so he could get into them. Daddy was twenty-two when he first met Mama, and he had tricked her, she said, with his worldly ways.

"The pain," Mama said, mumbling. "He about ripped me in two."

I nodded my understanding. She was a small woman, with delicate wrists and a thin waist. There was a look of fragility to her that had fooled more than one person. Daddy liked to say that she was skin and bones, but I thought she was more like skin and muscle. I reached out and stroked her arm, which was wiry and hard from working. A sliver of light came from the window. With the weight of the day off her, her face was relaxed, and I could see the young woman she was before Daddy got to her. I could see how beautiful she must have been to him, and how she was totally the opposite of me. I felt like a monster next to her.

Her head turned suddenly, the slackness gone, a furrow set into her brow. "You listening to me?" she demanded, her tone low and sharp in the small room.

"Yes, Mama," I mumbled, drawing my hand back as if from a snake. She kept that look on me, paralyzing me momentarily with the sudden flash of anger and fear I could see brewing inside of her. Though she had never hit me, I felt violence radiating off her, like she might lunge and throttle me any minute.

"Don't be me, baby," she said. "Don't end up in this house with your daddy like me."

Tears came in earnest now. I whispered, "I won't, Mama."

Her look said she didn't believe me, but that she knew nothing could be done about it. She turned her back to me and fell asleep.

Of course, Mama's warning had come too late. Neither of us knew at the time, but I was pregnant.

After she died, Daddy sat me down at the table. He leaned his elbows on the table, his hands clasped in front of him. I noticed that together, his hands were bigger than my head. He smelled of pipe tobacco and sweat. His beard was growing in though he was a man who liked to be clean shaven. Mama's passing had been hard on him.

"Now that your mama's gone," he said, "you gotta be the woman of the house." He paused, his broad shoulders going into a slight, almost apologetic shrug. "The cleaning, the cooking, the laundry. They's just necessary things a woman's gotta do."

There was true regret in his voice that sent shivers of pain through me. I ran from the table and vomited into the kitchen sink. Looking back, I don't know if it was the baby or Daddy's words that brought such a rush of bile up from my gullet.

Daddy was on a long haul about six months later when I started to have pains. It was just me in the house and had been that way for the last three weeks. I had stopped going to school and nobody had bothered to find out why. Being big anyway, carrying my weight in the front like I did, nobody remarked upon the fact that I was showing. I had no idea that I was pregnant and had taken the stop of my monthly flow as a gift from God rather than a sign of impending childbirth. I was fifteen by then, same as Mama when she had me, and with her gone, I was still naïve to the ways of nature.

The two hundred dollars Daddy had left for food was gone by the third week of his absence. I was a child and did not know how to buy groceries. There were packs of Kool-Aid in the cabinets and sweet tea was in the fridge but no nourishment to speak of lined the shelves. We were in the middle of an unseasonably hard winter, and except for the pecan shells I was burning in the fireplace, there was no heat. Between the cold and my hunger, I think I brought on the worst for the baby. I take responsibility for it.

That morning, I had taken Daddy's .22 rifle and shot a squirrel, but the meat had been sparse and I don't think I cooked it long enough. The pain hit me hard around six that night. At first I thought it was cramps from the bad meat, but soon the sharp contractions took hold. I thought I might die. I thought of Mama, and that seemed okay to me.

Night passed, then another day, then another night. Pain seized me so hard at one point that I broke a chair trying to get into it. We never had a phone in the house and even if we did, I would not have known who to call. I didn't know where Daddy was and I had no friends from school.

The baby came around one in the morning on the third day. She was a tiny little thing with only one arm and a knob where her left foot should have been. When I pried open her eyes, they were a deep blue, but that can be said of most babies. The cord was wrapped around her neck, which I suppose is what made her pass. I said a prayer over her head, begging God to accept her into His house, even though she was deformed and had no father.

The ground was too cold to bury her. I wrapped her in an old blanket and set her behind the cauldron in the pecan shack. At night sometimes I would wake, thinking I heard her crying, realizing it was only me. Two more weeks passed before the ground thawed, and I buried my baby next to Mama in a tiny little grave out behind the house. I put a stone on top of the mound and I prayed on my knees for them both to forgive me. I took it as a sign that they did when Daddy came home the next day.

I made him chitterlings out of a pig he had kept off the back of his truck.

"These'r good chitlins, baby," Daddy said, scooping a forkful into his mouth. "Just like your mama used to make."

His eyes watered, and my heart ached for him at that moment more than it ever had. He had loved my mama. No matter what the drink made him do or where his temper brought him, he had loved her.

"I remember you made these when your mama—" his voice cracked. He managed a smile for me. "Come sit on my knee, Peanut. Tell me what you been up to since I was gone."

I did not tell him about Laura Lee, my baby girl that lay in the back field alongside Mama. I made up stories for him about classes I had not attended, friends I had not made. He laughed with me, smoking his pipe, and when I put my head on his shoulder, he comforted me.

After a while, he moved me off of him, and I sat at his knee as he spoke. "Listen, honey," he began, using the same phrase he always used when there was something difficult that he was about to say. I remembered he had used those same words with me that first time. I was lying on the couch, Mama asleep in the next room, and Daddy came in, shaking me awake. "Listen, honey," he had said then, just as he said now.

"I met this lady," he said, and my heart dipped into my stomach. "She's gonna be coming by some." He gave a low laugh. "Hell, she might even move in after a while if things work out. Take some of the chores off your shoulders. What do you think of that?"

I wiped my mouth with the back of my hand as I sat back on my heels. I remembered Mama in the kitchen that day, washing her hair at the sink. I remember how angry I had been, hearing them the night before. He had promised me that he wasn't with her anymore, said the only reason he needed me was because she wouldn't let him touch her. And then I had heard them together in bed, snorting like pigs. And then I had walked into the room and watched him working his mouth between her legs until her body went taut and her hand snatched his hair up in a tight fist.

I clenched my hands now, and I could feel Mama's hair between my fingers as I jerked her head back. Daddy was due back that night, so I had acted fast, knowing even as small as she was that her hands were stronger than mine. The blade was sharp, but cutting a person's neck is a lot like cutting up a chicken. You have to whack it good in just the right place, or it won't slice all the way through. I hacked six times before her neck separated.

By the time I had taken off her head, the knife was dull, but not at the tip, and when I used it to cut out between her legs, the flesh folded in on itself like a piece of liver. I used the cauldron to fix dinner that night, giving Daddy the same thing to eat as he had had the night before.

Daddy scratched his chin, giving me a tight smile. "With Mama just taking off like that," he said, shrugging. "No note, no good-bye." He sat back in the chair, smiling apologetically. "I got needs."

"I know, Daddy," I answered, buttoning my blouse with shaking fingers.

"I mean, nothing's gotta change with us. You know you're still my girl."

"I know, Daddy," I mumbled back.

"That okay with you, baby?" Daddy asked, zipping himself into his pants as he stood.

"That's fine, Daddy," I said, forcing some cheer into my voice. I looked up at him, giving him my best smile. "Why don't you invite her over next Sunday? We can have her for dinner."

Licensed Guide

by

ERIC WRIGHT

OUR HISTORY TEACHER in grade nine was insane. He was an old man, "grizzled," I realized, when I discovered the word about that time, who wanted to be an athlete and got as far as the training camp of a professional football team. After he failed to make the cut he went in for teaching—physical education and history.

He still spent most of his time on the playing fields and in the gym, assisting the team coaches and generally getting in the way. He had a simple mind, and an equally simple code of life. He liked to see struggle, effort, self-discipline, the team spirit, and death in battle (he had a very distinguished war record, having fought at Ypres with the Princess Pats). His history teaching was a record of heroes and gallant failures. He couldn't stand liars, cheats, or boys who didn't look him square in the eye, all of which were standard behaviour with us. We were terrified of him.

On a day in May, he left the room for a few minutes, first warning us to be totally silent. We were quiet for thirty seconds, then someone said, "He's having a quick drag in the can," and old Baker reappeared in the doorway. "Who said that?" he asked. No one spoke. He was clearly already out of control, looking to kill. He went round the room. "Was it you?" he asked us, one at a time, and one at a time we looked him in the eye and answered, "No." All except Simpson, whose gaze wavered. He denied it a second time but he blushed and looked away. Old Baker hit him so hard that Simpson's head bounced off the wall. (He told us later that he was deaf for two days afterwards.) "I can always tell," Baker said, looking around the room.

What has this to do with the drowning of a man in a fishing camp, fifteen years later? A great deal apparently, because even now, thirty years after the drowning, I never think of one incident without the other.

THEY ARRIVED one afternoon late in the season, three of them, a man named Baxter and his wife, and his business partner, Crossley. Three was an awkward number because we were set up to guide in pairs: it was not possible to put three guests in one boat and uneconomic to allocate a guide to a single guest. There was nothing else for it, though. Bailey, the camp owner (Bailey's Circle Lake Lodge—"We Fly You In, We Fly You Out"), assigned them to Henry Goose and me, and the following morning Henry and I waited on the dock and asked them how they wanted to split up.

"We'll go with Henry," Baxter said, after a glance at me. You could see his mind working; the Indian was bound to be the better guide. I moved to put his partner's bag in my boat. "No, no," Baxter said, "*we'll go* with Henry. *You* take *her*."

His wife said nothing, simply leaned against the rail of the dock, smoking, waiting. I picked up her bag, held the boat steady for her to get in, and asked Henry where we should fish.

"Grassy," Henry said.

Grassy Narrows. I started the motor and headed across the lake. We would meet up with Henry at noon for shore lunch.

It took me half an hour to get to the first spot I wanted to try, and she kept her eyes on the landscape without attempting to connect with me until I anchored over a pickerel hole. She was a handsome woman, lean rather than slim, and she made it plain that she was there to fish. For the first hour with a new party you tried to sort out the kind of guest you had in your boat and planned the next three days accordingly. There were the chatty ones who wanted to get down to your level right away, laughing at any joke, wanting your approval. You had to be careful with these because they could turn on you when they got bored, and sometimes get nasty. Knowing little about fishing, they measured their pleasure in terms of the number of fish caught, and after two days a hundred five-pound pickerel a day wasn't enough. At the other extreme, and much to be preferred at the end of the summer, were the professional fishermen who knew that fish stopped biting sometimes. You had to work hard for these, but they knew what you were doing and appreciated it. Occasionally there were the third kind, the rich sportsmen who happened to be fishing in northern Canada on their way to a caribou hunt in Alaska. These people thought of themselves as bwana and treated you accordingly. They talked to each other as if you weren't there, sometimes even talked about you.

She was one of these. Being alone, she stayed silent. I tried her with a remark when her line was in the water. "I guess those guys want to fish together," I said.

"It was my idea," she said, and turned her back.

Which was fine with me. By this time in the season I was tired of it; I was burned black, my hands were covered in hundreds of little cuts from the spines and gills of fish I had handled, and I had told the same stories too many times to too many guests.

She fished hard all day, stopping only for shore lunch. Henry and I cooked while they drank and compared notes on the fishing, and on us. I didn't have to prick up my ears; these people talked in front of the servants, but she simply said I seemed to know my job. She knew I was listening and perhaps it did inhibit her slightly.

In the afternoon we fished for pike and bass, and she very quickly absorbed everything I knew. By the end of the afternoon, she could have guided me, needing only to know what the prey was in order to go after it with the right tackle.

At supper in the guides' dining-room that night, Henry said his experience with the two men had been that of a taxi-driver. "I drove, they fished," he said. "I don't think the other guy spoke to me once."

The next day they switched. Crossley went with Henry, and I took the Baxters. Baxter was not yet sure he had the best, so he was trying me for a day before he let his wife or Crossley have the guide he didn't want. "I'll try Duck Lake," Henry said. "You go to the falls. I'll meet you there for shore lunch."

That suited me. Meynell Falls was really a very steep rapids where Meynell Lake emptied into Ebb Lake, creating a big whirlpool where fish gathered to feed on whatever came over the falls. For some reason the pickerel here were darker, almost black and gold, and they put up a bit of a fight, which made for livelier fishing as long as you had good fishermen in the boat. The thing was that you couldn't anchor the way you usually did for pickerel because the water was too fast. You kept the motor going at half speed and the boat pointed towards the falls. It was good for a couple of minutes before the current caught the prow and you were swept around in a circle and came back in for another try. Three people had to work together to keep the lines clear as you circled, especially if there was a fish on the line.

The Baxters could see the way it was and we did a couple of passes and caught three fish. She was up front. Then, on the third pass, Baxter threw the anchor over the side. The anchor was a big piece of rock on a rope and it was between Baxter and me on the floor of the boat. I didn't see him throw it because I was turned around to watch to see their lines didn't cross behind us, but I felt the boat lurch and I heard the rope twang as it went taut. I had my filleting knife handy because I liked to clean the fish as soon as we caught them; otherwise you had to clean a sackful of fish at the end of the day in the fish hut, a stinking shed full of flies. I cut the rope just as the water started to pour over the back of the boat, and we stayed the right way up. I shut down the motor and we drifted while I scooped some of the water out of the boat, not wanting the motor to pull the stern down until I had lightened the boat a little. Then I started the motor and pulled over to the shore where we dried out and I explained.

"The anchor and the current pull against each other," I said. "If you put the anchor in, it pulls down the stern and we fill up with water. Can you swim?"

He didn't say anything. Nor did she. It was hard to tell if they realized what had nearly happened.

Henry appeared for shore lunch and I waited for Baxter to tell his pal, but he didn't say a word, so I helped Henry to cook the lunch and we went fishing again. I said it wasn't worth going back to camp for a new anchor rope, and we would spend the afternoon trolling.

"I'd like to try this again," Baxter said, as we left the falls. "Now I know how it works."

THE NEXT DAY Baxter went up north for three days to Bailey's other camp to fish for Arctic char. Both men were supposed to go, but Crossley pleaded too much sun and said he wanted to stay inside for a couple of days. While Baxter was away, I looked after his wife. Most of all she liked bass fishing, so I spent most of the time paddling the shore of Duck Lake. She still said almost nothing, indicating what she wanted with a word or a gesture, fishing hard until mid-afternoon, then gesturing me to pack up and take her home. As I say, that suited me. I wanted to go home, too.

Baxter came back a day early. The weather up north was bad and he flew in before supper. My boat wasn't in its usual spot so he asked where I was and someone told him they thought his wife and I were still out on the lake. He decided he was hungry and would eat by himself unless Crossley was around, and he went off to Crossley's cabin, but his pal was along the shore, watching Bailey's carpenters putting the first logs in place for some new cabins. So Baxter ate alone.

I ran into him as he was leaving the dining-room. He still had his bag with him, and I took it off him (the guides were also supposed to act like bellboys) and walked with him up to his cabin. On the path, we ran into his wife and Crossley, who had called in on Mrs. Baxter to take her to supper, and I left them to tell each other the news. I put Baxter's bag inside the door of his cabin.

TWO DAYS LATER Crossley drowned at Meynell Falls. It happened like this.

On Baxter's first day back I had him and his wife in my boat and Henry had Crossley. Then on the second day I had Mrs. Baxter to myself again while Baxter and Crossley went out by themselves, without Henry. When we had checked with them after breakfast, the two men hadn't wanted to fish, but Mrs. Baxter was keen so I took her out and Henry went into town. Then, according to Bailey, about eleven o'clock, Baxter had appeared and asked if he and Crossley could use Henry's boat by themselves. Bailey hated to do this; even new guides from another part of the country could get lost around the English River system, and people from New York City weren't to be trusted out of sight of the dock, but in the end he agreed if they just puttered around the shore line.

I had a pretty good day. Even without too many words, I was comfortable with her now; we communicated, and I was happy to stay quiet. She pulled in her line for the last time around three o'clock, and I came home the long way round and tied up at the camp dock just after six. Bailey was standing there, looking worried.

"Did you pass Baxter on the way home?" he asked me. Mrs. Baxter was already on her way up to her cabin.

I shook my head.

"They probably ran out of gas." He dropped a spare tank in my boat. "Go look for them, will you? They might have made it across the lake then missed the channel when they turned around. I'll send the other boys out when they come in."

I plugged in the full tank then headed for Ebb Lake and Meynell Falls. I found the boat as soon as I turned into the channel. It was upside down, so low in the water that only the front of the keel was showing, caught between a pair of rocks near the bank. I moved my gas tanks to the front of my boat to keep my prow down and went closer to the falls at half speed. Baxter waved from the other shore. He was soaking wet. I pulled in to take him off and looked around for Crossley. "He's gone," Baxter said. His teeth were chattering. "We did all the wrong things. The current took us and he threw the anchor in and we filled up right away. I never saw him surface."

I took him back to the camp and Bailey sent for the police. Henry's brother, David Goose, found Crossley tangled up in some weeds in a little bay not far from the falls. There wasn't much to investigate: Baxter hadn't even seen it happen. All he knew was that the boat turned over while he was sitting in it after he heard the splash of the anchor and when he came up he was close enough to shore to save himself, but he lost sight of the boat and never saw Crossley again. A coroner was flown in and he declared it an accident, and the Baxters left the next day.

HE'D KILLED CROSSLEY, of course, but I didn't speak up right away and then I knew I never would. The thing that made it certain was his story about the anchor. Henry didn't have an anchor; I'd borrowed his when he went to town because I still hadn't found a good rock to replace the one I had cut free, not one as good as Henry's. I'd left my temporary anchor in Henry's boat, along with the rope, but I hadn't tied it to the seat. The police were surprised that the anchor wasn't still dragging the boat, even though it was upside down, but they just assumed it came untied when it got wet, so that was that. I reckon Baxter threw it in, and when it disappeared he found another way to dump the boat, then decided to keep his story.

I also knew why Baxter had killed his partner. The night he came back from the north he had looked for Crossley in his cabin, then, not finding him, had gone on to his own. With his hand on the door he had heard sounds from within, guessed what they were, and backed off, returning to the dining-room for supper. Then he met Crossley and his wife coming to supper when he was on his way back. What he had heard was Mrs. Baxter, giving voice at last, crying out, maybe, because the bedroom door was open, and I heard Baxter open and close the outside door before I could shush her. At the time, I thought it was one of the maids, come to clean the room.

So you can see why, whenever I think of Baxter, I think of that old history teacher banging Simpson's head against the wall. Even now I still wake up feeling bad about Simpson.